BEWARE BLOOD VALLEY

THE
BLO
RUN

MARIE B. CAMBELL

CONTENTS

For the girls who think the villain should get the girl

Raiden

I turned the handle on the wooden music box, taking comfort in the tiny chimes that sounded so like the crackle of ice in a winter storm.

The fire popped and cracked within the grate, while the wind outside howled—a pack of wolves that tore at the roof and walls.

"Would you put that thing away?" my older brother, Beckett, snapped from the bed above mine.

I twirled another few notes from the box before answering. "I'm waiting for Ama to come back."

"Just go to sleep. She and Baba have to help with the sandbags, so the flooding doesn't get any worse."

I sighed, letting the hand that clutched the box fall to the mattress at my side. In the room beside us, I could just make out the soft snores of three of my other brothers. Further down the hall were the youngest two girls in the family. None of them cared when our fragile house barely held together in the wake of a storm.

Through the wicked wind, I could have sworn I heard screams.

A shiver spilled down my spine. Immediately, I picked up the box and spun the melody faster, wishing it was Ama who hummed it instead. Her warm and bright smile staring down at me until sleep claimed me.

But not tonight. The storm was relentless, flooding the village.

Shrieking rattled the ceiling, making me flinch. Through it all was an unmistakable scream pulled away by the wind.

I sat bolt upright. "Did you hear that?"

Beckett groaned. "It's just the wind, Raiden. Go to sleep."

But when it sounded again, this time from inside the house, the hairs on my arms stood on end.

Beckett sat up too.

Footsteps pounded down the hall before our door was thrown open and Ama tumbled in, her forehead wet and shining in the dark with something darker than her bronze skin. "Get up!" Her frantic cry rammed my heart up in my throat.

"What is it, what's wrong? Where's Baba?" Beckett asked, leaping down from the top bunk.

"You need to go!" She rushed forward, grabbing my arms and pulling me up to my feet. The music box clattered to the floor, and I jerked from her hold to grab it.

"Leave it! Get your siblings and *hide*! They're here. You can't let them find you. Go to the basement." She looked to Beckett. "You know where the board is in the back of the boiler room?"

He nodded.

"All of you hide in there. Wait until they're gone and then run. Don't stop running until you get somewhere safe, alright?"

"Ama," my voice quavered. I squeezed the small box in my hand until my fingers hurt. "What's going on? *Who* is here?"

She didn't answer, instead pressing a kiss to my forehead, then Beckett's. "You two are the oldest, so it's up to you to care for the others. Understand?"

Beckett nodded again, but I could only stare at the tears that soaked my mother's cheeks, and the dark, thick liquid that trailed her forehead to her temple. The fire in the hearth banked with another gust of wind, barely illuminating her features enough to glimpse the terror she couldn't quite hide.

"Who hurt you?" The words fell from my lips with numb detachment before my eyes flicked to hers.

More tears spilled over as a sob broke from her lips. "I love you more than every star in the sky."

The words I'd said a hundred times caught in my throat. *A million, billion.*

Before I could open my mouth to say them, the city's siren wailed, though it sounded faint through the blood rushing in my ears.

"Quick!" Ama pushed us toward the door, where Julius, Kiern, and Samael already stumbled into the hall, wide-eyed. Darling and Brixen let out mournful cries.

Beckett grabbed Samael and Kiern by their hands. "Come on!" He gestured for Julius to follow. "Raiden, grab the girls and meet us down there."

I forced my feet to follow down the hall. Ama rushed past me, into Darling and Brixen's room, scooping them up. She turned to me, a sort of desperation swimming in her eyes as she urged me to move faster.

We ran through the house, down the stairs and into the basement when shouts and screams grew louder outside. Something—or someone—was here to hurt us. To hurt Baba and Ama.

In the cold, dark space, we finally made it to the unfinished wall where Beckett helped squeeze the younger boys into the opening. Samael whimpered, turning to Ama.

"It's too scary," he protested in his small voice.

Ama's demeanor turned stern. "You *have* to be brave for your sisters, Sammy. Beckett and the others will be close. Hold their hands." Turning to me, she held out Darling and Brixen, their eyes drooping, and heads unsteady with sleep. I shoved the music box into the pocket of my sleep pants before taking the girls.

"I've given them a natural herb to make them fall asleep," she whispered to me. "If they make noise, you'll be found. Do you understand? None of you make a sound."

A loud bang erupted on the floor above us, loud male shouts speaking words I didn't understand. Ama closed her eyes, letting another tear slip free. "Don't come out for anyone or anything. Not until everything is quiet. I love you all."

More than every star in the sky, I wanted to say.

She shoved me toward the gap before sliding the board in place. The scratch of moving furniture settling in front of the wall, too loud, even over the thrum in my ears.

Then she ran for the stairs again.

Boots on the wooden stairs were like thunder. "I've caught another one!"

Ama made a noise that caused my heart to stutter in my chest. I leaned to peer through the sliver of opening left.

I could barely make out the massive, burly male covered in furs of all sorts grab Ama by her long black hair. She cried out, grasping for his hands as he began to haul her out of the basement.

Rage and fear churned in my gut.

Their struggle retreated up to the main floor, more desolate cries coming from my mother. I wondered where Baba was; if they'd already gotten him, whoever these people were.

"Take them." I shoved Darling and Brixen to my right, feeling their weight lift a split second before I yanked at the board.

"Raiden, don't," Beckett hissed. "Ama said to stay put."

I ignored his words, pulling harder until a gap large enough for me to slip through appeared.

My feet carried me up the stairs so fast, I barely felt them. That's when I heard the crackling. The roar of destruction before I felt the wave of heat. Hungry tongues of flame devoured the walls, slithering across the floor.

Smoke, thick and black darkened the air. I sucked in a deep breath and choked on the cloying scent of ash.

"Beckett!" I turned and raced down the stairs, calling to my siblings each by name until they emerged from their hiding place. "The house is on fire; we need to leave!"

Samael began to cry anew and Keirn joined in. Crouching low, I faced my youngest brothers. "Be brave now. We'll get you out."

To Beckett I said, "Take the girls first, I'll follow with the others."

He nodded, rushing up the stairs and through the house. The demonic snapping as our house was consumed grew louder.

"Follow me and stay as low as you can. We're going out the window." They nodded their understanding, and I turned, leading them up the stairs. Flames billowed near the hall, the heat sweltering, but we crawled away from it, back into the room I shared with Beckett. Each panting breath I took scorched my lungs, and coughs from behind me told me they, too, were affected.

The window, already ajar from Beckett's escape, brought minimal clean air into the room, and instead, fanned the flames that began to groan into the hallway. I got to my feet, finding Julius and Kiern behind me. But not Samael.

"Where's Sammy?" I demanded. They turned, matching looks of panic twisting their features. "Climb out, Beckett is there to catch you, I'll grab Sammy."

Julius hoisted himself up on the windowsill first, peeking outside to the ground below before he shut his eyes and let himself fall.

I rushed into the hall, the thick black cloud stinging my eyes. My lungs burned, but I forced out my brother's name. "Sammy!"

A slight wheezing breath sent me to my belly. I crawled along the floor, finding my youngest brother sprawled out, his eyelids dancing. *His asthma,* I thought with terror twisting my insides.

Grabbing him as best I could, I dragged his small form back toward the bedroom, keeping lower than the plumes of smoke.

Above, the ceiling gave an ominous crack. Something heavy fell in front of us, a spray of embers lapping over my skin, burning my face, my eyes.

I sucked in a breath, filling my lungs with flame. "Beckett!" My scream came out hoarse and muffled by the inferno we were trapped in.

Samael whimpered weakly in my arms. I curled myself around him, trying to keep the dancing flames from burning him.

"Beckett!"

Heat seared into me, ravaging my back.

A dark figure appeared just out of sight, then he was there, grabbing Samael. Beckett yanked me by my arm, pulling me awkwardly. Slowly.

"Get Sammy out," I croaked. The pain was everywhere, stealing my breath, and whatever was left was suffocated by thick, acrid smoke. Reaching for what was left of the clothing on my legs, I fumbled around for the music box Ama had gifted me. It was hot, but comforting in my hand.

"Walk, Raiden! Get up!"

I couldn't answer, but struggled to my hands and knees, fisting the music box as though it were a lifeline. Beckett charged for the exit with Samael, vanishing from view.

I crawled as fast as I could, knowing the end was in sight. But the pain. *The never-ending pain.*

Finally, I entered the room, chased by the demons of fire that reached for me, caressing me down to my shoulder blades. When I reached the window, I struggled to haul myself up, but once I had the momentum, I let my body fall to the other side.

My back hit first, and all I could do was stare up at the sky. Screams filled the night, though I wasn't sure if mine joined them or if it was just in my head.

The music box. My thumb stroked over the object in my hand, assuring myself it was still there. That the fire hadn't taken *everything*.

"They're taking everyone from the city and burning it." Beckett leaned over me, shaking while wounds on his face and arms oozed blood and other fluids.

It took too long to push the question out, but finally I rasped, "Taking them where?" I winced from the pain of speaking.

Beckett's eyes shut while he seemed to try to compose himself. When he spoke again, his voice broke on the words. "Out to sea. Then they're burning the ships."

There was no room for emotion. No grief came. Nothing could get through my barely hinged consciousness.

"We need to get somewhere safe," Beckett said after what felt like minutes, but it could have been hours when I blinked my eyes open.

Wordlessly I turned to my stomach and heard someone gasp. I gritted my teeth as I lifted myself to my hands and knees. "Sammy?" The word was barely audible through my scorched vocal cords.

"He's okay. You're in the worst shape."

I wanted to snort a laugh, but I'd expended too much effort already. Instead, I focused on getting to my feet. The punishing winter wind soothed the fierce burning pain.

My brothers and sisters huddled together in the snow, smudged with ash, but alive. Together we walked, searching for any place untouched by the attack on the city.

After what felt like too long, we came to a derelict shed of sorts on the edge of what was once civilization.

"Better than freezing to death," I said, my words barely audible.

Beckett nodded, opening the door with Darling and Brixen curled into his shoulders, their skin tinged with blue.

It was small and the wind threatened to tear the entire structure apart with each roaring gust, but it was all there was. A small cabinet gnawed on by some sort of creatures held enough moth-eaten blankets for all of us to bundle up in.

"We need a small fire, or we won't survive the night," Beckett said.

Just the idea of being near a fire made me flinch. My brother's eyes softened. "I'll keep it contained. Stay here."

I didn't tell him that I lacked the strength to move, even if I'd wanted to, but he was gone before I could even try.

"Raiden?" Kiern whispered in the dark.

I grunted, unable to manage words.

"Are Ama and Baba dead?"

The question hurt more than the burns covering my body, and my face. More than everything I'd lost. Slowly I uncurled my fingers, exposing the small music box. The sliver of light through the slats above allowed me to see that the wood was almost completely burned away, leaving little more than the metal mechanism.

My breath left me in a eruption of pain. Slowly, I tried to turn the handle, letting the discordant clinking sounds fill the small structure. A broken melody to fit my now ruined voice.

The answer wouldn't come, even if I'd been able to speak it. I let the haunting notes be the reply I wouldn't voice.

Chapter 1

Ferrah

Many Birth Tides Later

When the light breaking through the solemn gray sky above offered nothing by way of warmth, my mood soured further. The least the Council could do was inject a little extra heat into the atmosphere. *Or replace the thermal mechanism on my suit.*

Freeya was a hostile tundra for most of the birth-tide. Despite that fact, it remained a vital member of trade within all of Triste. Still, I often wished I had been born in one of the lower regions.

My numb fingers flexed around the long, heavy weapon held at my side. I scanned the horizon, walking quickly to keep blood flowing to my equally frozen toes. My thermal suit made a feeble attempt to thaw my limbs, shooting a burst of warm air into my boots and gloves. I groaned, deciding to put in a maintenance order once my shift was finished.

The sharp spikes that shot out of the ground at regular intervals in the distance surrounding the Freejian border, gave off a glimmer of violet light, barely visible to the untrained eye. The current of energy stretched high into the air, arcing well above the highest buildings in a dome that protected Freeya.

It kept us safe from the creatures that existed outside our borders. I let my gaze search the desolate land as far as I could see, my straining vision triggering the heightened magnification in my helmet. It allowed me to focus on the jagged rocks and hills. Velvety blue ferns sprouted every so often, their scaly leaves rippling in the wind.

That was the only movement I could see. My eyes narrowed. It was too quiet. No raids, nor a single tunnel collapse in nearly a handful of light-rises.

A flash of black and silver darted past my vision. I jumped, lifting my echo bolt, and peering through the scope until I spied what had startled me.

Ten long legs covered in fine silver hairs trembled near an indigo-colored bush. It curled its furry body into a cage provided by its legs. Through the scope, I could just make out a few of its lazy, blinking eyes.

"Don't do it," I whispered. The light was swallowed up by the dismal morning once more, and a blast of icy air buffeted my face, making me shiver. An errant lock of hair tickled my cheek, but I kept my attention on the pest.

As though the kwipai could hear me from such a distance, it leapt up, as tall as the curling ferns, and shot forward. For such large, spindly creatures, they were bloody fast. Grey eyes decorated its flat head, each of them fixed on the nearest post.

I couldn't help but watch it race toward the seemingly inviting city, knowing what was coming. Still, my muscles tensed when it impacted with the electrified Lufarium, exploding the creature instantly. The muddy sludge of its insides slapped the ground in thick, gelatinous chunks.

My nose wrinkled. Though the kwipai grew to about my hip height, far bigger and scarier predators lived in Blood Valley. Within a few rotations, the remains of the kwipai would be dragged away by another scavenger.

"What are you looking at, Fairy?" a familiar voice asked from behind me, and I started.

Whirling, I smacked Arlakai on the shoulder. "Don't creep up on me like that," I scolded, my heart still pounding in my chest. The focus on my goggles snapped back to normal, giving me a full view of my best friend's tall stature.

His wide grin was playful. Rusty-red curls tumbled over his forehead in the gust of wintry air. With his gun propped up on his shoulder, he looked far too relaxed for a Freejian Guard on patrol duty. If one didn't know him personally, they might chalk it up to the unnatural border silence as of late, but I knew that was just how Arlakai always looked. "Sorry, Fairs," he said in a tone that was not at all repentant.

I rolled my eyes. "What are you doing over here? It's not even high light yet."

Arlakai made a flourishing motion with his wrist before tapping the display screen he wore. The time projected above it for me to see as well. "I'm here to watch your post for your break."

I smirked. "Which is code for: I came to bother you for the next twenty snaps."

He didn't miss a beat, slinging an arm over my shoulders. "An excellent deduction, Lieutenant." Steering me away from my perch and toward the stairs, he continued, "With a mind like that, you're sure to be chosen for the Empire's most deadly race. The Scottomb will be helpless against such wit."

I ducked under Arlakai's arm, smirking. "I prefer to use my echo blades." My stiff, free hand patted the concealed weapon secured around my thigh.

He snickered. "Fiesty, Fairy."

When my cheeks couldn't quite manage a smile in the wicked cold, his own amusement faded. "Why don't you go warm up for a few snaps?"

I tried to wave away his concern. "I'll be on tunnel guard at lower light."

Arlakai shook his head. "You were already placed in the pool of contestants, Fairs. The Council isn't going to award you any more points for freezing to death."

I sighed, though it was broken up by my teeth traitorously chattering. Relenting, I nodded. "Just a few snaps. I'll be right back. Want anything?"

His grin returned, even as another punishing burst of chilling wind howled its warning of an impending snowstorm. He shook his head, shooing me away. I gave my friend a grateful smile before rushing toward the staircase that led down.

My legs were heavier than normal, but once out of the wind, the familiar stinging started through my skin.

At the middle of the tower, heat rose to greet me, and I sighed, wishing I could stay in it. Turning right to head to the commons, I peered over my shoulder, out the tall window behind me. The strewn kwipai wasn't visible, and I hadn't expected it to be, but my gaze still scanned the edge of the valley. Nothing roused.

I frowned, pausing once outside the surveillance area. The glass lifted with an audible whoosh, and I stepped inside.

The circular room was spacious, with display screens covering one part of the curved wall. Several soldiers wearing the same standard Freejian uniform—thin, but well-insulated, tan-coloured cargo pants, the bottoms stuffed into padded white boots, while a white, multi-layered jacket, lined with fur, hugged their torsos.

The Freejian insignia was embroidered into the front with silver stitches, a three-headed, snarling white bear. They were said to be extinct now, but still the bear was seen as a sign of loyalty and strength.

A few faces turned in my direction, some gazes lingering when they deduced who I was. They each held up a palm before touching them to their chests. I returned the salute, then carried on toward the automated server. The bot stood still while I tapped my selection on the floating screen, a message of confirmation flashing before it began to make a soft whirring noise. The mechanical limbs with chipping, buttery yellow paint reached for its port when a small door slid aside. It gripped the steaming cup with an odd sort of gentleness for a machine, before extending it to me.

"Thanks, Bernard," I said to the old piece of equipment. Its answering chirp brought a smile to my face before I lifted the warm beverage to my lips and inhaled the sweet, cinnamon scent and groaned with delight.

Taking a long sip of the pale red liquid, I savored the smooth, spicy flavor. Warmth seeped into my bones where the cold lingered, never fully leaving.

Ugh, I hate the cold. The thought of going back out for the rest of my shift made me groan inwardly.

A series of beeps came from the monitors on the wall. The attention of everyone in the room snapped to the screens. One of them flashed, a blur of figures racing through one of the tunnels as dust and dirt rained from above.

My heart shot up in my throat, and I was already moving for the door, tossing my cup into the vacuum vessel that took it to be cleaned, when one of the guards shouted, "Tunnel breach!"

The city-wide siren began to wail outside the tower. I flicked a button on my wrist communicator which flashed with the section and alert level of the collapse. It was a summons, but even if it hadn't been, I was going. There was no way I'd miss a chance to face the Scottomb. I clicked the finder for my transport, not looking up in time to see someone coming for me, until a hard body collided with mine. Arlakai's arms went around me to keep me from stumbling. I pushed away automatically.

"Tunnel collapse," I said before he could speak. The words were barely out of my mouth before I sprinted toward the open window. The faint whirring sound told me my communication was successful. I didn't stop, my foot catching the last few inches of stone that I used to push off.

And hurled myself out of the window.

The bitter chill lashed my face as I whooped, falling through the air. Arlakai's frantic shouts of panic followed me down, nearly drowned out by the piercing scream of the siren. A gold and white bullet whooshed toward us, and my heart tumbled in my chest.

Five.

Four.

Three.

Two.

My back hit the plush seat that squealed as it deflated to its normal size. My smile of triumph greeted the boy who dropped in beside me. His face was painted with terror in response, a few beads of sweat appearing on his forehead. He balled his hands into fists on his thighs to keep them from shaking.

"You know I hate heights," he complained.

With a laugh, I closed the steel top before steering the pod around the cluster of tall buildings. The steady flicker and pulse of violet energy arcing high above us illuminated the dull grey sky. Our pod hummed louder, pulling toward the active Lufarium like a magnet. I steered it lower, feeling the rush of its current like a shot of adrenaline. We sped toward the eastern border, a dozen or so matching pods rising to rocket alongside us.

The thrill of a fight against the terrifying Scottomb had my blood singing. I couldn't resist the urge to send my pod into a tight spin, angling it down toward the ground.

Arlakai gripped the overhead strap, his jaw tight. Flying was as much a phobia for him as heights were—in fact, he rarely took a pod, favoring walking to the delights of cruiser craft.

At the last possible click, I leveled out, bringing the pod to the ground with a gentle thump. Arlakai's entire body remained tense beside me, and I snuck a glance at him before smirking.

"Shut up," he grumbled, making me laugh outright.

When the top folded open, we rushed out, my echo bolt slung across my back, its weight knocked against me rhythmically. Dozens of Freejian Guard poured into the mouth of the tunnel. I paused, glancing out past the charged forcefield that gave off low vibrations this close to it. Out in the barren stretch of Blood Valley that separated us from our eastern neighbors, Kondez, I could just barely make out the collapse. Like a giant fist had struck out of the sky, the ground sunken into a crater.

It was one of two trade routes to the east. Our tunnels were the veins of Triste, carrying lifeblood through the nations and ensuring our survival. The Scottomb managed to isolate us by driving our borders back and seizing stretches of territory between us. If ever we attempted to cross the fingers that belonged to Blood Valley, they attacked and slaughtered us without mercy. The invisible monsters.

We survived by digging our tunnels and lining them with electrified Lufarium. But the Scottomb figured it out and often targeted the tunnels, trying to cut us off. And occasionally—rarely—they shut down the tunnel's power source and attempted to raid the bordering cities. Only two raids had been successful in my lifetime. But I was too young to remember much of them.

Arlakai tugged on my sleeve, and I lifted my eyes to his. "Ready?"

With a nod, I straightened my spine. Soldiers continued to rush in, while others filtered out, covered in dust and dirt, pulling loaders that overflowed with rubble. Singe marks marred their uniforms but looks of determination set their jaws and filled their eyes.

"Clearly no Scottomb got in," I said, bringing my pace up to a jog. There would have been screaming.

There was always screaming when the Scottomb attacked.

Inside the tunnel, the light faded out quickly, save for the torches attached to the soldier's wrist communicators. I lifted mine and said, "Light."

A beam of golden light poured from the device, illuminating our path. The end of the tunnel came into view, and many of the soldiers worked to begin clearing it.

"Did any of you run a scan?" I called out. Each of the tunnels were dug deep enough so the Scottomb couldn't easily burrow down into them, and the lethal current of Lufarium ensured they couldn't use their handy little disappearing trick to just slip through the ground and into the tunnel. But the electric current was lethal to us too. Digging near it was beyond hazardous.

A familiarly tall, sparrow-like woman turned to face me, scowling. "Of course I scanned it already," Erina—Captain of the Eastern regiment, and technically my boss—said matter-of-factly. "And I contacted Control to switch the correct arches off."

Arlakai clapped his hands together before rubbing them excitedly. He practically bounced on the balls of his feet, eager to clear the tunnel. He was only ever this energized when danger was involved. "Where should we start, Cap?"

Though Erina was only five or so birth-tides older than us, she certainly looked like she was beyond that. Probably because she only ever frowned.

"I've ordered a tunnel bot. Just move the stone slabs and get back to your guard posts." She turned and stalked away, clearly happy to leave the babysitting to me.

I sighed, bending down to lift a smaller chunk of hard, curved stone. We all worked to clear as much as we could, the dirt continuing to shift and dropping small chunks of rock in our paths.

When my wrist device chirped to announce the tunnel bot had arrived, I called to all the soldiers, letting them know to evacuate.

Arlakai walked beside me, whistling like he didn't have a care in the world. But I knew better. He glanced sidelong at me.

"Zeichra for your thoughts?" he asked.

I smirked. "Are my thoughts only worth a measly zeichra? A hot pastry is at least a hundred zeichra. Surely, they're worth at least that."

He snorted. "How about I sweeten the deal and throw in a hot pryani after work?"

I made a wistful sound, recalling the beverage I'd had to discard before the collapse. Shaking my head, I sighed. "Can't. I have to get home to help Nona and Charle."

Arlakai's jaw tensed, but he nodded. "If you're chosen for the Blood Run, they'll have to make it without you for a whole lunar shift, maybe two."

At the edge of the tunnel, I saw that the light was halfway in the sky. My stomach kindly knotted itself in a mess, but I forced a smile up at him. "That's why you and Daria should just come stay at my place. You'll be able to keep an eye on them." I batted my lashes the way that usually made him cave, but he only scowled. The light peeking through the clouds cast his features in sharp lines and deep shadows, pronouncing his displeasure.

"And if we're both selected?" he asked without an ounce of his usual, light-natured charm present.

The stomachache I was rapidly developing worsened. "I don't know," I answered honestly.

We both needed the hefty payout that came with competing in the most dangerous event our world had ever known.

It was simple—in theory. Each of the eleven nations were powered entirely by Lufarium. A violet crystal that could only be mined in the heart of Blood Valley. The nations selected two of its citizens to compete in a race to mine the most Lufarium. Whoever returned with the minimum amount first, won the highest honor in all of Triste—as well as a wealth so great, they were treated as royalty themselves.

My family needed that money.

But so did Arlakai and his sister, Daria. She, like my brother Charle, was faced with a handicap that required more money than either of us made with the guard to sustain.

And when their welfare cost became a burden on a household, the Council stepped in to perform a "compassion release."

I couldn't let that happen. To Daria *or* to Charle.

"Where are you stationed next?" Arlakai asked, snapping me out of my morose musings.

The tunnel I was meant to be stationed at had collapsed. Lifting my wrist, I checked the schedule on the projected screen.

Ferrah Zunnock

Report to east tunnel- section 4

I groaned. "Section four."

"In Dumiski?" His brow lifted, and I nodded. Arlakai repeated the action of checking his own station. Then he sighed. "Tower 34." Gesturing to the tower we'd been in before the collapse, he gave me a look that went from disappointed, to mischievous—his lips curling to one side. "Wanna trade, Lieutenant?"

I pretended to consider it, setting my chin in my hand, and humming. "The windy, frigid tower, or the warm, cozy tunnel?" Tapping the side of my face playfully, I drew out my sarcasm, ignoring Arlakai as he rolled his eyes.

I clucked my tongue, straightening, and gave him a grin. "Nope, I'm good. But I could give you a ride in my pod to the tower?"

He reached out to ruffle my hair like he did when we were young recruits, which I ducked away from, smacking his hand. Arlakai laughed, the sound warm and bright. "See you later, Fairy."

I stuck my tongue out at my best friend, but he'd already turned and started walking away. Shaking my head, my smile remained. Finally, when he was out of view, disappearing between the towering structures, I strode to my pod and climbed in.

When the top clicked shut, I settled into the seat and gave the automated system my destination. It lifted into the air with only a slight hum, zooming above from the city of Kilner and leaving the border behind.

Chapter 2

Ferrah

Tethering my pod to my window ledge, I used my communicator to lift the glass pane before climbing inside.

Nona hated that I used the window instead of the main entrance, but that would mean leaving my pod in the hovercraft bay, and I didn't trust that something wouldn't happen to it, like with my very first hover board when I was thirteen. It wasn't one of the compact ones that could be folded up and carried inside, so I'd been forced to leave it in the bay. When I'd come out to ride it the next light-rise, I'd found it shattered into pieces against the wall. A much larger multi-transport had taken the spot and crushed my board in the process.

Since we now lived on the top floor in our building, I just tied it up right outside.

A clatter came from one of the distant rooms, followed by a stern voice. "Don't you dare try to get that."

I smiled but hurried toward the metal door, which slid to the side with a hiss. In the meal room, I found Nona and Charle. Both of them turned to face me.

"Ferrah!" My smiling younger brother steered his chair around the counter-top. The bag that housed his medication suspended behind him, sloshed side to side. He jerkily opened his arms to me, the effort causing him to grunt. I smiled, extending my own arms toward him. I waited for him to come to a complete stop before I wrapped his smaller body in a tight hug, his weak grip around my neck making my smile dissolve like the sweetener Nona illegally purchased.

My gaze met Nona's over Charle's shoulder, and she gifted me a rare, small smile.

"We heard about the tunnel collapse," Charle said, letting me go.

I straightened, nodding. "It was just a little one," I assured him, though it was more for Nona than for him. "And nothing got in."

He nodded; no doubt having read all about it. The likelihood was he'd managed to analyze the footage already and would have notes regarding the structure itself. My lips twitched at the thought.

"It was considered a major collapse, since it knocked out four barrier arches," he retorted, though he didn't seem convinced.

"Three, apparently," I corrected him.

Charle frowned, brushing his shaggy dark brown hair out of his eyes, though it simply fell back into place a click later. I needed to give his hair another trim. "No, there was another on the other side of the collapse."

I blinked. How had Erina missed that in her scan? "Well, either way, the tunnel bot will have it all fixed by now."

Nona cleared her throat. "No more guard talk you two. Come now, the table won't set itself."

Nodding, I stalked toward her, wrapping her in a hug before working to set the table. Though Charle's condition—which affected his muscles—was medicated, he needed reconstructive nervous surgery which cost an absolute fortune. I watched him try to lift his arms to the open the steel compartment that stored dishes, and they wobbled, looking like they were too heavy for his body. My heart ached to see him struggle, but I knew better than to help unless he asked.

The bowl that had clearly been knocked to the floor when I arrived, had spilled something thick and purple on the floor that our service bot noisily sucked up, while Nona whipped up a new batch. Two of the three meals each light-rise were delivered as nutrition bars through the chute above the counter, while the final meal came pre-prepared in individual servings based on the height, weight, and nutrition requirements of each citizen.

Since I was a little girl, Nona had taken the delivered foods and made them something *more*. She liked to experiment and turn the boring, bland meals into an altogether otherworldly experience, even if that meant finding and purchasing illicit ingredients. I couldn't complain; she made the most delectable food I'd ever tasted.

"Take this to the table, Charle," Nona ordered, holding out a little white pot filled with steaming gravy.

He wheeled toward her and slowly extended his arms to take it. Just as she released the dish to him one of his arms failed, falling limp, and sending the jug to the white stone floor. It shattered, the hot liquid splashing up Nona's exposed legs. She leapt back, muttering a curse.

Charle made a noise that sounded like a half-sob, half growl of frustration. I rushed forward to help clean up. Even if the bot would get to it in a click, I couldn't just stand by and watch.

I grabbed a cloth from the counter and wet it, before kneeling to wipe off Nona's legs, then Charle's.

Before I could finish, his eyes flew open. His golden-hued eyes shone with angry tears. I wanted to pick him up and wrap him in my arms like I did when he was much younger.

"Don't." His voice was hard.

"Charle it's okay, I don't mind—" I started, but he cut me off.

"I'll do it." With his other arm, he held his shaking hand out for the cloth.

I swallowed hard against the lump rising in my throat. "Charle," I said quietly. "Please let me help."

"I made this mess; I'll clean it up. Even if I'm here all night."

Debating whether to fight him further, I opened my mouth, but Nona laid a hand on my shoulder, telling me to drop it. Since he was small, he'd insisted on forcing his limbs into submission. Back then, he was able to walk. He lost sensation in his legs entirely when he was just eight, but I couldn't afford his hover chair until I graduated training for the guard the birth-tide after. The lunar shifts I'd endured watching him crawl from place to place had been gut-wrenching, but he only let me carry him when his arms had grown too weak.

I handed Charle the cloth and walked out of the meal room, heading back through the chambers until I reached mine. The door slid aside without hesitation, and I marched inside, locking the entrance, ensuring neither Charle, nor Nona, would immediately know that I'd left.

Snatching an empty bag from the floor, I allowed a single tear to fall. *This* was why I had to be chosen to compete in the Blood Run.

And I needed to win.

For Charle.

No one should have to live like that, I thought bitterly. *If he doesn't get the surgery soon, it'll be too late.*

I swung the strap over my shoulder and ordered the window open again before dropping onto my waiting pod. As quietly as I could manage, I switched the transport device on and steered it toward the border.

Finding a few harmless bushes, I stowed my pod behind them and began my trek, leaving my echo blade inside, though it pained me to do so. Even if it was highly unlikely, occasionally a tunnel breach left behind artifacts or armor buried long ago. Items found were often sold to collectors, or a select few that studied the items. My compensation as Freeya's Elite Guard was enough to support the three of us, and afford Charle's medication, but I needed to save up in case my name wasn't called at the draw in a few light-rises. I'd scour every inch of Freeya if I had to. *Monsters below*, I'd find a way past the barrier and risk Blood Valley on my own if I had to.

Something about what Charle had said about the number of barrier arches made me think that Erina's scan had been faulty. It was possible she'd misspoke, but either way, I was going to see if there was anything to find.

The city was illuminated with lights that wound around the lookout towers as well as other buildings. Of course, the dome that enclosed all of Freeya sent bolts of dull violet light arcing between the massive pillars that lifted high into the sky.

The wind picked up, lashing my body with its icy breath. The incoming storm would hit soon unless the Council dissolved it.

I reached the wide tunnel mouth and glared at the crosshatching electric barrier that blocked my way. My eyes slid to the panel on the right that controlled it. Biting my bottom lip, I considered how long I'd have between the moment I disabled it before either a security bot arrived, or worse, Captain Erina Jillcolm.

Five snaps. Maybe ten, if I was lucky.

But if I disabled the reporting system as well, I'd get close to fifteen. Steeling my spine, I stepped toward the panel, pulling out an old, decorated blade that Nona had gifted to me when I completed my training for the Freejian Guard. It was designed with flowers twining up the handle. Another of her illicit dealings, no doubt.

"Tsk, tsk, I knew you were a rebel at heart," a familiar male said behind me, and I whirled.

Arlakai grinned at me, his green eyes glittered with pride. Instead of wearing his guard-issued gear, he wore simple black pants that lacked the pockets and straps required in our line of work—donning instead a sleek black hooded coat. It didn't look as warm as what we usually wore, but he was never as affected by the cold as I was.

I *really* hated snow.

Licking my wind-blistered lips, I replied, "I wanted to look for relics."

His eyes scanned my expression, reading something in it that I wasn't sure I'd been displaying until he nodded, smile vanishing. "Let's do it."

"Where's Daria?" I asked, wondering if he'd left his little sister alone. Charle and I, at least, had Nona. Arlakai was able to leave Daria in the care of a disability bot across Kilner during the light, but there was no one during the dark except him.

"I had a similar idea, and Fenley agreed to stay with her." Fenley was Arlakai's neighbor. Since Arlakai was not a Lieutenant, he was not afforded the same luxuries I was, including top floor living quarters.

The lower levels were split into two, resulting in a much smaller space, which was one of the reasons I kept trying to get him and Daria to move in with me. Nona was up in birth-tides, becoming more tired than usual, but Daria's ailment wasn't as severe as Charle's, and I knew the three of them together would be beneficial.

Arlakai examined the panel and made a rumbling noise of contemplation, then pulled a small maintenance tool from his pocket and clicked it open. A small, narrow blade shot from its tip just before he slid it in between the display panel and the outer casing, prying it apart in one swift motion. I gasped, looking around wildly for a beat. Part of me expected to see guards shouting and running through the streets to tackle us; instead, the peaceful silence of curfew remained intact.

"Please state which command you require," the robotic voice chimed.

Before the alarm could sound, Arlakai found the tiny compartment that housed the thin wires and cut through the entire bundle, silencing the automated help service.

The bright barrier of light dissolved in an instant.

"We won't have long," Arlakai stated, pulling me into the tunnel at a slow jogging pace. We kept on the balls of our feet, so the Scottomb weren't as likely to sense the vibrations, but the collapse itself had already caused a stir above ground. They would be watching. Waiting for an opening. Any weakness that would grant them access.

Every so often in the tunnels, my skin prickled; and though we were well below the surface, I could almost swear I sensed them above me.

It was probably just paranoia, but when I'd mentioned the theory to Arlakai, he hadn't laughed at me like I'd expected him to. Instead, he brushed it off, leaving the conversation behind in the frozen air.

When we were far enough in, we switched on our torches, granting us much needed light. Slowing, we scanned the walls, coming to the recent collapse where it was no longer stone, but a reddish-brown dirt supported with beams. There was freshly installed stone where the tunnel bot had begun its repairs, leaving a few segments unfinished. In the gaps, the violet pulses of Lufarium hummed away, keeping the possibility of another breach next to none.

But that also meant if anything had settled from the surface, we'd make a killing. Every so often the glitter or gleam of rock caught my eye. Some were as black as the Scottomb's veins, others were the deep green of a sacred lake—though I'd never seen one in person to know for sure. I collected each of the stones I found for Charle. They were only worth a few dozen zeichra, which wouldn't be worth it even if I managed to find a hundred in each tunnel.

My light passed over the shine of something silver, roughly as big as my thumb, and I paused only a click before whipping back toward it. Brows furrowing, I took a step closer before brushing my gloved fingers over the object.

"I think I found something," I whispered over my shoulder.

"Me too," Arlakai answered. I could hear the thrumming excitement in his voice.

A smile tugged at my lips, and I gently began to massage the packed dirt away, revealing more and more of the dull, silver beneath. My breath caught when I registered what it was, the words escaping on a gasp, "It's some kind of armor."

"Fairy, come here. I think I found a helmet," Arlakai said with so much enthusiasm, the echo sounded throughout the tunnel, freezing us both in place.

I turned right as he pulled it free from the dirt. More rained down at the disturbance before settling.

It was only a portion of the old piece of armor, crinkled in places and damaged to the point of appearing more like a scrap of discarded metal.

"That'll fetch a fair price," a voice said from the darkness beyond.

My gaze snapped toward the intruder, gut twisting at the familiar drawl.

Isak Fairway stepped into the light, one of his minions at his back. His grin was all teeth, green eyes glittering with mischief.

I groaned in mock disgust. "Oh, so *that's* what the smell is. I thought someone had mistakenly deposited the refuse into the tunnel."

Isak's cruel smile didn't falter. "No, little warrior, that's just how all of Freeya smells when it warms up."

I rolled my eyes.

Isak was from Kondez, one of our neighboring nations. While none of the Feejian Guard liked the Kondez Battalion, trade between Freeya and Kondez was vital. Their climate was more temperate. Food sources and livestock thrived there, whereas Freeya rarely thawed long enough to see what laid beneath all the snow.

"You wouldn't last more than twelve snaps in Freeya," Arlakai snapped. "Maybe that's why Kondez hasn't won a Blood Run in thirty birth-tides."

Isak's grin did slip then, his stocky body lurching forward a step before his friend caught his shoulder, stopping him from whatever punishment he planned to exact this time.

"I'll be taking those artifacts," Isak sneered, holding out a thick hand.

"Get frostbite, Isak." Pulling what looked like a large piece of wrist armor from the tunnel wall with more force than I meant to, I didn't wait for Isak's response before turning on my heel and stalking back toward the Freejian border.

"Too bad your name won't even place in the top five, *Fairy*." Isak tossed my nickname at my back like it was an insult, but I merely chuckled.

"We'll see, Kondez. We'll see." I didn't want to admit it, but his comment rattled me. There were many within the Guard that possessed greater skill and rank than I did, but since I was twelve, I'd fought for my spot in the draw. Not to mention that I'd held the record for the fastest echo blade skills test for five birth-tides.

"You're going to get chosen," Arlakai said quietly, keeping pace with me. I didn't bother to answer, my teeth grinding.

"Do you think we'll get caught?" I asked instead.

He checked his wrist communicator yet again, then said, "We've been down here for fifteen snaps."

I swore low, picking up my pace. Arlakai did the same, and we made it back to the mouth of the tunnel a few snaps later. It was still open, mercifully, but the faint whirring of an alarm in the distance had us hurrying faster.

We peered left and right, making sure there were no officers directly outside. The surveillance system would have a hard time identifying us with our heads down and our guard issue-weapons nowhere on our persons.

A service bot raced toward the tunnel, and I grabbed Arlakai's hand, pulling him after me. When we made it a safe distance away, I heaved a breath of relief, leaning against a building to let my heart return to its normal rhythm. Arlakai sent me a grin that I couldn't help but return.

After a moment, we carried on around the outskirts of the city. The only trader on this side of Freeya was Marcus, and we'd have to make it before he shut up his less-than-savory shop font until the light returned. I did my best to conceal the gauntlet inside an interior pocket within my jacket, but the bulge would no doubt be noticeable.

The wind had calmed like I suspected it would, leaving a bitter cold that nipped at my nose. Each border tower gave off a modicum of heat, the softly hissing electric current that caged in all of Freeya capturing my attention every so often. The way it seemed to whisper as we passed made the hairs on the back of my neck stand on end.

If Arlakai heard it, however, he didn't let on. Ever since I was young, I felt inexplicably drawn to the border. And not just because the occasional crackle and pop resulted in showers of brightly colored sparks that made all the children gasp in awe.

"Ferrah." My name was a barely hissed breath in the air, though it sounded as though the barrier itself tried to speak. Whirling, my gaze snapped to the border. The darkness beyond only shimmered in the glow of the barrier.

I felt it though. A presence. One that I couldn't see, despite the tower lights.

"Fairs?" my best friend queried with caution, his words failing to fully register.

Stepping out from between the two high-rise apartment buildings, I tilted my head to the side.

"Little flower," the voice breathed again, and this time I knew it was for me. Only one person had ever called me "flower."

My heart catapulted into my throat. I tried to swallow it back down as I drew closer, the barrier's heat penetrating my thick jacket. A deep thrumming in my veins began, seeming to pulse in tandem with the barrier. Its power made me step closer still.

The urge to touch it was nearly overwhelming, but a single graze was lethal. Still my hand lifted, despite the warning bells sounding in the back of my mind.

Just a little closer...

A shimmer just before me took shape, blurred and warped as it was through broken glass. Sharp edges on a face that I barely recognized, the man clothed in black.

And eyes carved from brutal, silver ice. I jolted at the sight, realizing my mind hadn't conjured some false image. There really was a man standing on the other side of the border!

"Flower." The sound was garbled and rough, but there was no denying I'd heard it.

My heart beat against my ribcage as my feet carried me forward another shuffled step. My hand that was still raised, ached to touch the figure, to trace those sharp edges and see if they cut. Before I could, however, he vanished from view. A gasp slipped from my barely parted lips.

I didn't know his name. Couldn't call out to him like he did to me.

"What in the burning light are you doing?" Arlakai hissed, yanking me back by the collar of my jacket.

I blinked, my mind catching up with what I'd undoubtedly looked like. "It was…" Swallowing thickly, I tried again. "There's someone out there."

Arlakai whipped around, scanning the warped land through the violet haze. "There's no one there."

I opened my mouth, closed it again, then said, "You didn't hear my name?"

He watched me for a moment, likely gauging my mental fortitude before glancing out at Blood Valley again. Arlakai shook his head. "I heard the crackling sound the barrier makes."

There was no sense in trying to prove I'd heard my name, followed by a word I hadn't heard in many birth-tides when I couldn't actually prove it.

"Come on." He grabbed my hand, leading me back toward the city. I let him, glancing back for only a click in hopes of catching a glimpse of the figure. But nothing lay beyond the static. Nothing but barren wasteland.

Even after both of us left the old historian's house a thousand drekels richer, I couldn't shake the rough quality of the voice that had spoken my name. The boy who'd saved my life so long ago had slipped into distant memory, but came crashing back the moment I'd heard him call to me. It had to be him.

I'd told Arlakai about that event when we were younger, but he hadn't been convinced that my savior had been from Blood Valley. The only people that lived there hated all that dwelled within the Empire. If not for the gift he'd left me, I might have believed it was all just a trick of my imagination or a dream I'd conjured to replace my parents' absence.

I'd gone back to the border to call out to him, but when Nona caught me sitting so close to the lethal energy, she'd banned me from going near it again.

Even after joining the Freejian Guard, I'd mostly stayed away—the childish notion that anyone out in Blood Valley existed and watched over me banished from my mind.

But I'd clung to the memory of the boy who shoved a wooden box into my hand and told me I'd save *him* one light-rise after he rescued me from being trampled to death. I reached into my pocket and pulled the worn trinket out.

The large, fierce-looking bird holding a flower in its beak sat atop the lid, a golden latch securing the box. It had intrigued me since the moment it was gifted to me. The boy had called me 'flower', making me think the carving had been made just for me. But it was the soft, haunting song the box played that had held my attention all these years. Even when I'd heard it for the first time, it felt familiar.

I wanted to return to the edge of Kilner now to look for the voice that had said my name, but if there *had* been someone there, they'd most likely already gone.

Still, as we passed along the outskirts of the city, I found myself trying to peer through the translucent wall from a distance yet again. I wasn't surprised when nothing stirred, though the pang of disappointment still weighted my chest.

After climbing into bed a while later—with Nona and Charle fast asleep and temporarily sparing me the apology I needed to issue for storming out earlier—I fell into a restless sleep chasing those silver eyes and the hushed murmurs of my name.

Chapter 3

Raiden

I shouldn't have gone to the border. Then again, I hadn't expected to see anyone so close. Especially not her.

Stranger still, I knew she'd heard me speak.

No longer the small girl who'd ventured too close to the border, she was a soldier now, and all woman. Capable of defending herself, and skilled enough to rise quickly through the Freejian ranks. That thought alone allowed me to walk away.

She would be safe without me. Safe in the cage the Empire kept all its people in.

My trek was quick and swift and only a few kwipai braved the utter darkness laid over Blood Valley like a stifling cloak. Distantly, Scottomb bayed their unending hunger. Two figures appeared in the distance, seeming to rise from the rocky slope.

I stopped far enough away from the Kondez border so as not to be spotted, letting the two men close the distance.

Isak halted, a smirk curving his lips. I didn't particularly like him or his companion, Zek, but I tolerated them both since they were always reliable with their information.

"I'm assuming Sequoia made it through since there were no lockdowns," I stated, the grating rasp of my harsh voice sounding as bored as I felt.

Zek nodded, but Isak wasn't about to let him get the first word in. "She's in as far as we can tell. It's just two light-rises, they're not gonna catch her." His infuriating grin remained in place, and though I wanted to slap it off, I forced myself to focus on the mission.

"If you'd like, I can point you toward the two dozen soldiers who thought the same thing and were violently mistaken." My words were clipped, and my mind was back at the Freejian border even though Ferrah was likely deep inside the city, sleeping soundly.

Isak rolled his eyes. "If Sequoia gets caught, then that's on her."

My feet moved without my permission, my fingers so easily slipping around Isak's thick neck. "This mission is too damned important," I hissed, squeezing his throat tight to make my message clear. "For all our sakes, you better hope that Sequoia *doesn't* get caught."

"Or what, the *Phantom* will finally leave his mythical hiding spot and finally do something around here?" My grip increased and Isak's eyes widened. He clawed at my covered forearms, unable to break my hold.

Leaning in, I whispered, "Be careful what you say. The Phantom hears all. He sees all. And he knows all." I didn't give him time to scoff or argue, flicking my wrist and releasing the brute. Through his panting for breath, he shot me a glare that I returned with a twisted smile.

He didn't have to believe in the name spoken throughout Blood Valley. Many had begun to doubt the Phantom still lived.

But the rumors of an army that had formed in the furthest parts of the south, sent whispers that their wicked ruler remained and was growing restless. Through those utterings, a revolution began. The Scottomb outnumbered the citizens of Blood Valley six-to-one while resources dwindled.

It was time for change.

"Psh, if you believe that, then you're deluded. It's just us out here. Freak."
Isak retreated with his words, and I let him.

He had a part to play, as did I.

This Blood Run would be the last. We would all make sure of that.

Chapter 4

Ferrah

I was up before first light to gather the ingredients needed to make the little cakes Nona taught me how to make. With a metal skewer, I flipped them in the bubbling oil. They looked a little darker than they were supposed to, but my culinary skills were basically non-existent, despite Nona trying to teach me.

My talents were reserved for my blades, and for protecting Freeya, but I knew that the best way to sweeten Charle up after my outburst last night was through his stomach.

The whoosh of a door sliding open made my lips lift. Charle's mechanical chair whirred as he picked up speed, entering the meal room.

I glanced in his direction but found him watching the pot filled with oil.

"It's too hot," he said stiffly.

I didn't answer, turning the heat down a notch. "After breakfast I thought you and I could watch the delegates and contestants arrive." My olive branch went unanswered, and I knew he was still mad about how I'd acted. I spooned out the cooked puffs with a sigh.

When they were all safely out of the pot, I leaned back against the counter, staring my brother down.

"I'm sorry, Charle." Still, he didn't meet my gaze. "It's so hard for me to watch you struggle to do everything without helping. Helping is in my nature, especially where you're concerned."

Finally, his eyes that reminded me of the light, bitter drink Arlakai so enjoyed, flicked up to lock onto mine. "If they pick you, I'll be on my own, Ferr." His voice was barely audible, but still I felt the broken sound shatter my frozen heart.

I turned to hide the tears that welled, grabbing the small canister of sweet, crystallized granules. Pouring it over the pastries, I blinked away my guilty tears. They wouldn't help anyone.

When I turned back around, I held out the plate of coated puffs. "We don't know if I'll get chosen, Charle. There are thousands of other soldiers vying for one of two spots. The odds are slim at best."

Saying those words out loud made my heart ache. I needed to be chosen. Charle needed me to be chosen. Without the surgery, the Council would likely only give him another two or three lunar shifts before they decided to intervene.

Charle lifted one hand with single-minded concentration, the limb trembling, but he managed to pinch a puff between his fingers. I turned away again, unable to watch him struggle to get the treat to his mouth.

"I'll do whatever it takes, Charle," I whispered.

There were a few beats of silence where he chewed the pastry, then, "I know you're tough and all, but if you died out there, it would all be a moot point. I think you should withdraw your name from the list."

I steadied myself, my hands gripping the countertop. "You know I can't do that Charle."

"I figured you'd say that." With a sigh, his chair whirled around, starting back toward his sleeping chambers. "I'll meet you out here in ten snaps. Then we'll go."

I left the mess to be cleaned up by the bot and headed straight for the washing facilities. The control panel on the right chirped, illuminating a hovering touch screen. I swiped a finger over the options, selecting what I needed.

When I stepped into the warm spray of soapy water sans clothing, a groan of pleasure slipped from me. The jets lined within the rectangular space—which was large enough to accommodate Charle's mobility chair—blasted me from head to toe, suds coating my skin.

The only times when the bone-deep ache of Freejian cold felt as though it began to thaw was in the heat of the water. My eyes closed while I rubbed the lightly scented soap up and under my arms, savoring the feel for a moment. While I knew that a part of me would always belong in the tundra, with Nona and Charle, another part of me couldn't help but wish for a transfer to one of the other ten nations.

Maudeer and Werea-Haot were both desert climates. They had longer light-rises, and it was always hot. It sounded *amazing*. Not that I'd experienced hot weather before. But as part of the Freejian Guard training, it was mandatory to study each of the nations that made up Triste as well as our overall history.

And now I'd get to see delegates from all over Triste before Freeya made their final selections tomorrow. In one more light-rise, I'd find out who would run for my nation.

The overhead jets turned on, squirting cleanser onto my hair that I worked into my unruly brown curls. When it switched back to water, I rinsed it out, scratching my scalp a little harder than was necessary.

I'd barely managed to work the nourishing oils into my hair before the water cycled one last time, then turned off.

Water was controlled in Freeya to five snaps per wash. Barely enough time to enjoy the process, but I was used to it. Besides, out in Blood Valley, there would be no washing facilities. From what I knew of the previous broadcasted runs and my own research, it was mostly desert. Any water sources found along the way were toxic.

When I was dressed in the only formal-wear I possessed—attire similar to my standard uniform with the exception of extra beige fur lining the neck and sleeve cuffs—I exited my quarters. Charle waited by the sleek, metal door and I smiled at the way he'd attempted to comb his messy locks.

"Ready?" I asked, looking around for Nona to say goodbye, but the apartment was silent. *She's probably meeting her supplier,* I thought grimly. I didn't want to know what would happen if the Council ever found out what Nona was up to.

He grunted in acknowledgement, clearly still frustrated with me for refusing to withdraw my name. I fought back a sigh and called the lift to our floor with the button. It took only a few moments before the door slid open, and we entered the cage.

The footpaths were heaving with civilians making their way to the Council's palace. We filtered into the throng, excitement thrumming from every passing citizen. A light dusting of snow and ice covered the walkways and crunched underfoot.

Though most made way for Charle's limited mobility, I still found myself angling slightly ahead so as to part the crowd. My brother seemed not to notice the stares that came his way, but I did. Charle rarely left our quarters. His education was through the virtual learning portal, and he wouldn't enter the workforce until the end of the birth-tide.

If he survived that long.

My gaze scanned ahead, up the steep incline of Kilner to the massive, glittering palace. The light above reflected off its carved-gem walls, giving it a slight blue hue. Nona had once said the palace was the highest point in Kilner so the Empress could glower down at the rest of us when she deigned to spend time here, but I thought it embodied all of Freeya. It looked like the ice our nation was known for. It was beautiful in a haunting sort of way.

As early as I could remember, I wanted to be a member of the Freejian Guard, sworn to protect the Council's palace and the people of Freeya. And from the moment I qualified to run in the most important and deadly race known to our world, my life had been dedicated to proving myself the soldier Freeya needed.

A loud humming streaked by from above, the silver ship stamped with Freeya's white insignia. People pointed excitedly, speculating on which nations' contestants were inside.

"Did you see the video of Maudeer's contestants training last night?" Charle shouted as we continued to shift forward little by little.

I glanced down at him. "No."

His lips quirked mischievously. "You've seen stills of them though." It wasn't a question.

I sighed. "Spit it out, Charle."

His smirk didn't dissipate. "In traditional Maudeer fashion, their contestants are giant, but the girl, Imani, is especially skilled with an echo blade. She managed to hit all thirty targets in the training ring without taking more than five steps. Broke the record speed too."

I gritted my teeth but didn't respond. He couldn't scare me into withdrawing, but he knew that an echo blade was my weapon of choice. The record she broke wasn't just any record.

It was the one I set five birth-tides ago.

I wanted to see this Imani and her wicked-fast skills.

Charle chuckled at my silence, no doubt sensing the competitive side of me was rearing its ugly head.

"Fairs!" A voice called from behind me. "Fairy!"

I turned towards Arlakai who wound through the mass of people.

"Hey Charle," he greeted my brother with a nod.

Charle lit up with a wide smile, looking more himself than he had in light-rises. "Arlakai!"

I bumped my shoulder against my best friend's. "Aren't you supposed to be on duty, soldier?"

His grin was sly. For someone meant to conform to Freeya's every wish, Arlakai retained the most of himself of any other Guard I knew. "I'm on my way there. I have palace patrol."

I nodded. "I have tower patrol at half-light."

"So, did you see that video of the Maudeer girl?" Arlakai asked, sending my mood into a further nose-dive. "She broke the training record with an echo—"

I held up a hand. "Yes. I heard." My response was clipped.

Arlakai exchanged a knowing grin with Charle. "Gonna challenge her when you get selected?"

"Absolutely," I countered. "In fact, I'll challenge her now."

Arlakai threw his head back and laughed. "I love how feisty you are. Surely you knew you weren't going to hold the echo blade record forever."

I swallowed down any further retort. Of course I knew. And as a general rule, I never thought of other women as my enemy, but when I broke the training record as the youngest guard member to hit every target in less than seven clicks, I knew it would give me a much-needed boost in the Blood Run selection process.

I sighed. "I know. It just means I need to practice more."

Arlakai shrugged. "The selection is tomorrow. You're not going to re-break your old record in one night."

I didn't answer, focusing instead on helping Charle's hoverchair scale the stairs leading up to the palace courtyard. Another massive council ship passed overhead, blocking out some of the light. It flew through the open crystalline gate and floated just above the dunes of snow, beside the other ship.

Flurries of white swirled in the air, the bitter chill buffeting us all. I shivered, glancing down to make sure Charle's fur-lined jacket was keeping him warm enough. He rubbed his gloved hands together as best he could, and I wished I could give him my jacket. It didn't have a built-in warming system like my standard uniform, but it was insulated to withstand long periods spent in the cold.

People congregated everywhere, trying to catch a glimpse of the foreign delegates and contestants still inside the metal containers. We were lower than I wanted to be, but when the projected image of the scene hovered in the air for the entire crowd to spectate, cheers erupted. Arlakai scooped Charle up out of his chair and onto his shoulders, making him laugh. Despite my worries that he might fall backwards, I smiled at the rare sound of my brother's laughter.

One of the Freejian Council members, Venedikt, stepped into the clearing. His skin was as pale as ice with eyes to match. He wore the traditional council robes in white with silver stitching throughout the extravagant fabric.

When he spoke, his voice was light and melodic. "Welcome, Freeya, to the 212th opening of the Blood Run."

I stomped my feet in the snow and roared my approval with everyone else gathered. Some howled the old bear call until he held up his hands to draw silence from the eager crowd.

"As you all know, each of the eleven nations of Triste relies on Lufarium for our walls, our energy, and our weapons. Without it, we would succumb to the Scottomb—the scourge of Blood Valley."

An image of the nightmarish creatures attacking the border replaced Venedikt and the Palace grounds. Their translucent skin, hairless bodies and pure white eyes were enough to make a baby somewhere in the throng cry. I hated their gaping mouths and the way you could see their organs inside their body through their skin. Their veins were black. And I knew firsthand that they bled like spilled ink.

"Through Triste's long history," Venedikt continued, "we have attempted to quell the hatred within Blood Valley using pure militant force, but were met with bloodshed and cities taken. Our borders were pushed back each time we tried to fight for the Lufarium we so desperately require."

A somber air fell over every person. We knew what came next. I knew the history of our world forwards and backwards.

My lips moved, forming the words that Venedikt spoke aloud. "A bargain was struck with the ruler of Blood Valley. He agreed to allow passage of two citizens from each nation once a birth-tide to collect Lufarium in exchange for an end to the war that ravaged our lands for too long. Thus, the founders of our nations proposed a race. Whoever returned first to the hosting nation with the minimum required weight would be honored by all of Triste. A hero forever more."

Though Venedikt didn't say the rest of what we'd all learned in guard training, I replayed the words in my head. *The ruler of Blood Valley was called the Phantom. Having not been seen since Triste broke with Blood Valley, many believe that the title of the Phantom is passed down when one is too old to continue, but others speculate that he is truly a ghost, watching over his people from afar.*

Even with the Phantom's permission to pass through Blood Valley, the Scottomb are wild creatures that hunt without mercy. Then there are the elements which are just as lethal. There's a reason it's called the Blood Run.

Though twenty-two people set out in search of Lufarium, never has that many people returned.

Through the raucous applause, my gaze clashed with Arlakai's, who seemed to have recalled the same speech to mind. On the screen, Venedikt stepped back with the other Council members.

The first ship's door slowly lifted, and three people stepped into the opening. I saw a man, short, but well-built beneath a thick, green, woolen jacket, and matching trousers with an orange stripe down the outside seam. He donned an orange hat tipped to one side of his otherwise bald skull. His lips tilted into a charming smile that he sent the crowd, then the Freejian Council who stood at the entrance to the palace.

"Lockard Brulle, first chairman of the L'Ogustian Council," an unseen, robotic voice announced. When he stepped forward, two more people took his place.

They were younger, though their uniform was the same. I recognized them, even from an image projected into the sky. The girl, likely nineteen or so, had pale hair but a broad jaw. Her companion was slightly older, possibly twenty. He had golden brown hair and bushy eyebrows that detracted from the rest of his attractive face.

"Kesper Hermann and Lialette Fuchs," the announcer stated without inflection. "Contestants from the L'Ogustian Legion."

Like automated bots, they marched out of the ship and followed their representative. One by one, the three of them shook hands with the Freejian Council members.

"Kesper had incredible training scores in the compiled rankings," Charle mused just loud enough for me to hear him.

Nearly everyone held their breath as the second ship's door dropped. Two perfectly built people stared across the grounds at the other ship before they assessed the Council members, and lastly, the frozen tundra that was Freeya.

I recognized Imani's dark, silken mane of waves and her cold stare without the announcer sending her name echoing through the whole of Kilner. The male contestant beside her, who I think was called Daveed, scowled out at the palace with distaste. Both of them wore loose, sleeveless tunics that were blood red, edged with an orange ribbon that reminded me of flames. Neither of them shivered from the cold, but it was clear they didn't enjoy it.

An even larger man with bulging biceps on display, guided them down the platform to where the Council waited.

Arlakai leaned close to me. "Something tells me they don't want to be here."

I nodded, watching their stiff exchange. When they disappeared inside the castle after the L'Ogustian contestants, the procession seemed less tense.

Or maybe it was my own curiosity at Imani's prowess with an echo blade that had made me watch her with bated breath.

Nimua was next with their airy purple and gold uniforms, followed by Roffair.

Each nation's style of dress and customs such as bowing or clasping hands and bowing their heads fascinated me. We'd studied the nations in depth, and I'd seen the live broadcast from my living quarters almost every birth-tide, but still, seeing so many different people in one place was almost magical.

Charle spouted random facts about some of the contestants or their homelands, but when the last contestants emerged from the furthest ship that faced us, my stomach twisted.

Isak from Kondez, and a female that looked shockingly like a relative of his, smirked out over the crowd. And though I knew it was impossible, I could have sworn his gaze lingered on where I stood for just a moment.

Then he was walking toward the palace.

My focus on his back wavered for only a moment. A girl caught my eye in the crowd. She had her back to the palace, staring out at the border.

Only then did I feel the slightest rumble beneath my boots. I whirled just as the city-wide siren shrieked out its warning.

Boom!

The explosion rippled through the crowd, even so far from the border. It was hard to see what had happened, but I knew *who* had caused the disturbance.

Scottomb.

Resounding cries of shock rang out as I pushed my way through. Over my shoulder, I called to Arlakai, "Get Charle home!"

Then I was running, sliding between bodies, and moving faster than I ever had. There were units already stationed at the border, but I wouldn't let a single vile creature step foot inside the city.

Other soldiers who were attending the arrival ceremony thundered after me. I didn't have time to look over my shoulder and make sure that Charle was safe. Not that I needed to. I trusted Arlakai.

The electrified barrier ahead pulsed a deep shade of violet as several large shapes collided with it. My stomach flipped as I recognized what crashed into one of the charged towers over and over.

Old, abandoned airships. How they flew without Lufarium, I didn't know.

They were dented and dinged but their shields were visible. It was a physical impossibility unless someone on the outside had harvested Lufarium to power the ships.

My feet pounded over the snowy walkways, the edge of the city drawing closer. The only weapons I had on me were two echo blades which would do nothing for long range.

Soldiers in the towers rained down lethal blasts on the ships. But I knew from the past two raids that the Scottomb weren't just in the ships.

They were on the ground, waiting for a weakness to present itself.

The barrier flickered again, but my view was blocked while I raced between several buildings. When I reemerged, the border was close. Soldiers stood like a secondary wall, echo bolts aimed and ready.

A rumble shook the ground, harder this time, and vibrated the soles of my boots. The ships made a garbled noise, shaking like a frond in the breeze. I held onto the hope that their engines would soon give out.

The assault from the towers wasn't doing enough with the barrier up, but the alternative would result in a blood bath.

"Hold fire!" someone shouted. It sounded like Erina. "They don't have enough power to knock this tower down."

Just as she said the words, I peered over one of the on-duty soldier's shoulders. The ground churned in a single channel, moving toward the tower at a speed that was too fast to be human or creature.

A machine.

I opened my mouth to scream the words when someone else bellowed, "Tunnel digger!"

There was nothing anyone could do to prevent the inevitable. The rumbling grew louder, and I felt it boring into the frozen ground, tearing right underneath our defenses.

Yet, there was no deafening boom, no explosion. The curved rod that towered high above us tilted slowly, casting a shadow directly over me. I shot to the left, along with at least a dozen other soldiers.

It groaned, cleaving through a building before crashing to the ground. The force of it sent me scrambling.

The city-wide siren changed, a monotone voice stating, "*Border breach detected. Civilians are to follow evacuation protocol. Border breach detected. Civilians are to follow evacuation protocol.*"

I heard the first choked scream less than a breath later. Echofire erupted on the Scottomb now invading Kilner. Bouncing on the balls of my feet, I held my blades at the ready which crackled with lethal energy at my sides.

They materialized like ghosts becoming corporeal. Their taut, translucent skin wrapped around grey bones. Elongated skulls with empty white eyes that had haunted my nightmares popped up before the frontline.

I adjusted my grip on my right blade, preparing for the first Scottomb. My wait was short, the telltale shift of air that rushed at me forcing me to swing. With a hiss, the blade sliced through what felt like nothing, but it wasn't empty.

A shriek that made my ears ache rent the frigid air. It dropped to the ground, solid and grotesque. Its jaw gaped; blackened, broken teeth exposed.

A thin hand covered the wound on its side which leaked thick, dark liquid. Droplets stained the thin layer of snow.

Its pale eyes met mine. With a fierce scream, it lunged. My blades crossed in an arc, slashing for the monster. In a breath, it vanished.

"No!" I bellowed, swinging through the air left, then right. The spray of blood hit my jacket sleeve and coated my hands. It was cold and oily.

Two thumps sounded on the ground beside me, the creature sliced clean in half. I didn't spare it a glance as I faced the battle.

There were at least a hundred Scottomb visible, which meant there were likely half as many trying to fight their way through the ranks, unseen. The two airships had grounded due to mechanical failures, but the tunnel bot continued to bore under Kilner.

My heart pounded. Never had a breach been this successful.

Something hard crashed into me, sending me sprawling on the icy dirt. I grunted, feeling the Scottomb's weight before it appeared, straddling my hips.

Gritting my teeth, I thrust one of my blades forward. With lightning-fast motions, it snagged my wrist, knocking the blade from my hand before it pinned it above my head. It bellowed its fury before rearing back to take a bite out of my neck.

I flipped my grip on my remaining blade then plunged it sideways into the creature's neck.

The Lufarium crackled and sizzled while the Scottomb's eye sockets widened. It tilted sideways, allowing me to slide its hefty weight off me.

A human scream had me scrambling to my feet and searching the sea of monsters and Freejian Guard.

Erina writhed in a Scottomb's hold. Another had its wide mouth latched over her thigh. Blood soaked her trousers. I grabbed my second echo blade and ran.

Clearing my path with brutal slashes, I just managed not to trip on a Scottomb gutted from neck to abdomen. The putrid smell invaded my nostrils.

Erina's weapon laid in the bloody snow just out of reach. I leapt between two guards and let a blade fly. It hit the Scottomb holding Erina, knocking the beast back. She used her fist, pummeling the other's oblong head until it finally released her leg. The torn flesh and tissue were exposed, drawing the attention of every Scottomb in the near vicinity.

I reached her side a moment later, plucking my blade from the fallen creature's skull.

"You're creating a gap, soldier," she snapped with a tightness that I knew meant she was in a great deal of pain. "We cannot let any through our ranks."

"Yeah, no problem for helping save your leg. Any time, Erina," I replied sarcastically as I flicked my wrist, sending another blade into the chest of a Scottomb that tried to use its disappearing act.

The captain huffed. "I'll thank you when they're all dead and our border is sealed."

"Fair enough," I called back, slicing into a creature's back as it attempted to run. It dropped with a strangled scream.

Finally, I reached her echo bolt and snatched it just as a Scottomb lunged for it. With my other hand, I buried my weapon between its eerie, empty eyes.

I stood, wielding the gun just in time to fire a shot directly into a bony creature whose face was splattered with crimson. Passing the echo bolt back to Erina, I turned the hilt of my familiar blades over in my palms. Their heat was near blistering, but soothing.

I slashed through body after body, fighting beside the woman who barely tolerated me until my face was sticky with foreign blood. Somehow, I didn't need to *see* them. I could feel them move. Feel their breaths on my skin. My mind barely registered their faces as I slaughtered them. Instead, I remember the breach from when I was only six birth-tides. The soldiers cutting through the monsters with skilled ease.

Swipe.

Duck.

Kick, jab, spin.

I could feel the raw sensation of screaming in my throat even with my lips pressed into a thin line. My chest heaved with each breath as I looked around, finding the last few visible Scottomb falling to the ground.

Instinctively, I looked out into Blood Valley. Movement behind one of the fallen, smoking ships had my feet moving.

Erina shouted my name, but I didn't stop. My fingers flexed around my blades as my arms pumped in time with each step. Echofire blasted past me, the raw energy heating the side of my face.

The further from the Freejian border I got, the warmer the air grew.

I rounded the side of the ship, poised to strike. Nothing moved that I could sense. My gaze scanned all around while I waited for them to attack, but whatever had caught my attention remained was somehow gone.

Chapter 5

Ferrah

The bots arrived to repair the border almost as soon as I crossed back into Freeya. Luckily, the tunnel digger was able to be accessed and controlled remotely, which stopped its path beneath Kilner.

We spent another rotation collecting the Scottomb's bodies and loading them into the airship that took them for disposal.

By the time I was walking back to my housing quarters, I felt a sharp sting under the band of my wrist communicator, making me suck in a breath. The device chirped, and I swiped a finger over the screen to read the message.

10 agm of aetharus administered

The booster shot was given whenever there was a border breach or anyone ventured outside of Freeya since the air in Blood Valley was considered dangerous, containing pathogens that our science had conquered.

When I secured the pod to my window and climbed inside, Nona rushed in through the door to my sleeping quarters.

"Where is Charle?" she demanded. "He never made it home after the attack! You know better than to leave him alone—"

My heart shot into my throat, and I thought I might puke it out. Opening the menu to my wrist communicator, I selected Kai's contact.

It buzzed once. Twice. Three times. Then the error flashed: Arlakai Monius is unable to answer your communication. Please try again later.

I swallowed hard, still drowning out whatever Nona was saying in favor of turning toward the window. One hand shoved into the pocket of my heavy coat and wrapped around the comforting wooden music box. I held it tight, as though it would keep me from drowning in the tumultuous sea of panic raging within me.

"He might be at Kai's place," I offered by way of placation, then jumped back into my pod, cutting off whatever response she might have given.

Soaring through Kilner faster than I ever had, I made it to the building my best friend lived in within record time. It was just as tall as the one I resided in, but the white paint that coated the outside was beginning to chip off, and the structure itself looked like it was in need of heavy maintenance.

The lift—similar to ours—clanged and jittered as it took me up to the fifth floor. My thumb feverishly stroked the carving atop the music box. The bird's head was smooth from my incessant rubbing. When my thumb reached the sharper point of the flower held in its beak, I pressed down hard enough to hurt, even after I rushed through the hall to the last door on the left. My fist lifted, and I heard the sound of happy laughter.

Swallowing down my nerves, I knocked. The time that it took for Kai to answer the door had my heart thrashing against my ribcage.

It zipped open and Kai's eyes widened to find me standing before him. "Fairs—"

I pushed past him. "Please tell me Charle is here, Nona said—" my words cut off when I saw Daria's reddish-brown curls leaning over a makeshift tabletop from old crates, Charle watching her hand move freely with awe. My grip on the music box eased, and slowly I pulled my hand from my pocket.

At my entrance into the room, his gaze lifted, meeting mine.

"Why didn't you let Nona know you were safe?" My voice was filled with harsh anger, though it broke on the last word, betraying the surge of emotion.

Kai's brows pinched. "I sent you a communication to let you know I'd brought him here. The way to your building was blocked off with ships."

I frowned, checking my device, but there were no missed communications. "I'd tried to call your device as well and it said you were unavailable. I thought something bad happened."

Kai grabbed my arms and pulled me to his chest for a tight hug. "I'm sorry to have worried you. Maybe you should have your communicator looked at to make sure it isn't faulty."

I nodded, pushing away from him.

He flashed me an apologetic smile. "Stay for dinner?"

My eyes went to Charle and Daria who laughed at something she said, and a smile tugged at my lips. "Sure, just let me send a message to Nona."

After scanning our ID's, the chute delivered our prepared meals. I got a soup with meat and vegetables while Kai got some sort of meat log.

"I know it doesn't have that extra flair like your Nona does," Kai said a little sheepishly.

A smirk played on my lips. "I wouldn't trust you adding anything extra to my meals, Monius. Not after you managed to set a batch of sweets on fire."

We both laughed, then settled into discussing the contestants, and who was most likely to freeze to death, or die from dehydration.

"Nimua is always the weakest nation," Charle pointed out. His dinner had gone mostly untouched, and my heart constricted. I knew he didn't want Daria to watch him struggle.

Kai's younger sister put her spoon down, looking only at Charle. "I'll be shocked if Kondez lasts more than a handful of light-rises."

"Isak is clever and conniving. He'll use the rest of them as shields the whole way, as long as it means he makes it back alive." The words spilled out of me before I had time to stop them.

Both Charle and Kai gave me a hard look.

"Is he still bugging you?" my brother asked. I'd told him about the various run-ins I'd had with Isak in passing. Charle had been the one to point out that it was weird that Isak—a fairly low-ranking Kondez soldier—was the one to come to Freeya for delegation business, sometimes in the stead of the Kondez Council, but I was fairly certain that he weaseled his way into Freeya at every opportunity just to torment me.

My gaze snapped to Kai's, a warning in my eyes. I didn't want my brother to know Kai and I went scavenging to sell artifacts. Fortunately, my best friend seemed to be on the same page and inclined his head before taking a sip of his canister of water.

"Only when I have to see his ugly face," I answered Charle, smirking as everyone laughed.

My brother's amusement turned into a hacking cough that made my stomach clench. He wheezed, struggling to draw in enough air.

I stood up suddenly. "Let's get you back before Nona drags us home," my voice stayed light for Daria's sake, though I wouldn't take any arguments from Charle.

Fortunately, he relented, his lungs rattling with each labored breath. Kai helped load Charle's chair into the pod, and we flew home.

I glanced in my brother's direction, finding his head resting against the glass dome, his attention on the city below us. "You okay?"

He stayed silent long enough to make me think he wasn't going to answer, before he said, "I'm going to die, Ferrah. No surgery is going to stop that."

My heart constricted; my lungs unable to draw in air. "Why would you say that?" I asked, my voice laced with anger and hurt.

His shoulder lifted just enough to make out a shrug. "I've looked at the statistics. Even if you could get me the surgery next lunar-shift, it would likely only add a few birth-tides to my life. And that's if the Council will approve it. I'm a drain on society. They don't let people like me live for long."

A burning sensation in my throat had me swallowing hard. "Don't say that crap, Charle. I'll do whatever it takes." I met his gaze, making sure he knew I was serious.

He turned his attention to Kilner again. "I know." His answer fractured my heart, but if he thought that would discourage me from competing in the Blood Run, he was mistaken.

It solidified my purpose. I wouldn't let Charle die.

The Council would have to break me into a thousand pieces before I let them touch him.

Chapter 6

Ferrah

I met Arlakai at the base of the palace ground's steps. His jaw was tight, and his eyes red, dark smudges lining underneath. Whatever had happened after Charle and I left, he didn't voice it.

"You should have had some pryani," I teased lightly. When he didn't smile like he usually would have, I bumped my shoulder against his. "Did you sleep at all?"

He ran a hand through the rusty curls piled atop his head. "I doubt it."

My hand found his, our fingers weaving together. I squeezed gently, offering silent reassurance. I hadn't slept much either, and when I'd left Nona and Charle this morning, they'd both had a hard time looking me in the eyes. It was as if I were facing a death sentence, not a chance at restoring Charle to a better quality of life. No matter what though, I wanted to assure Arlakai that we would still be best friends, and I would do whatever it took to keep Charle and Daria alive.

The courtyard steadily filled with hundreds of soldiers that all faced a raised platform in front of the palace that must have been erected sometime before this light-rise. A massive screen twinkled in front of one of the icy walls with the symbol of united Triste—a tree with hundreds of branches that wove around the spaces which represented the unified nations.

Long, lethal-looking icicles hung from the dips and peaks of the palace roof while a fresh dusting of white coated the entire structure.

If not for the tense atmosphere among those gathered, I would have thought the place serene. My own pulse spiked when the doors opened, and the Council members filed out in their fur-trimmed robes.

Arlakai squeezed my hand in return, seeming to sense my growing anxiety. Chatter among the hundreds of guard members fell silent, as the Council took the stage.

The woman that stepped forward—Council Lady Ellitebet—was tall, her robes a pale cream color with fur spotted white and brown around the collar. But it was the gems sewn throughout the entirety of the fabric that made it glitter and sparkle. Her hair was white to match the snow, falling behind her slender shoulders in tight curls.

She was beautiful, despite her lips pressed into a hard line. Even her eyes were a pale, icy blue. She looked as though Freeya itself created her. Cold and harsh, yet breathtaking.

My communicator vibrated, letting me know a broadcast had begun.

Just before her lips parted, the door to the palace swung open again, the audible groan of its weight echoing through the silent courtyard. Each of Triste's selected contestants strode out onto the stage, lining the crystalline wall closest to where Arlakai and I stood.

As much as I tried to ignore the Kondez contingent, I found Isak staring right at me, a smirk pulling at his thick lips. My eyes narrowed on him before I pulled my gaze back to Council Lady Ellitebet.

"Now that we're all here," the ethereal woman said in a voice that was magnified, echoing off the palace walls. "It is a longstanding tradition that the host nation of the Blood Run draws their contestants last, to allow a sense of unity with those racing for their own nations. So, without further ado... the random selection from the Freejian Guard."

The screen showed names that came and went too fast to read. My chest tightened as I held my breath, staring up at the screen. Arlakai stepped closer, sliding an arm around my waist. I felt eyes on me and flicked my attention back across the stage to where Isaak stood, still watching me.

My heart felt as though it would rip through my chest at any moment. Still the names scrolled, slowing, but each click felt like it stretched out into snaps.

For Charle, for Charle, for Charle...

Finally, it stopped, two names illuminated brightly on the screen.

Domivit Leer- Gaerf

Henny Zjarg- Elemen

I barely had time to read the names before the screen flickered to black, static scratching through the speakers on everyone's communicator. The lump in my throat threatened to choke me.

"No," I breathed. *It can't be. Charle. Oh, sacred tree, Charle will die.* Tears stung the backs of my eyelids.

A gasp rang out, forcing my eyes open again. The names that blinked back into view looked large enough to jump off the screen and ram themselves down my throat.

Domivit Leer- Gaerf

Ferrah Zunnock- Kilner

Deafening silence stretched through the courtyard. I blinked at the screen; certain the names would cycle again. When they didn't, and a hesitant applause began, I finally heard Arlakai's voice.

His lips tickled the top of my ear as he said thickly, "Don't worry, Fairy, I'm not letting you go out there without me. I'll fix this."

Council Lady Ellitibet's smile was brittle. "Congrats to this birth-tide's runners, I know you'll serve Freeya well."

My wrist communicator chirped, a message shining brilliantly. I stared at it, uncomprehending for several moments.

Congratulations, Ferrah Dunnock. You were selected for the 212th annual Blood Run. Please collect your belongings and report to the palace by 08,79 dark.

Arlakai's grip on my shoulder tightened as he hauled me through the crowd. I glanced behind me, up at the stage to where Isak stood, a grin curving his lips. Soldiers watched us go with something like hostility on their faces.

Whoever Henny was, if she'd seen that her name had been drawn first, she would no doubt be furious at whatever had happened. The glitch was odd enough, but the way the Kondez contestants had their eyes on me the entire time made my gut twist.

"I wasn't chosen," I said to no one, but it came out sounding as guilty as I felt.

"All that matters is that the Council now recognizes you as a contestant," Arlakai responded. He was practically dragging me down the steps until I finally dug my heels in, yanking myself out of his hold.

"Kai," I snapped, forcing him to look at me. Soft, puffy flakes of white fell from a darkening grey sky, nipping at my cheeks and dusting my best friend's red curls.

He shoved his fingers through his hair, turning to look out over Kilner. His silence made the knot in my chest double in size.

"What in the sacred tree was that back there?" I asked, knowing he didn't have the answers I wanted. Hysteria built in my chest, swelling and choking off my breath.

His green eyes locked with mine for several long beats. The war of emotions going on inside him played easily across his handsome features. His brows pinched together as he released a ragged breath. "I don't know, Fairs. Clearly the system malfunctioned. But for a moment I..." He swallowed audibly, his Adam's apple bobbing. "I genuinely thought you were safe."

But in the split click that Henny's name had been on the screen before mine took her place, it wasn't relief I'd felt. It was cold, sheer terror for Charle.

Yet, now all I could think about was the fact that I'd be running with Domivit. Not Arlakai.

Of course, I'd considered what would happen if only one of us was selected, but the reality was as harsh as the winter air.

"I thought it would be us together," I said. "Even though we were up against thousands of other Freejians, I had this perfect scenario in my head. But now—"

"Stop." Arlakai's voice was cold. "I'm not letting you do this alone."

"Kai…" I reached for his face while storms brewed in his eyes. He stepped back, forcing my hand to fall uselessly to my side. "It's going to be okay," I finished lamely.

He nodded stiffly. "Yes," he agreed, but the single word felt less like a promise and more like a threat.

Without any further chatter, he stalked down the steps. I followed after him, my mind and heart racing.

Tonight, I would leave my family to enter the contestants training. And in two light-rises, the Blood Run would begin.

My first step into the apartment was met with Nona and Daria standing near the gate, their arms crossed. Arlakai crossed the space to his sister and swept her up, twirling her around into a tight hug.

The young girl with wild, fiery red hair wrapped her arms around her brother's neck. Beneath her loose woolen trousers were metal casings around her legs, secured at the hip. The robotic appendages were able to help her walk and stand upright, unlike Charle.

Nona didn't move, her eyes boring into me while I watched Arlakai and Daria. Charle's chair whirred to a stop in the entrance way, a grim expression curving his lips downward.

"I'm guessing you all saw the draw," I said with as much levity as I could muster.

Nona harrumphed. "Of course we did, child."

I lifted my gaze to meet hers, finding a look of accusation staring back at me. "All of it, going by that loving look you're wearing." My voice had more bite than I'd intended.

"I suppose you think you're going to just march into Blood Valley, grab as much Lufarium as you can, and skip your way back home?" Her cool tone had everyone watching us now.

My chin tilted up, defiance surging through me. "No, Nona, I've seen the broadcasts. We've watched every Blood Run since I was a child. I've poured over the archived broadcasts of many more. I don't expect this to be easy."

"Good," she snapped. "Because that's how you'll end up *dead*." Turning on her heel, she stormed through the apartment, disappearing behind her door that slid shut.

I looked to Arlakai for support, and he cast me a knowing expression. Finally, I focused on Charle, realizing in that moment just how much I wanted him to accept this. To be happy that I secured this chance for us.

My brother offered no such sentiment. "When do you leave?"

"Charle, you have to know I'm doing this for you. For all of us." I wanted him to see reason, but before the words were even out of my mouth, I knew I wouldn't get that.

He nodded slowly. Then to Daria, he said, "Want to help finish the jel?"

She smiled, stepping away from her brother before turning jerkily to face me. Her long, golden lashes fluttered, and she said, "I think you're really brave, Ferrah."

I returned the gesture with the best smile I could manage. After she and Charle retreated into the cooking room, my shoulders sagged.

"So much for honor and glory," I muttered.

Arlakai reached out a hand to me, and I slid my calloused palm over his. "What did you expect their reaction to be?" he asked.

I shrugged, the two of us heading into the media room to sit on the padded seats, our legs brushing. Taking in the sight of our hands still clasped, overwhelming sadness washed over me. Soon I would not get this time with him. Not for many light-rises, assuming I survived.

"At least acceptance, I guess. They've known since I joined the guard that my only hope was to compete in the Blood Run. I have to, Kai." My voice lowered. "For Charle."

My friend nodded. "I know. Give them both a few snaps to adjust to the news. Then enjoy these last few rotations with them. And with me."

I let my head rest against his shoulder. The only projector, supplied by the Council, played a loop of old Blood Run footage along with announcers discussing each tactic and pitfall, though the sound was switched off. I tried not to focus on any of it, but when a band of Scottomb ambushed a young girl, the clip of her stabbing them with her blades over and over until she was coated in gore, I couldn't look away.

Soon, every device in Triste would be playing footage of *me* in Blood Valley. Every slip. Every kill. Each element of the next lunar shift would be scrutinized and watched as pure entertainment. Those of us that didn't make it would be forgotten.

But I had no plans to be one of them.

CHAPTER 7

Raiden

A rare smile tugged at my lips when Ferrah's name was announced. I had no doubt her country would choose her. And soon, she'd be in my realm.

The land of monsters.

I didn't know what I'd say or do when we eventually met face to face, and she saw who had watched over her from afar.

It was something I'd spent far too much time imagining. Hearing her laugh. Being the one to make her smile.

A familiar burn in my shoulder blades had my muscles twitching. I tilted my head to one side, then the other, trying to ease the discomfort. With a long sigh, I turned away from the border that had been wide open for several rotations. If I'd wanted to slip inside Freeya, it would have been alarmingly easy.

But there was no need to sneak into her world. I'd patiently waited to properly meet her for most of her life. A few more light-rises wouldn't make any difference.

Besides, I had things to do. Duties that couldn't be ignored no matter how much I sometimes wished to.

Sweltering heat bared down on me, while a huddle of kwipai scuttling in the distance to forage for food. Only the sound of my boots crunching on brittle rock kept me company during my trek.

Sweat dampened my cloak, but I didn't dare remove it. Any exposed skin in Blood Valley was a feast for the insects that were roughly the size of my hand—fingertip to the edge of my palm. They flew in hordes, scenting out their prey.

The light faded to brushes of gold and red in the sky as I made it into the village. My stomach grumbled, the aromas of savory delights seeping from the dining house.

Within an enclosed, reinforced building, workers peered through the windows to watch me pass. A tall figure rushed up the road in my direction, his hood lowered to shield his face, but I knew who it was anyway.

"Devlin," I greeted when the man was close enough to hear me. My ruined voice was just another reminder of everything I'd lost—of the things I fought to change.

"Raiden, just in time," he said with a tinge of excitement. With one hand, he pulled his hood back, revealing one yellow eye as well as an empty socket. His scalp was free of hair, but symbols were inked around the sides, disappearing down his neck. "There's a meeting in the hall in a rotation. Whispers carried this far north say that the Phantom may make an appearance."

I snorted a laugh. "Wouldn't that be a sight?"

Devlin smirked. "Blood Valley is finally uniting. If the Phantom still exists, he or she'll have to take notice."

"*If* he exists, there's no way he hasn't already noticed how Triste shut us out and murdered millions of our people." My words were tight, but Devlin nodded in agreement.

"Was your journey long, *diyon*?" he asked, guiding me back toward his housing quarters which was barely a shack. The word 'son' in the old language of Krovaya constricted the barely beating organ inside my chest. So few of our people were left to remember the old way of life—our forgotten traditions, or our language.

Despite the gnawing hunger in my gut and the effects of the heat having worn me down, I shrugged. "I've endured far longer."

Already the heat was slipping away, fading into the darkness where cold reigned. We wove through the cone-shaped homes, the villagers bringing in their washing so it didn't freeze, or heading to the main hall where they all ate.

Devlin stopped at his hut, the wide, bluish leaves that made up the exterior walls were hardened with morjil sap. It was a seamless waterproofing that had been used throughout Blood Valley for eons.

He lifted the door on the ground, revealing steps that led below. I listened for sounds, but beyond the stirrings of villagers around, I couldn't sense anyone else. Descending the steps into a dark room, I didn't wait for Devlin before crossing the room with practiced ease. Not that it mattered, my vision adapted to both light and dark seamlessly. The crack of a match turned to a fizzle. A single flame flickered to life, Devlin set it in the lantern, allowing light to spread. I surveyed the small living space with a sense of fondness.

A bed spanned across the wall to my left, a bronze chest beside the head which held nearly all of Devlin's personal effects. To the right was a circular tub used for bathing and washing clothing. It wasn't the lavish washing chambers I'd encountered in other places, but it did the job.

In the center of the room stood a cylindrical heating unit that stretched up into the peaked roof. It began to hum, the deep red glow inside emanating between the rows of slits that decorated the tube. From there, a trickle of heat started to combat the cold that was descending on all of Blood Valley.

The dirt floor was a muddy red color, but as Devlin pulled a bed roll from his chest and spread it out on the floor perpendicular to where he'd sleep, I offered a smile. "Of all the places I've crashed, this is my favorite."

The older man grunted. "Liar." Straightening, he turned to the tub. "I'll let you get cleaned up and bring some food back before the meeting begins."

"Rewards heaped upon your head, Devlin." I intoned the saying of thanks, meeting his one eye.

He bowed his head, then wordlessly vanished back up the stairs, ensuring the door was locked before I heard his steps moving away from the hut.

The water that poured into the silver tub was cold, but I didn't care, letting the icy temperature pull away the sticky heat that still clung to my skin. I sank under the surface, letting my thoughts get away from me. The moment I saw the young face of a woman with hair so black it was almost blue, and a man with stormy grey eyes, I fought to clear my mind.

No matter how hard I tried to dismiss the recurring memory, I still heard her screams of pain while watching men haul her away. The lick of flames devouring my flesh as I crawled with Sammy to the window. I could recall her terror so clearly, though the rest of the details were more hazy now. Instinctively, I put a hand to my cheek, tracing the scars that had faded over time.

The ever-present pressure within my chest grew, an ache spreading through my veins like a toxin. Alone, the shadows pressed in, ready to attack. They hungered for my blood.

Softly the melody of the music my mother had created for me trickled in, bringing with it a determination to bring justice to my people.

My eyes opened, the water rippling above me slightly as I let the air in my lungs go in a steady stream. I broke the surface, sitting up with my back against the edge of the cool tub.

Shoving the sodden dark locks of hair from my eyes, I grabbed the bar of soap from the metal edge.

Being alone was a curse I lived with, but people like Devlin eased that pain. People that deserved better than what they had.

And I planned to help them get it...with Ferrah's help.

The girl who was much like me.

Alone despite being surrounded by people.

Roughly a hundred people were packed inside the dining hall looking like caged animals ready to claw their way out. Not because they didn't want to be here; no, the tension in the air was solidly to do with the rumors of the Phantom making an appearance.

Before the excitement got to be too much, Devlin took to the stage and a respectful hush fell on their gathering.

"The eleven nations' runners will leave Freeya in a matter of light-rises. Dissent has spread throughout the whole of Blood Valley, and for once our forgotten people have joined together. Now is the time to end the Blood Run once and for all!"

An explosion of pride surged through the room in a cacophony of cheers and applause. A larger, bulkier man with a bushy beard took the stage as well before clapping Devlin on the back. He grinned out at the people, dark eyes snagging on where I stood in the shadows.

Finally the hall began to quieten, and the man that looked familiar some-how began to speak.

"My village out west has been preparing for this time since the last Blood Run. We have enough volunteers for a convoy to strike once the runners are far enough away from the Freejian border, but we're asking any villages nearby to help as well. These soldiers are deadly with their advanced weaponry. However, we will have the element of surprise."

More cheers erupted. Ice slid into my gut like a hefty brick. I got to my feet, and the man on stage paused "They will have their hover bots that will be watching," I let my voice carry over the din, and silence from everyone around me followed. "If you attack while still inside the cradle of the eleven nations, they'll all launch their own counterattacks. The level of war that will descend is beyond anything you could possibly comprehend."

A smirk twisted the man's features. "And what would you know of it, lad?"

My jaw clenched. "The nations are far more powerful than we could ever hope to be when divided. If you wait for them to get further south and pick them off one-by-one, then they'll just see it as part of their game. Better yet, just ensure that none of them can get their hands on Lufarium."

"If we simply deny them Lufarium, their armies will converge on the mines and they'll take it all," a man in the crowd shouted.

"Maybe we should *let* them take it all," another called. "If they don't have any reason to come into Blood Valley, then they'll leave us alone."

"They won't stop!" My voice boomed through the hall, abruptly halting any other unsolicited opinions. "When they run out of Lufarium, it'll just be something else that they continue their game for. Who knows, maybe one light-rise it'll be to hunt us all down. They're barbarians and it's time they remember that Blood Valley will not stand for it any longer."

"Here, here!"

The man on the stage raised his hands to call for silence yet again, though it took a moment or so for the voices to abate. It was clear that he was having a hard time keeping the attention of everyone in the hall, and I couldn't help but smirk at that.

"Our convoy will take out the cameras first, then we strike. Any that wishes to join us need only be at Jatal Village the light-rise after tomorrow by sunrise." His cold eyes swung back to me, daring me to challenge him again. "With or without the elusive Phantom, it's time that Blood Valley put an end to the Blood Run!"

I slipped out of the hall, unable to listen to roar of excitement building within. They were all fools if they thought that starting a war unprepared was their best chance at ending the race that slaughtered so many of their kind.

Besides that, I wasn't about to let Ferrah be killed the moment she stepped outside of her walled prison. Which meant, I had a convoy to stop.

Chapter 8

Ferrah

I'd hugged and kissed Charle and Nona until my eyes burned with tears that I refused to shed in front of them. Arlakai walked with me to the palace, silence sitting heavily between us.

My breath rolled like a storm cloud from my parted lips. Guards stood like they were sculpted from ice, but their eyes were on us. Kai shuffled a boot over loose snow, seeming as reluctant to say goodbye as I was. My gloved hand twirled the wooden carving tucked into my pocket, feeling all the once-pointed edges that I'd worn down over time.

Just as I thought of something to say, my words were cut off.

"Lieutenant Zunnock, you must be shown to your temporary quarters," one of the eerily still guards said.

Glancing at Kai again, he finally lifted his head, but the sadness I expected to find in his expression was absent. Raw determination tightened his features.

"I'll be back soon," I said with a forced smile.

Wordlessly, he pulled me into a tight hug. Not the kind of hug that said goodbye, or see you soon. No, it felt like a normal, quick hug that made my chest constrict.

The guards moved in tandem to either side of me, directing me to the grand double doors. I told myself it was better this way. That I'd end up crying on the palace steps, which wouldn't do anyone any favors. I managed only a glance back at my best friend, hoping he could read in my expression all the things I hadn't had the chance to say.

He watched me go with only a slight incline of his head, which I took to mean, he understood. That he would take care of Charle and Nona as best he could in my absence.

They'll be safe, I told myself as I followed the nameless men. They ushered me through a dimly lit hall, and into an opulent glass lift. As it began to move, the awkward silence between the three of us dissipated. Beyond the glass were at least half a dozen landings filled with people. Some of them sat in darkened spaces with glasses in hand, watching something I couldn't see.

Others milled through the hall, heading for some unknown destination. It all flashed by so fast I barely had time to catch the minimal details, but I doubted I'd have time to explore the palace before the run began.

The lift finally stopped, and the taller guard gestured to the open hall with a grunt to get me moving. It was lavish—the small, golden carvings atop the wainscoting made to look like the three-headed wolven our nation had emblazoned into our emblems.

When I'd gotten to the room I was meant to stay the night in, the guards turned and left unceremoniously. I'd barely shut the door behind me before finally letting the tears fall.

Panic swelled like a dam ready to burst. I hadn't said a proper goodbye to anyone—not only that, but at first light, I'd be subjected to all the horrors of Blood Valley for at least one lunar shift.

My breaths came in labored bursts while I attempted to rein in my emotions. Then, my communicator dinged.

I wiped away the snot and tears, forcing several steadying breaths through my nose as my brother's face filled the projection. His eyes were red-rimmed, just like mine.

"Fairs?" he said tentatively.

I had to be calm for him, even if I didn't feel it. "Yeah?"

"I know you'll win. I love you. Nona too, even though she seems upset."

I nodded, holding back another wave of emotion with the final threads of my frayed resolve. "I love you too. See you soon, little brother."

After Charle ended the communication, I cried some more. The sounds of Nona cooking, preparing some old-fashioned dish that would no doubt be followed by another and another until she used up her stockpile of illegal ingredients had been the only heartfelt farewell I'd receive.

I hoped Arlakai and Daria would help Nona and Charle eat all of the delights that Nona prepared as her way of working through her emotions. I'd tried to call him to ask if he'd check on her tomorrow, but the communication wouldn't go through. After trying several more times, I abandoned my communicator beside me on the gaudy mattress stitched with Freeya's wolven emblem.

My gaze fixed to the ceiling, letting each snap pass me by while mindlessly glancing at my silent communicator over and over to see if Arlakai was trying to contact me. In the passing rotations I waited for any sort of instruction about tomorrow, but the snaps turned to rotations and my eyelids grew impossibly heavy.

I fought their pull, but in the end, I gave in, knowing I needed the sleep.

Explosions rocked the ground beneath my shoes. My small body went flying, the doll I'd been holding careening out of my hold. I opened my mouth to cry out, but the air was caught in my lungs. My ears rang so loudly I couldn't hear anything else. Dirt and specks of something dark floated to the ground as if in slow motion like snow.

A face peered over me—a boy's face. He was young but quite a bit older than me, with something black smudged across his cheek.

"Are you okay?" The boy's voice was rough, like rocks, and sounded like it was far away.

I blinked once. Twice. Then nodded. He reached out a hand to pull me up, and I accepted it. His grip was firm as he pulled me away from the chaos, behind the cover of a building before he released me.

"Where are your parents?" the boy asked.

"Gone." I wasn't sure if I whispered or screamed the word.

His expression changed, showing he understood. It was just me and Charle. "You have to get somewhere safe. The soldiers have weapons."

I looked around, frowning. "Weapons?" I'd never heard the word.

"Echo bolts," he corrected.

I shrugged. "They won't hurt me. The monsters will." All around us people shouted and ran for the hole in the border. Some of them fired at things I couldn't see. But for some reason, I didn't want to run away. I wanted to stay with this boy. He was nice.

His face screwed up like he was hurt. "Neither one is good. What's your name, flower?"

"No, it's Ferrah," I answered. My hand grabbed him again, hoping to pull him the rest of the way to my quarters, away from all the noise and danger, but his feet stayed rooted in place.

"I can't go any further, Ferrah," he said gently.

I frowned. "What do you mean?"

He smiled sadly. "I don't belong in Freeya. But I'll stay by the wall and if you ever need me, I'll sit with you, okay?"

I nodded, still not understanding why he was here if he didn't belong in Freeya. When his hand released mine, I felt terror taking hold of me. He pulled a wooden figurine from his pocket and held it up. It was a carved bird carrying a single flower in its beak atop a box with a metallic bar sticking out of the side.

Wordlessly, he pressed it into my hands, a small smile curving his lips, and this time, it wasn't sad. I liked that he wasn't sad. "This will keep you from feeling so alone."

I frowned. "Where are you going?"

"Home," he answered. Then he slipped away from me, back into the chaos.

"The number one threat to each of you will not be the Scottomb, it will be the elements." Nuhelle—the leader of the United Empiric Guard—paced atop the raised platform before us. "You will be equipped with a manual Aetharus injector should your bands fail or be broken. If you fail to keep your Aetharus status up to date, your health will fail. Those of you from northern nations will be given an extra immunity booster since you will be faced with vastly different climate changes which may make you susceptible to illness."

I glanced down the row of contestants to see if any of them found that chunk of information strange, but when Isak caught my gaze and shot me a smirk, I focused my attention back on the information I needed to help ensure my survival. Still, I had questions, but for now at least, they would go unanswered.

Disease and illnesses were eradicated thousands of birth-tides ago. So why would we suddenly be vulnerable to such weaknesses? I knew our daily injections were what kept us in perfect health, but I wanted to know more. Call it simple curiosity.

Nuhelle pulled a roll of tablets from a standard guard-issue bag in front of her. She popped one from the casing and held the white, oblong shape up for us to see. "Everyone will have a hundred water tablets which, if rationed properly, will last you well to the end of the race." Next, she grabbed an empty canister, unscrewed the lid, and then demonstrated crushing the tablet before dropping it into the canteen.

"Despite the arid climate you will be faced with, each pill pulls water molecules from the air, which is then filtered, creating enough drinking water to last you a few rotations." She shook the canteen slightly, and water sloshed around inside.

My eyes widened. I had assumed the contestants in previous runs had simply found fresh water sources to drink from that weren't toxic, but with such handy tablets, this would speed things up.

"Any water you find in the valley will most likely be poisoned, even to the touch. As you know from watching previous races, even the rain can be deadly. Which brings me to your only form of shelter." She pulled out a large, square device that snapped up into a tent-like structure complete with metal rods for support. Her voice faded in my mind as I recalled one particular clip that I'd seen from my studies of past years.

One where the rain that fell was pure acid, burning through the tent that Nuhelle demonstrated closing back up into a neat square to stuff inside the bag. The acid rain had sliced through flesh and bone, leaving the few contestants who'd been caught in the storm to burn in agony until their hearts exploded.

It was a gruesome way to die.

Not that dying in the valley was ever a pleasant experience. Beside me, sweat beaded on Domivit's forehead, his face taking on a greenish hue. I didn't know him beyond our basic introduction, but I couldn't help feeling the need to reassure him. With a nudge from my shoulder, I cast him a smile that I hoped would help settle his nerves, but instead, a tremor began in his hands that he wrung together as though he could squeeze the anxiety visibly taking hold of him from his body.

I swallowed hard. Clearly my partner was having major life regrets. Such behavior would get us both killed.

Leaning close, I snapped, "Pull it together. You signed up for this."

His eyes went wide, stunned that I'd gone from trying to calm him gently, to resorting to anger. He sidestepped further away from me, his throat working before he appeared to have somewhat mastered his palpable fear.

"The bot that will be trailing you is programmed to your tracking device. As with all Blood Runs, your moves will be recorded and televised—some of it will be live. It is how we ensure the citizens in Blood Valley don't violate the treaty, but also to bring glory and valor to each of the nations. This birth-tide is a little different, however. The Empress herself assigned you all a specific task which you will find on your communicator once the race has begun. For some, your message won't arrive until you're deep within Blood Valley."

"Why not now?" A boy from Tiau called out.

Nuhelle huffed, like the answer was obvious. "So that everyone starts with a fair advantage. Your missions will likely take you to different parts of Blood Valley, so your messages will be staggered based on calculations of time it will take to travel to each location."

Murmurs rustled the stale, recycled air in the room. *We are all going to different locations? Does this mean we aren't mining Lufarium?* That was the whole point of this race.

Someone else beat me to that thought, asking it aloud.

"Yes, if at all possible, you are to return with the one-hundred vecks of Lufarium. As a reminder, your backpack has a built in scale that will tell you if you've harvested enough."

Panic soured my gut, thinking of Henny's name who'd flashed before mine. What if I wouldn't get a task because it was supposed to go to her? What if they discovered this was all one big misunderstanding?

"Only you are to know what your individual task is. Your bravery and courageous drive have brought you to this moment. Let it lead you to our Empire's slowly dying heart, and back again. Because of runners like you, we can sustain our nations with an energy source that cannot be bested by the Scottomb. On behalf of the entire Council, we thank you for your sacrifice."

Nuhelle crossed her hands, entwining her fingers into the Empire's salute, and we all echoed the gesture. The silence that followed rang in my ears.

Individual tasks.

"Proceed through the door on your right where you will receive your packs. The race will begin in one rotation."

My pulse kicked up its pace. Excitement and nervousness thrummed through me like the static hum of a border tower. In a matter of snaps, we'd be placed at the edge of Freeya, and I would cross into the Valley for the second time in two light-risess. Only this time, I wouldn't be going back until my mission was completed.

You may not come back at all, my dark, inner voice quipped. Steeling my spine, I silenced that thought and followed the others through to the next room.

It was smaller than the one we'd been in, with benches and lockers where bags and uniforms hung beneath a small golden plaque with a name engraved on each. I went down the row until I found mine.

Others had already begun to strip, putting on the provided jumpsuits.

"I hear your echo blade record was the one I beat," a haughty feminine voice said from behind me.

I turned, finding Imani standing there, already suited up, with her backpack already secured. She looked lean and deadly in the outfit.

"Guess so," I answered, trying not to sound like a petulant child. Extending a hand and a small smile, I added, "The sacred tree has favored you."

She snorted a laugh, somehow still managing to make it sound musical. "Hard work and dedication are why I beat you. And it's how I'll win this race."

I offered her a sickly-sweet smile while silently hoping a kwipai would eat her the moment we stepped into Blood Valley.

"Your confidence is so inspiring." I placed a hand over my heart in mock awe. "I just hope it's not misplaced."

Her look of smug satisfaction wilted. "Don't worry," she hissed, stepping so close I could see my reflection in her dark brown eyes, "it's not." Then she spun on her heel and started stretching by the exit, which was guarded by statuesque soldiers whose eyes watched her lithe form with more than just cautious interest.

I sighed to myself before changing into the lightweight material of the jumpsuit. When I lifted the pack and buckled the straps in place, I looked around for Domivit. The other nations' contestants were beginning to congregate near the door that would lead us out, but he was not among them.

I worried my lower lip, wondering where he had gone in the few snaps it took for everyone to get ready.

"Contestants to the exit," a robotic voice crackled through the room. "Your transport vehicle will be leaving in five snaps."

My stomach did a backflip as the door whooshed open and wickedly cold air assaulted us all, stealing our breaths. The light material suddenly felt like far too little, but before I could contemplate grabbing a jacket to stuff in my pack, warm air rushed along my limbs and torso from the suit itself.

Thermal adjusting bodysuits, I grinned. *Nice.*

Outside was a jetport, which was used to move large numbers of guard members on different assignments. I took the last place in line, wondering where Domivit was. Just as I moved to question one of the guards, a figure rushed out into the blustering wind with their hood drawn down to protect their face.

Relieved, I headed into the transport and took a seat. Domivit shuffled in after me, taking the seat across from me. He kept his head down the short flight to the border, but at least he'd stopped shaking.

Crowds had gathered on the streets below us, waving and smiling as we passed. I scanned their faces, looking for Nona and Charle, even though I knew they planned to stay home and watch the projection. I hoped that Arlakai was among the gathered people though, even if I couldn't spot him.

My leg bounced nervously, and I gnawed on my thumbnail like a wild animal tearing apart its next meal. What if I didn't get to see my best friend before I crossed into Blood Valley?

Just the idea that I wouldn't see him again for a lunar shift had my stomach in knots.

"For Charle," I whispered to myself, letting out a long, steady breath. *For Charle, Nona, Arlakai, and Daria.*

We landed far too soon, disembarking when the door rushed open. Glittering silvery flakes tumbled lazily through the air, melting as soon as they touched my heated face.

Around us, the civilians of Freeya cheered and waved. I scanned the faces closest, expecting to see my best friend. But every click that passed without spying the only face that could put me at ease, my throat burned with the disappointment.

"Contestants take your positions!"

We lined up, Domivit beside me. The technicians approached, each carrying a bot the size of my hand that would film our journeys. A boy with heavily freckled cheeks paused before me.

"Communicator?"

I held out my wrist for him to scan the ID, then pushed my sleeve up for him to scan my tracking device. The softly whirring bot came alive with an almost inaudible chirp.

"She's activated," the technician said.

I grabbed his arm before he could walk away. "Is there any way to make its tones silent? If it dings while I'm trying to stay hidden, that could cause some issues."

He looked at me as though I'd asked if he would switch places with me before clearing his throat. "Um, no. But it only makes the noise when it starts and ends recording."

"Great," I grumbled, facing the starting line.

The technician doing Domivit's bot had to scan his ID three times before deciding the bot was defective. Just as she went in search of a new one, I turned to him. "Bad luck, eh? It's usually me that fries the technology."

His head bobbed in acknowledgement, but he didn't respond. I took to scanning the crowd again, hoping to spy Arlakai one last time.

First light washed over Blood Valley, and though it was difficult to see through the barrier without my goggles, I squinted, trying to detect any movement beyond. The massive device that would momentarily part the barrier and let the contestants through waited in front of us—a wide circle we'd all have to jump through.

The projections playing on the side of a few shop fronts cycled with live footage from each of our cameras. Everyone's but Domivit's.

The technician returned, harried, and panting before scanning his communicator and tracking device. This time the bot chirped merrily, and all twenty-two cameras were finally ready.

With a flicker on the many screens, Empress Divina's face appeared, smiling, and lined with each of her many birth-tides as Triste's figurehead.

"I'm sorry I can't be there with you all, I was called up north for some other duties, but just know that I'm counting on you to secure the Lufarium we need, complete your chosen tasks, and continue to keep all of Triste safe. Your families will be honored and cared for in your absence, and if you should perish, your memory will be immortalized forever." She straightened, her surroundings blurred while her regal lips twisted into a demure smile. "And whoever wins the race will be rewarded beyond all measure. May your feet carry you swiftly, your journey be short, and your mission a success."

Her visage winked from view, and then the Council rose from the dais.

"Contestants to the starting line."

I didn't even bother to see who had called out the order, my feet moving automatically while a clawing sense of trepidation scoured my insides. There was still no sign of Arlakai. I knew that if he was able, he would have pushed his way to the front to wish me luck.

The machine that would allow us to pass through the barrier without injury began to whir. A countdown began overhead while the crowd cheered it out in unison.

"Five... four... three... two."

Domivit grabbed my hand. I whipped my head in his direction, but instead of telling him off, I tried to pull myself free. He gripped me harder, refusing to let go as the siren whirred.

And the electrified border parted.

Chapter 9

Ferrah

Domivit's hold on me didn't lessen as we sprinted hard across the line that switched abruptly from snow-covered ground to desert-cracked rock. I tried to pull free again, but to no avail. The heat that washed over me sent its blistering fingers down into my lungs, trying to squeeze the breath from my chest.

"Let go, it'll be easier to run!" I called.

He didn't have the chance to answer, however, because a wicked *BOOM* knocked us both back, finally breaking the connection. My ears rang and one of my shoulders felt like the skin had been ripped off my body.

Domovit's face appeared over me, although it looked different. Not the boyish roundness and blond hair I had seen earlier. His jaw was sharper, eyes greener.

"Arlakai?" I blinked up at him, dazed.

His answer was too garbled for me to make out. Hands fisted my jumpsuit, then he was pulling me upright, taking off at a run while I struggled to keep my feet beneath me.

Another explosion rocked the ground. In the distant recesses of my mind, I thought it odd that there were bombs going off. There were never explosives so close to the border.

"What's happening?" I asked, trying to clear my mind.

"Scottomb attack," came a gruff response from a voice that was entirely too familiar. His hood fell back, revealing his mane of rusty red hair, and his worried expression.

"Arlakai?" I asked, my feet suddenly forgetting how to work. The ground rushed toward my face, and I braced myself for impact. Only my best friend's hand jerked me upright just in time.

"We can't stop here. We have to keep moving," he said, looking back at where our nation's barrier was now sealed. Those within watched the destruction and carnage unfold, but did nothing to intervene. I looked too, seeing the bodies of several competitors lying on the ground, some of their limbs at odd angles while others were torn apart completely. The scene turned my stomach.

"What about them?" I asked. Even as I said it, Isak and Olivia of Kondez ran past us, veering far left.

Arlakai grimaced. "There's nothing we can do for them, Fairs. Come on."

We began running again while my mind raced even faster with questions. But I'd have to save those for now. My suit pumped cool air over my skin, everywhere but at my shoulder where the fire grew in intensity.

I slowed my jog, blinking at the injury. The suit was torn, but only a small slit that wove itself together while I watched in fascination. This technology surpassed anything the Freejian Guard had.

"Kai, I need you to look at my shoulder." We were far enough away from whatever had happened near the border that only the clicking of the insects filled the air—their drone almost deafening.

He stopped but didn't turn right away. When he did, his expression was grim. "Sure," he mumbled, motioning for me to turn.

I did, and he slid the zipper down with care before gently prying the fabric from my sticky wound. A gasp of agony escaped me, and my communicator chimed just before I felt the pain inhibitor injection which was likely laced with an antibiotic in case of infection. The effects were instant.

"Will I live, medic?" My tone was light and teasing, despite the ebbing pain.

"Yeah," he replied hoarsely before zipping the fabric back up. "You should wash it though."

I spun around to face him. "Great, now what in the sacred tree are you doing here? Where is Domivit?"

His jaw tightened. "He was in no state to run with you. If I hadn't found him when I did and convinced him to trade tracking devices with me, he'd be dead right now."

I glanced over my shoulder at the stealthy, hovering bot, wondering if it was recording this interaction live. Not that it mattered much now. I had a job to do on top of now keeping my best friend alive. "Your tracking device pairs with your DNA. It's only a matter of rotations before the switch is discovered, if it wasn't already. You'll be disqualified." My eyes widened. "What if they discharge you? Who will care for Daria?"

Arlakai put a hand on my good shoulder and squeezed. "It's going to be okay, Fairs. As long as you cross the finish line first, that's all that matters."

My answering smile was half-hearted at best, but the reminder of the special task I was meant to complete had me focusing on my wrist communicator. There on the notification slider was the Triste symbol with the words: *Special Task* floating above it. I touched the icon on the projection and read the first line.

My stomach bottomed out, and I felt sure my legs would give out.

"Fairy?" Arlakai asked, steadying me when I swayed.

I read it again just to be sure.

Execute The Phantom

Message will self-destruct in ten clicks.

The countdown flashed and I watched each number, too stunned to react.

"Fairs, what's going on?" Arlakai asked, sounding more and more worried by the moment.

I turned to him just as the projection switched off, unsure of what I was allowed to tell him. My head jerked toward the bot at my back pointedly.

"We were each given a... special task," I said in a whisper, knowing that if the bot was recording, it could still hear my words. "And we can't share what the task is with anyone," I added when he opened his mouth to no doubt ask what mine was.

His lips pinched into a flat line. "So where to then?" he asked.

I didn't have the faintest idea of how to find the Phantom. He was in our history, but I assumed he was dead. Just a scary tale to tell children at dark. *Stay away from the border or the Phantom will grab you.*

For a moment, I contemplated asking Kai what he knew, but it was too likely that I would give it away. Not to mention the fact that he'd drag me south to get the Lufarium we needed and back to the border kicking and screaming if it meant he could keep me from hunting down someone that our Council clearly believed was still alive and a threat. No matter the consequences, my best friend had been unable to let me do this race without him. There would be no completing my mission if he got wind of the danger it posed.

I pulled up the map on my communicator, a small black star indicated where the Lufarium mines were. The eleven nations of Triste made up the full, luscious foliage atop a gnarled tree while Blood Valley was the trunk and writhing, curling roots.

It would take weeks to journey to the southernmost tip of Blood Valley. Already the light crawling up into a sky that was painted with pinks, purples, oranges, and reds was testing the capabilities of my suit. Sweat trickled down the valley of my neck and soaked into the top of my suit.

I'd have to wash and dress my wound once we got somewhere less out in the open. We walked in relative silence. Since I didn't know where I was supposed to find the Phantom—or if he even existed—I decided I'd go to the mines. But I had to wonder what special task everyone else had been given and what would happen now that some of the runners were dead.

The sole purpose of these races was to gather enough Lufarium for our nations to survive. However, in the end, it was the Council that decided how much each nation got, regardless of whether or not they had any runners complete the race, which meant that the minimum required amount was likely more than Triste actually needed. And with special missions, it stood to reason that there was a possibility we'd all die out here in the valley and Triste would go an entire birth-tide without Lufarium.

My eyes scoured the horizon, taking in the gleam of what looked like water. I knew to heed the warning we'd been given by Nuhelle and veered a little to the right in order to give the oasis a wide berth. Whatever creatures lived in the area would likely flock to that watering hole and I didn't want to be anywhere near them when they did.

A distant scream rent the air, halting us both in our tracks.

"That sounded human," Arlakai said.

I nodded, debating whether or not to check it out. "I think it came from that oasis."

Without another word, Kai sprinted full force toward the area that I had absolutely *no* desire to go near, but with a resigned sigh, I chased after him.

Something bright blue writhed, holding a dark shape that screamed. As we got closer, I saw that it was one of the many carnivorous plants that lived in Blood Valley, and in its jaws was the male runner from Roffair. The other Roffair runner had his companion's arms and was trying to wrest him free while someone, who I guessed was from Ontecurial from the brief glimpse I had of the nation's badge on their sleeve, held onto her to keep her from getting snatched by the plant too.

Arlakai whipped his pack off his back and dug out his echo bolt, and fired three shots so fast I barely had time to register them.

The plant quivered and groaned before its spiky indigo jaws went slack, and Mog tumbled to the rocky ground, the plume of dust sticking to his mucous-covered body. He let out a string of curses I couldn't quite make out.

"Where are your echo bolts?" Kai demanded.

All three of the runners faced us, the two girls looking sheepish. Giesele, the other Roffairian contestant, tugged at the blond braid over her shoulder. "The plant knocked it out of my hands, and it fell into the water."

My wide eyes went from her to the water and back. "If you fashion a net from the non-poisonous fronds, you might be able to pull it out."

Giesele's cheeks turned red, and she nodded. "That's a really great idea."

The Ontecurial girl, Meegs, folded her arms over her chest, looking defensive. "We don't need some Freejian bossing us around. We would have sorted it out for ourselves."

Arlakai snorted a laugh. "Yeah, you three absolutely had it under control. My mistake."

She shot him a glare. "You're not even supposed to be in this race. What happened to the other guy?" It was clear she was embarrassed that she hadn't thought to take out her own echo bolt, but I wasn't going to rub that in her face. If she didn't want our help, then I'd happily leave them to their fate.

Kai flashed her a smirk. "I think he was busy fainting when I relieved him of his burden."

I blew out an impatient breath. "I'm sorry for offering to help. It won't happen again. But if you're so wise, stay away from the water like Nuhelle said. Every foul beast that lives within twenty snaps will be drawn to this place."

I turned and began walking back on course with the map, but not before calling over my shoulder, "Oh, and you better get that mucous off. It can cause severe rashes, fever, and vomiting."

The mad scramble that ensued after sounded as though they'd taken my warning to heart. Arlakai chuckled beside me.

"See, you and I are a pretty great team."

"You were supposed to stay and take care of Daria," I said in a barely audible whisper. When he didn't answer, I looked over at him, finding him still carrying his echo bolt, but looking contemplative.

"She's with Charle and Nona," he said at last. "I told your grandmother only that I was going to keep you safe. And in return I asked that she keep Daria safe."

The silence between us stretched out like a yawn, but there was nothing I could say to that, so I settled on, "I'm glad you're here with me."

His lips twitched at the corners, the beginnings of a smile. "We should stop for water soon. I'm not keen on drinking any of the water around here though. Especially if they're surrounded by human-eating plants."

Remembering that he hadn't been in the briefing with Nuhelle I nodded. "There are tablets and a canteen which filter out any toxins in the air." I shared everything I could remember, adding in a few random bits of information that I thought would be relevant to our journey.

We stopped so I could show him how to activate the water pills and we each took a bite from the meager rations we were given. Eventually we'd have to hunt game because the food we were given would last maybe half a single lunar shift if done carefully, but until then, I'd focus on getting as far as possible on foot.

Chapter 10

Raiden

I'd managed to stop most of the convoys, but the mines that had been placed under the ground had somehow escaped my notice. Fortunately, Ferrah was a soldier through and through. She'd survived the blast while at least five of her competitors had taken the brunt of the explosions. Their lives were a small price to pay for her safety, however.

I trailed behind her and her comrade from a distance. Part of me wanted to make her friend disappear, but I knew her well enough now to know that wherever she went, he was sure to follow.

The pulse of heat that stirred in my veins every time he snuck a glance in her direction was sure to drive me mad before I could reveal myself to her naturally. I tried to convince myself that she didn't need me to protect her, but no manner of convincing could pull me away from her. She was even more magnetic now that she was in my realm. Even more beautiful with the light reflecting off her dark brown hair and casting an ethereal glow around her. She wore the vile Triste jumpsuit like the lethal weapon she was. The only question was, was she in control of her own power, or would the traitorous nations try to wield her against me and my people?

I wanted to know her the way her companion did. And I wanted her to finally know me. To see me properly without a barrier between us.

For now, I'd keep my distance and if she needed me, I'd be there. Just as I always had been.

Chapter 11

Ferrah

When the bright orb in the sky began to descend behind craggy mountains off in the distance, I heard the first howl. A warning cry that the dark would be even less safe than the light.

My limbs were sore, especially my shoulder which I'd cleaned and bandaged after the human-eating plant incident. I wanted to wash the sweat from my body, and finally lay down.

When we came to an outcropping of rocks and I began to set up my tent for the night, the bot at my back chirped, the shutter on the camera sliding closed at last. It continued to trail us, its soft whirring the only sound out in this open expanse of desert. Arlakai noticed it too and let out a breath of relief.

"Does this mean we can talk freely?" he asked.

I eyed the idling bot warily. "I doubt it."

His lip puckered into a disappointed frown, but instead of pulling out his own tent, he scanned the horizon, then all around us. "There's at least two other groups around us."

"How many do you think died in the blasts?" I asked.

He shrugged. "I was too busy getting us out of there to count."

My stomach twisted painfully. Their journeys were over before they'd even begun. "It still surprises me that no one did anything to help with the attack."

"It wasn't an attack on the border, and once the race begins, no one can interfere with the contestants or the race itself. It's part of the treaty." Arlakai pulled his canteen out and snapped another pill, dumping the contents inside before taking a long swig of water.

"I know, but that's never happened before. They were waiting for us to cross. Isn't *that* a violation of the treaty? No one in Blood Valley is supposed to attack us while we race."

"Except the Scottomb, since they can't be controlled," Arlakai pointed out. "And I didn't see anyone there, which meant the ghostly bastards were probably hiding."

I frowned but let it drop. "Aren't you going to set up your tent?"

"We should stay where we can see each other in case something attacks. Strength in numbers, yeah?" He tossed his pack inside the tent before I could respond, then turned to look at the light descending beyond the flat, yawning stretch of desert.

It was incredible how it colored the sky in a display so breathtaking that I couldn't look away at first.

"The temperature is starting to drop. I'm not sure a fire is the smartest move though. It'll only attract predators."

That had me glancing out at the two camps that we could see. Both had small tendrils of smoke pointing to their locations. If they'd managed to kill and clean game that they needed to cook, then a fire might seem worth the risk, but even with half a rotation of light remaining, drawing attention to yourself anywhere in Blood Valley was almost always a death sentence.

I nodded. "Best not to risk it. Between our suits and the tent, we should be fine."

After splashing some water from my canteen on the parts of my body that needed it most, I crawled into the tent, shivering. Without the climate control that Triste had, the desert swung from scorching heat to bitterly cold in a matter of snaps.

The bars that gave the tent some of its rigidity glowed a deep violet—not bright enough to be blinding inside the tent—but the small bit of Lufarium would help stop a silent assassination from any Scottomb.

The dim lighting guided me to the sliver of bedroll not occupied by my best friend. I laid down with an exaggerated huff to cover the strange fluttering sensation taking flight in my gut at being in such close quarters with Arlakai. It didn't make sense, since we'd shared a bed many times since we were kids.

We laid in silence for a moment, our shoulders touching.

"How's your wound?" he asked, voice stiff.

"It's fine," I answered. "I rewrapped it after cleaning it again."

I felt him moving his head in what I assumed was a nod. Silence settled over us again, and I gnawed on the inside of my cheek. Why was this weird? By the sacred tree, we'd even seen each other in various stages of undress during guard training. And sometimes our guard duties required us to sleep wherever we'd been working, which meant using each other as something soft to rest our heads on.

"Ferrah," he rasped.

"Yeah?" I could barely get the word out, my throat constricting while I waited for him to say whatever it was he needed to say. My gut told me it wasn't going to be a light-hearted conversation.

"When we get back..." he paused. "I was wondering if you'd...I think we should..."

A howl shattered my stupefied silence, jerking me into an upright position. The sound was incredibly close. The sound came again, this time followed by the chorus of three or four other baying calls of hunger.

I scrambled for the mouth of the tent, tearing out into the bitter dark. The cold stole my breath, but I pulled an echo blade from the stealthy pocket at my hip. Screams came from one of the camps nearby, the flames of their still-lit fire guttering.

I ran without knowing what I'd find. The types of beasts that lived wild in the valley were nothing short of deadly.

The brilliant red crackle of an echo bolt firing lit my way and illuminated a dark creature that reared back on its hind legs. It was a monstrosity of fur and muscle. But it wasn't alone.

At least three others swiped giant paws at their opponents. Another few rounds fired from an echo bolt, and one of the creatures thudded to the ground. The smell of charred flesh burned my nostrils.

I recognized Isak in the fray, but whether this was his camp, or he'd come to help like I had, I didn't know. Arlakai sprinted at my side, taking aim at the biggest beast.

He hit his mark, the sizzle spreading around the fist-sized hole that had been punched through its chest. Swaying, it stumbled before landing on all fours.

A growl puffed plumes of white from its foamy maw. I halted, pulling Arlakai to a stop with me. The creature's eyes were an eerie yellow, but the stench of blood and death that emanated from it gave it an undead quality that sent goosebumps up my arms.

It looked from me to my best friend, probably wondering if it could take us both out in one move. Arlakai jerked away from me, taking aim at the beast again.

It lunged with a thunderous roar. The crackle of the echo bolt's fiery blast kept me rooted in place, but whatever the terrifying thing was, it kept running—not at Kai this time, but at me—even with most of its chest exposed.

I slashed my blade for its throat, but it reared its head back before wicked claws tore into my side. It swiped its other paw out, catching my weapon and sending it flying. A scream caught somewhere in my chest, dissolving when my back hit the ground and the creature's bloody jaws loomed over my face. Its rancid breath had my stomach turning violently.

I felt around frantically for the blade, fingers sliding over empty, craggy stone.

Arlakai shouted something, and I heard the blast of the echo bolt once more. Another round of howls followed. The snap of jaws sent my hands up to protect my face. I gripped the creature's snout and a fistful of its lower jaw, attempting to wrestle its head away from me. But it was beyond powerful. Inching toward my neck, it snarled, then shook itself free of my hold.

I glanced to my right, trying to search the dark encampment for my blade when something sprang out of the shadows, a blur of light.

The creature above me jolted, then lilted to my left, hitting the ground with a sickeningly wet sound, its torso rolling in one direction while its back end veered another way.

A crouched figure rose to its feet between the two pieces. I finally located my blade—it glowed a bluish-purple in the stranger's hand.

They were tall and imposing, wearing loose-fitting clothing that looked nothing like the Triste-issued uniforms.

Taking a step toward me, I caught the sharp angles of a masculine jaw, skin smudged with dark lines, and even darker eyes. My stomach flipped. I'd seen this man before. He looked almost exactly as he did in my memory—like nearly ten birth-tides hadn't passed since then.

He was impossibly beautiful, despite the silver patchwork of scars marring one half of his face, from forehead to chin. That dark gaze smoldered with familiarity and something else I couldn't quite place. With several graceful steps, he stopped before me, handing me my blade.

I couldn't speak, even as he extended a hand to help me to my feet. The moment my hand slid into his, the shock from the contact created a visible arc of light—there and gone in a flash.

He pulled me up effortlessly. "Are you hurt?" His voice was low, raspy and lightly accented, but even that struck a chord of memory within me.

"It's you," I whispered.

His throat bobbed, while he seemed to be absorbing every inch of me like I was doing to him. After so many birth-tides of wondering if I'd ever see the boy that had saved my life again, he was here in the flesh.

"Yes," he answered.

"Ferrah?" Arlakai said, a menacing quality in his voice that made me turn.

"I'm okay, Kai," I said, still reeling.

"State your business, savage," Arlakai demanded.

A wry snort came from the man behind me. "I just saved your lives."

"Why were you following us?" Kai didn't lower the echo bolt, keeping the barrel pointed at the boy from my childhood.

I stepped in front of the weapon, forcing my mistrusting friend to lower it slightly. "I know him, it's okay." A smile curved my lips. "The one I told you about."

A crease appeared between his brows while he considered my words. When it finally clicked who I meant, his eyes widened. "The outlier from the breach?"

My smile dissipated. "Yes. He saved me from getting trampled or turned into Scottomb food." Isak glared at the newcomer with his arms folded over his chest.

"I can assure you, I'm no threat out here," the man offered in that husky voice that reminded me of scorched honey. "You have far more to fear from the beasts that roam wild out here. My name is Raiden."

"What business do you have interfering with Triste runners, *Raiden*?" Isak sneered. "No one in Blood Valley can interfere with the race."

My head felt like it might float away in the frigid night. I blinked, trying to clear my hazy vision when Raiden answered.

"I wanted to make sure young Ferrah was okay when I was passing by and heard the screaming. I'll be on my way once I know she is unharmed." He looked to me expectantly.

"I'm fine," I answered, waving my hand at his words like that might dispel the attention on me. "Was anyone seriously hurt?" I took a step forward and halted at the jarring pain that returned to my side with a vengeance just before my legs gave out. Kai rushed forward but Raiden already had an arm around my back, lowering me to the ground.

My hand came away from the area sticky, the mess of dark liquid already cooling thanks to the outside temperature.

Raiden's gaze turned intense, while his fingers gently pulled the slashed fabric of my suit aside to see the damage. With it already beginning to mend, I didn't feel like having anyone strip my bodysuit off me in order to tend the wound.

"K-K-Kai, can you help me b-b-back to the tent?" I suggested, my teeth chattering for some reason.

"Yeah, let's—" Arlakai cut himself off when Raiden lifted me into his arms in one fluid motion.

I sucked in a breath, my arms wrapping around his neck instinctively.

"I'll carry her." Raiden's tone was like metal—unyielding, yet cutting when wielded like a blade.

Kai's hands clenched into fists before he followed behind us, walking in silence to the tent.

The already cramped space was made worse when Raiden laid me on the floor of the tent, followed by Kai who pressed in, glowering at my savior.

"You should wait outside while I tend to her wound," Raiden said in a way that sounded less like a suggestion and more like a command. A muscle feathered in Kai's jaw.

"*I* will tend to her injuries. *You* can get lost."

"Kai," I said, trying to keep my tone soft. "It's okay."

His eyes narrowed on me with blatant anger. "You don't *know* this guy. So what if he saved you? That doesn't mean anything."

I wanted to defend myself and the instinctual belief that Raiden was... *safe*. I hadn't spoken to him in almost ten birth-tides, and we knew nothing about each other, but he'd saved my life a second time. That had to mean something, right? It sounded insane, I knew. All my life I'd been told to never trust anyone from Blood Valley.

Raiden seemed to sense the battle I waged in my mind because he laid a hand on my arm. "I'll grab some kometai leaves. They help fight off infection."

Unable to rise to his full height in the tent, he crouched at the exit that Arlakai still blocked, arms folded over his chest. The two stood silent in some male standoff that had me rolling my eyes.

"Don't mind me, I'm just bleeding out," I wheezed.

Kai finally squeezed to the side and let Raiden pass. Once the flap was secured in place once more, he bent down beside me.

"Do you want help getting your jumpsuit off? The hole is repaired already."

I pressed my lips together, trying to hold back what I truly wanted to say before nodding. He moved into action robotically, keeping his gaze averted when the snug fabric slid down my chest, leaving my abdomen and up bare besides the strip of breathable fabric that held my breasts in place.

His fingers moved around the wound, assessing how deep the slice was. "This might need stitches, Fairs."

I swallowed hard. "Get my medic kit and I'll do it."

His head shook side to side, the floppy strands of his reddish hair shielding his eyes from me. "You can't trust him, Fairs. He's an outlier."

"He's not a Scottomb, and besides, he saved my life twice. We have no reason not to trust him. He knows the valley far better than we do."

Finally Kai's eyes met mine. "Maybe, but you're basing your beliefs on something that happened ten birth-tides ago. People change. Especially ones raised in Blood Valley. They're taught to hate and attack us."

"And we're trained to kill them the click they get too close," I shot back, surprised by the fire that laced my tone.

Frustration sharpened his features as he sat back on his heels. "And what do you think the bombs were, Ferrah? A friendly welcome committee?"

The tent's flap shot open, and Raiden stepped inside, a bunch of leaves clenched in his grasp. "This should be enough."

"She's not going to put those anywhere near her cuts," Kai snapped. "They're probably filled with toxins."

For a brief flash, Raiden's greyish eyes seemed to shine a metallic silver. Everything about him sharpened in the blink of an eye before he reigned in his anger. "Those wonderful bands you lot wear will protect her from any *toxins* you may encounter out here. These are kometai leaves that have been used since before the ultimate war. I swear to you, they help."

"She needs stitches," Kai protested again.

I grabbed my best friend's hand and squeezed it gently, turning his attention back to me. "Trying won't hurt anything. The bleeding stopped a while ago, so it's probably not that deep."

Raiden's attention dipped to the cuts on my side, his throat bobbing as he strangled the leaves in his hand that showed a slight tremor. "If the tojergoat released any venom, she will die without proper treatment."

After a long moment, Kai released a breath, relenting, before storming out of the tent. I didn't think he would go far if Raiden and I were left alone.

He didn't waste a moment, kneeling beside me and carefully keeping his gaze from wandering while he ground the leaves up between his long fingers like he'd done it a hundred times before. I hissed at the first stretch of skin, causing Raiden to pause.

"I'm okay," I assured him.

He nodded after a moment, then kept working until all the leaves he'd brought were slathered over and into the cuts, including the one on my shoulder, though he didn't ask how I'd gotten that injury. "They'll dissolve and help the cuts close. I daresay you won't even have a scar to show off to your friends."

I laughed, gingerly pulling the suit back up before slipping my arms inside. "Thank you for your help. It was lucky you were nearby."

He nodded slowly. "Yes, luck certainly favors you."

I scoffed. "I doubt that very much."

As he moved to rise, I grabbed his arm, a sudden idea forming in my mind. Flicking my gaze to the tent's entrance, and back to Raiden, I bit my bottom lip. Asking him about the Phantom was probably my best bet at finding him if he still existed, but no one was allowed to know my mission, save myself.

His larger hand covered mine where it still rested on his forearm. "What is it, flower?"

The term of endearment made my cheeks warm. "Have you heard of the Phantom?" The words came out in a rush, as if that might prevent me from facing whatever consequences Triste would have me face for sharing my mission.

Raiden jerked away from me as if I'd burned him, his eyes wide. "Why would you ask such a thing?" He demanded.

My heart stuttered in my chest for a moment as I tried to find the words to answer. "I-I was just curious. He's a bit of a legend where I'm from."

Raiden's posture relaxed slightly. He ran a hand through his dark hair, tousling the shiny strands which somehow made him look even more beautiful. "We don't speak of him out here. It's too dangerous, even if most people believe he died long ago. Sort of like invoking the evil spirits of your lore."

In truth, there wasn't much lore left in Freeya. Only the truth that was written in our history books about how the world came to be. A collision of particles that created a barbaric civilization that rose and thrived but ultimately destroyed itself with war and conflict, leaving the remaining humans to build up a new world which became Triste. We created peace, cured most illnesses and diseases, and perfected life for humankind.

But some of the southernmost nations of Triste like Maudeer and Werea-Haot still observed supernatural deities, even if all of Triste recognized the Empress and the sacred tree as their supreme beings.

I nodded anyway, sitting up as best I could, ignoring the twinge of pain. "I'm sorry. I won't ask again."

Raiden's silvery eyes searched my face, as though he were trying to read what I left unsaid.

But before he could question me, the tent flap opened again, Kai filling the opening. "The light will rise soon; we need to get some rest." He didn't so much as glance in Raiden's direction, probably pretending he wasn't even there.

Raiden got to his feet. "Be careful when you wash not to soak the leaves, or they'll dissolve too fast. You won't need to wash the wound at all, it'll be self-cleaning."

I nodded, thanking Raiden again for his help. He bowed his head and moved past Kai so fast it almost looked as though he wanted to escape being in this tent with me.

Kai didn't speak as he closed the flap, securing it and laying on his back on the bedroll. Exhaustion pulled my lids down, but when he spoke, they fluttered open again.

"I'm glad you're okay."

I hummed in agreement. "I'm glad everyone is okay."

Another beat of silence. "Hey, Fairs?"

I yawned before answering. "Yeah?"

This time the silence didn't seem to end. Rough fingers stroked a few errant strands of hair away from my face, followed by a murmured, "Tomorrow."

My lids felt like they were soldered shut, and sleep dragged me down, taking me prisoner in its hold where dreams of the silver-eyed boy from my past haunted me.

Chapter 12

Ferrah

My side was almost entirely pain-free when I woke before first light. Halfway through breaking down camp, I chanced a look at Arlakai. He broke a ration pack in half before extending it and a full canister of water.

"Thanks." I drank deeply, feeling as though I hadn't had a drink in far too long. "Too bad they don't have pyrani capsules. That might make the cold more bearable."

A laugh of acknowledgement came from Kai whose back was to me. He stuffed the pop-up tent container into my pack before zipping it shut and rounding on me, his lips parted.

I waited.

He snapped his mouth shut, a muscle ticking in his jaw before he finally said, "We need to get moving before the other groups get too far ahead of us."

Suspicion twisted in my gut, but I nodded and got to my feet. After shouldering my pack, we started off at a slow jog, though it didn't take long for Arlakai's longer strides to set him ahead of me.

I ran harder to keep up, but it was clear that something was bothering him.

As the light began to lift out of the hazy darkness, looming up and setting the sky ablaze, it warmed my skin. The suit switched from heat to cooling, but not even that could keep the sweat from running down my forehead. Kai's pace didn't relent, and the stretch of desert blurred by heat lines ahead of us dulled any signs of others. The hovering camera bot followed faithfully behind.

Up ahead, a shadowy swarm floated in the air, the drone of buzzing getting louder. I pointed to it, and Kai nodded, veering so as not to attract the insects.

The arid heat felt like it had burned away any oxygen left in the air, causing my lungs to ache. That, combined with our pace made me finally call out for a rest.

We slowed to a stop, both of us breathing hard. I turned my bag to grab my canteen as Arlakai did the same. The water was hot and tasted like dirt, but it turned my thick, rubbery tongue back into a useful part of my anatomy.

"Whatever you need to say, Kai, you can say it. I can tell something is bothering you."

He took his time screwing on the lid of his canteen, then placing it back in his bag before he said, "You know how Triste law states that you have to be bonded by nineteen birth-tides?"

My stomach dropped at his words. "Yes." The reply came out weakly.

He kept his eyes locked with mine, while his fingers fiddled with the strap on his bag nervously. "Well, I've been thinking for a little while, and I think we should be bonded." The words came out so quickly it took me a moment to even process what he'd said.

Before I could reply, he continued. "And before you shove it off and say I'm not thinking clearly, just remember that if you don't find yourself a match, the Council does it for you and you could end up with someone older and hideous." A sheepish smile pulled at his lips. "You and I have always gotten along well, and it just makes sense for Daria and Charle..."

My mouth opened, though I couldn't formulate a response.

Kai held up a hand to stop whatever I might have said. "Don't answer me right this click. Just... think about it, okay?"

I could only nod, dumbfounded that my best friend of seven birth-tides had even considered the bonding ritual required when all Freejians came of age.

Being bonded would mean that we would be mandated to provide Triste with two offspring, thus ensuring the incline of the population. I was certain there were a thousand other things bonded matches did, but I hadn't given any of it a moment's thought. The only thing that had been on my mind since I was eleven was competing in the Blood Run.

As he'd pointed out, to protect Daria and Charle as well as Nona, it made sense, but did Kai think of me in a romantic way as well? It wasn't necessary to have any romantic notions toward your match, but Nona had loved Opa, and part of me had wanted that too.

Could *I* love Arlakai in that way? Immediately the answer came to me as a resounding *no,* but that didn't mean I wouldn't come to love him beyond our friendship, did it?

"Come on," Kai said, snapping me out of my jumbled mess of thoughts, "we have to keep moving."

For several rotations, the only distraction from the bomb Kai had dropped was the steady rhythm of my boots on chipping stone. I focused on the sounds around us alone, drowning everything else out.

Thud, thud, thud, thud, thud.

The sound seemed to grow louder, echoing in my ears. I slowed my pace, wondering if someone else was running behind me.

Craning my neck, I glanced over my shoulder. My breath caught between a scream and a gasp.

Thundering after us was a giant creature with black eyes and a long, twisted horn protruding from its wrinkled snout.

"Kai!"

He whirled, his frown of confusion morphing into shock. "Again?" he bellowed.

"I'd rather not fight this one," I called, my side and shoulder giving a twinge at the most inconvenient moment.

Arlakai looked around wildly, trying to find a place to either lose the creature or hide from it. Blood Valley, was, for the most part, barren. And infested with bloodthirsty creatures such as this angered beast. That was how the valley had gotten its name.

I saw a raised stony mesa not too far off, surrounded by some sort of vegetation. "That way!" I pointed for good measure, and Kai adjusted our trajectory.

The stamping beats shook the ground, rattling rock and sending a kwipai scuttling back the way it came. My breaths sawed in and out of my lungs, threatening to split them at the seams, but I didn't stop.

I couldn't glance back, but I knew the creature was gaining ground from the heat of its foul-smelling huffs assaulting my back.

"Don't stop!" Kai ordered.

I didn't bother to respond to such a silly request. The mesa—closer than it had been before—looked larger than I had initially thought and would require a moment of climbing that I wasn't sure we'd get. But if we weaved between the large, green forked columns decorated in glinting spikes, we just might slow it down.

I pulled ahead of Kai, the stampede of thick feet falling behind and I nearly whooped, but I'd celebrate when we were both safely on the rocks.

Finally I made it to the cover of thorns, weaving in and out to avoid being stabbed by a single needle. Partway through I noticed the sounds had all but faded, heading a different direction.

Peering around the trunks I tried to see where Arlakai and the creature had gone, but they were out of sight.

"Kai!" I screamed, making my way back into the open. Off in the distance where the telltale gleam of water sparkled like an inviting jewel, I saw the toppled animal. But Arlakai was nowhere to be seen.

Something like laughter came from the Oasis and I rushed toward it. Jeers and clapping reached my ears when I was close enough, followed by splashing and grunts.

I halted around the rocks blocking my line of sight where Isak held Kai's head in the pool of tainted water. A shocked scream tore from my throat, most likely alerting every predator within a light-rise's walk of here.

Kai's arm finally snagged around Isak's waist, his leg swiping out in a blur and dropping the Kondez boy into the water.

I rushed to Kai's side, my stomach trying to turn itself inside out with worry. Black wriggling creatures the size of my fist had attached themselves to his face and neck. He lifted a hand to touch one, but I spoke before he could.

"Don't just rip them off, they'll rip through flesh and muscle! You have to relax them." I stopped in front of them, grimacing as I stroked a hand over the back of one that covered his eye, offering a silent plea to the sacred tree that it hadn't taken his eye.

It quivered, its slimy skin coating my fingers but when I did it again, it unlatched with a sickening squelch before dropping to the water around his ankles. Isak shrieked, clawing at the waters as if he could fend off the flesh-eating leeches.

Arlakai followed my lead, gently caressing one on the top of his skull. I refused to look at the damage until all six of the slimy, horrid creatures had swam away. Pulling Kai out by his bloodied hand, I checked him for more, spinning him while hysteria pulled at me.

I wouldn't let it show though, clenching and unclenching my hands to fight away the tremor.

Kai reached for me, and I spun, training my glare on Isak and his posse of guys which included Mog from Roffair—who had clearly abandoned Meegs and Gisele—plus Leo of Demiwind as they attempted to crawl away. Isak had taken to tearing the creatures off, and blood poured from gaping wounds.

"What in all of Triste is your problem?" I demanded, storming around the water until I'd blocked their escape. "Isn't this race bad enough with everything trying to kill us? You have to try your hand at it too?"

Isak glared at me as best he could, though he looked moments away from fainting.

"For what you did, I refuse to give you medic care. When you came to help last night, was that meant to be a murder attempt as well?"

His jaw flexed, but he didn't answer, continuing to look up at me like *I* was the monster here. With a scoff, I toed loose dirt, sending it flying up at him before I turned to march away.

"The Phantom ordered your companion be killed!" Isak called at last, halting not just my feet, but my heart as well.

All of me suddenly felt like I'd been suffused with ice.

"He wants to meet you, but he said that you would go to him before long."

I spun. "He's real? Have you seen him?"

Isak's grin was cold and cruel, despite the gashes filling with pus on his cheek and shoulder. "He's as real as you and I, even if he doesn't show himself. If I were you, I'd run back to Freeya where it's safe. No one survives when the Phantom chooses his prey."

Goosebumps spread over my skin, and I retreated another step from the water's edge, as though the ghost I hunted lurked within its dark depths.

Somehow the Phantom knew about me.

Did he know about my mission? Is that why he was certain *I'd* go to *him*? If he'd ordered Arlakai dead, it stood to reason he wanted me dead too. Or if he didn't now, then he would when he learned I was sent to execute him.

The bombings at the beginning of the race made sense now.

The Phantom wasn't merely a tale the adults told children to keep them from the border. He was real and had already tried to kill us.

I wondered if Raiden knew. If he had ever met the Phantom.

Kai grabbed my hand, pulling me on. "We gotta go, Fairy."

I nodded, numb, putting one foot in front of the other, unsure if each step was taking me closer and closer to my last breath.

At least now I knew two things I hadn't before. Yet I couldn't help but wish I'd been stuck in ignorance, because the rest of this race was sure to be a bloodbath.

Chapter 13

Ferrah

Kai watched me. I could feel his eyes on me, and while he didn't voice it aloud, I knew he was wondering if Raiden had been sent by the Phantom to lure me to him or to spy on me.

I knew, because that's what thought kept playing over and over in my mind. It plagued me to think our friendship might be exploited in some way by the mysterious ruler of Blood Valley.

Raiden was my childhood hero. I didn't wish to think of him as a pawn, nor my enemy. But the way he'd recoiled when I'd mentioned the Phantom had seemed like genuine shock. Shock that I'd brought up the Phantom at all, or shocked that I might know something I shouldn't?

It made me leery of the boy I'd placed on a pedestal—the hero who'd saved my life and sat in silence with me. The more rational part of me said that I should ask him for honesty, while the other favored the idea of trusting that the coincidence was just that.

I'd been so focused on my emotional dilemma that I hadn't noticed that we'd wandered near a village when people wearing dusty, simple clothing turned to stare. Their houses were small and made from stone and what looked to be packed mud, then layered with fronds or sticks. There weren't many people present, but the cone-shaped huts were lined up in clusters that had to be close to a hundred.

Perhaps the others are inside their homes?

I offered a small smile and a wave to a young boy half-tucked behind a graying woman that might have been his mother.

Every adult face was lined from the oppressive heat and lethal cold brought in the dark. But something fiercer touched their hooded eyes. It was a hardness that came with resentment. A resentment for what, I wondered? Their circumstance? The ruler of Blood Valley that neglected them? Or was the hatred for us?

They murmured words I couldn't understand, a few turning away until the little boy sprinted toward us.

"Daifyre!" the woman called after him, but he didn't stop, eyes twinkling with a light that hadn't been forged into anger just yet.

The boy tugged on Arlakai's pack. "*Trujur*!" He rasped in a voice that was as dry as the stone beneath our feet.

"Daifyre," the woman chastised again, but the boy only turned to me and repeated the word.

I slipped my pack from my shoulders and knelt. The canteen was still half-full. "You thirsty?" I asked.

"No!" The woman cried in alarm, rushing to the child, and yanking him away.

I frowned. "He sounds like he needs a drink. I have some to spare, it's alright."

"We want nothing from *your* kind. The price is much too high." She pushed the boy behind her, causing him to whimper in frustration as he fought to move between me and Kai again.

"What do you mean?" I asked. "I don't want anything in return. He sounds hoarse, I wanted to help."

Someone in the crowd barked a laugh. "When has the Empire ever helped *us*?"

I didn't bother pointing out that their leader had chosen to leave the United Nations of Triste, so the Empire didn't owe them anything.

Kai, however, had no such reservations. "Shouldn't your king provide for you?"

"Our king *does* provide for us!" Several called the words out in unison, the sentiment echoed by many others that had gathered.

Dread coiled low and tight in my belly. "Can you not petition the Empire to become a nationalist of Triste?" I'd never heard of such thing, but it didn't sound impossible.

The woman before me gave a wry laugh. "If anyone dares get near your precious borders, we end up with our heads blown clean off our necks. We're seen as a threat, even starved, and dying as we are."

I reared back, the words coming like a slap to the face.

"Come on, Fairs, we don't have time for this," Kai said with gentleness. His hand came to rest on my shoulder, but I shrugged him off.

"I'll mention it to the Council when I return," I vowed. "Anyone that wishes to live in Triste should be allowed to do so."

"Aye," a man sneered, "that way our children can be brainwashed by the likes of the Council. *Ach*, we're better off food for the kwipai."

The little boy began to cough, the sound rough as rocks. It shook his whole frame and he leaned into the woman I assumed was his mother for support.

I ignored the man's jab, focusing on the little boy instead. "May I offer him water? Please?"

After another cough that racked his whole frail body, she nodded, lips pinched in displeasure.

I extended the canteen to the boy whose face had paled. He looked at it, uncertain, then to his mother who nodded, smiling though the gesture pulled her lips tight.

His small hands wrapped around the cylindrical bottle before he lifted it to his lips and took a sip. Then another.

And another.

His mother pulled the canteen away, muttering words to him that made him nod. Slowly she allowed him one last drink and handed the container back.

I took it with a friendly smile, hoping that the child would survive these harsh conditions.

"Do you have water for him later?" I asked, almost in a whisper.

The woman worried her bottom lip, then answered. "Some. Enough to get by."

I undid the zip on my pack again, tearing of a segment of capsules from the roll to give to the woman.

Kai's hand covered mine. "You only have enough for the lunar shift we may be here."

"It's five pills, Kai," I answered. "They need it more than I do."

His jaw clenched in disapproval, but he didn't answer.

Once I demonstrated to the woman how to break them and let moisture from the air—little as it may be—fill whatever container they had, the woman thanked me with less reluctance than before.

A few people around us pressed closer and a current of unease rippled through the group.

"What of food, we wouldn't want the boy to starve?" The taunt came from a row or two back. I looked up, finding the looks of disgust had morphed into hungry expressions.

My stomach dipped, and slowly I got to my feet.

"We need to move," Kai whispered, tugging my arm.

I nodded, wishing to offer some words of comfort for the boy and his family. But as we moved back a few steps, the crowd pushed closer.

"If we had one of their weapons, we'd have better luck hunting for our own food," a man called out and sounds of ascent rang out.

Kai and I turned as one, his fingers lacing through mine before we began sprinting. Their shouts and rapid footfalls chased us. The first impact at my back had me craning to look over my shoulder.

Most of the angered people had picked up stones and were hurling them in our direction.

"They're throwing rocks!" I shouted, appalled.

"They's acting on pure survival instincts," Kai called back. We ran harder, dodging whatever rocks we could while others pelted our backs. I heard something ping against one of the hover bots as well, but didn't dare look back to see if it was okay.

Only when the angry sounds dissipated did we slow to a walk. We trekked on in silence until the village was out of sight and the light had begun to nestle away beyond the horizon yet again.

"You're too nice, Fairs," Arlakai said, but there was little reproach in the words.

"You wouldn't have let him die either," I countered.

"True," he admitted. "But if you could have given those people everything in your pack, you would have. If they didn't steal it and kill you first."

I shrugged. "We got away."

He released a long breath. Our pace slowed even further, my feet aching so fiercely I contemplated using my echo blade to saw them off.

"Should we stop to eat a bite or two then make camp, or make camp then eat?" Kai asked.

"Let's stop now before my feet fall off."

He chuckled in response, halting his steps. There was nothing but brightly colored ferns, the occasional cacti, and jagged rock formations that stretched up to the sky like fingers reaching to grasp the light above.

We stopped at the first stretch of even ground, pulling supplies from our packs. I wasn't surprised, however, when Kai didn't pull out his tent.

"You won't have to bend your legs so much if you sleep in your tent," I said, deciding to state the obvious.

"And if you're attacked, there's two layers of material between us." He didn't look up from his ration as he spoke.

I snorted a laugh, accepting his explanation, though I couldn't help but remember how Raiden had smelled so close to me inside the four walls that popped up with a mechanical whirr. Part of me hoped he'd stay away, but a deeper part of me hoped he'd come back, and not just so I could ask him about his king.

The rotation's heat lingered while we set up and cleaned off. We sat outside the tent to eat our rations and I watched a large bird swoop and peck at a kwipai that hissed and reared up on its back legs, making it nearly as tall as me.

Arlakai shivered. "Nasty creatures."

I chuckled. "They're more afraid of you than you are of heights."

He nudged me with his shoulder, smiling through a bite of the freeze-dried nutrient bar. "If one decides to try to suck off your face, I'm not going to help get it off."

This time I openly laughed, startling the bird that had managed to grab the kwipai's arm, but dropped it back to the ground where it raced for cover near a large, carnivorous frond.

"You're thinking of leeches."

He choked on a disgusted noise, coughing loudly. I patted his back and offered my water. When his voice returned, he said, "Don't remind me."

"Isak is even uglier now than he was though," I pointed out.

He grinned, but the expression slipped when the kwipai's savior snapped its bright yellow leaves around its body, squeezing while it shrieked.

My hand automatically when to my echo blade, stopping halfway from the holster at my side when Kai's hand halted mine. I glanced sidelong at him, annoyed that he wouldn't let me save the creature.

"Blood Valley has an order to it, and despite your desires to save everything that lives here, you can't. You have a race to win."

I shoved the blade back into the pocket with a huff. "You're just saying that because you don't want that kwipai burrowing under our tent."

He shuddered again. "Do they do that?" His eyes were wide.

I smirked just as the chime of the hover bot going to sleep sounded, and the little ball sunk gently to the ground.

My wristband communicator chirped next, followed by the sharp pinch of an injection.

Vitamin Injection Administered

Kai checked his too, pulling up the menu.

"Do you have a special mission?" I asked, trying to keep the overwhelming curiosity from my voice.

"Not so far," he said. "The mission probably would have still gone to Domivit's communicator."

After a moment he turned his wrist, showing me the video playing.

"It's the live recap," I breathed. Faces flashed across the screen of the fallen competitors. Eight names I'd memorized. One of them was Imani's Maudreer companion, Daveed. Goose and Niahm of Tiau, Tecla and Serkis from Nimua, Gisele who we'd seen at the Oasis the first light-rise, Flad of Auktraise, and Meegs from Ontecurial who I was pretty sure was with Gisele. Had they both been poisoned by the water, or had they befallen another fate? Mog was with Isak last I'd seen him, which meant, at least for now, he was still very much alive.

It soured my stomach to know the vile serpent that Isak was had survived after what he'd tried to do to Kai. But never in Blood Run history had eight runners fallen so quickly. Many more would still be lost to the elements as well as Scottomb attacks.

The video changed to a wooden contraption rolling across the sand pulled by shirtless men whose faces were positively wild with bloodlust. More people spilled out of the back of the rickety wooden thing they used for transportation.

When the camera panned to Meegs and Gisele running and firing their echo bolts, my chest tightened.

The attack was over before it had truly even begun. Blood sprayed over the lens, blurring almost everything. But the second hover bot caught sight of the savages that rammed blades into the fallen girls' chests over and over, their mouths agape in triumph as they butchered the girls' bodies.

My stomach revolted, the protein bar I'd eaten coming up and landing at my feet. Kai shut off the video feed and pulled me away from where we'd been sitting.

"I'm sorry," he murmured, wiping the sick from my lip and handing me a full canteen. When he'd refilled them both, I didn't know.

I took a long drink and sighed, my gut cramping again from the sudden intrusion, but I didn't throw it up. "Not your fault."

Propping my back against a medium-sized stone, I closed my eyes and tried not to think about how much Nona and Charle had seen already. How they must be worrying constantly.

Arlakai pushed something into my hand, and I opened my eyes. The mouth care kit was more of a luxury out here, but I thanked him anyway. Deep blue that almost seemed to mingle with black painted itself across the sky, and thousands of brilliant dots seemed to ignite within. Despite the cold chasing away the light's heat, I found that I couldn't stop staring up at the little flickers of light.

"I never saw those freckles in Freeya," I whispered. "Or the big sliver of white light." Reaching up, I pointed to the partially round shape.

Arlakai nodded. "Not even in the footage from previous runs did it show the dark."

"Strange," I whispered.

A chilling breeze rushed over us, stealing my breath, and making me shiver.

"Let's get in the tent," Kai said, and I could hear the reluctance in his voice. Feeling a strange sadness twisting up in my gut, I let him lead me inside.

The smell of mildew and urine filled my nostrils. I wanted to choke on the scent, but stranger still was the room I stood in. It was almost too dark to see anything, save for the faint light of the dark peering in through a window high up on the wall to my right.

"Kai?" I called. Taking a tentative step forward, a plume of dust stirred around me, concealing the floor ahead. Another step closer revealed long bars caging me in.

My heart rammed against my ribs before beating a pace that no beast could outrun. I gripped the bars, trying to see what lay outside the cell, but there was only black nothingness. "Kai!"

"Why do you call for the fool?" A deep, silky voice spoke both behind me and far away.

I whirled, eyes searching the darkness all around me. "Who are you?" I demanded. My hand went to the holster at my thigh, but it was empty. I patted my jumpsuit, only to find that I was entirely stripped of weapons, even my communicator gone.

The answering laugh was darkness incarnate. A devil that lounged on the throne of depravity. That was the only way something so beautiful could sound so wicked. "I believe you and I have a bit of a problem, reickunteel."

A crease formed between my brows. "And what is that?"

The slight warm tickle down the nape of my neck had me spinning the opposite direction. Still nothing stood near me in the shadows.

"The Council wants me dead. And they sent you to be my executioner, did they not?"

I could have sworn my heart ceased beating in my chest for several long beats, the air stalled in my lungs. When at last I sucked in a sharp breath, it came out in a gust that formed the words, "You're the Phantom."

"That's right, reickunteel," the sinful voice purred, and I could have sworn I felt his breath against the shell of my ear. My fist swung out to strike, but sailed through empty air, just as I guessed it would.

"Did you know your people are starving? Dying without water?" I couldn't keep the anger and resentment from my tone. "You're letting them die."

The temperature around me dropped so suddenly, I saw my breath curl before me.

"You think I am to blame for their suffering?" the Phantom's voice was an even, deadly calm, but the silence felt ominous—filled with a cataclysmic rage that needed only a spark to explode.

"What have you done to help them?" I demanded, stepping closer to the bars where I was sure the devil hid his face.

"EVERYTHING!" The gust of wind knocked me on my backside, tearing some of my hair free from its tattered, dirty braid. "You know nothing of what goes on in my land. And that is why, when we meet, Flower, you will help me. You will be the reckoning Triste deserves."

The wind settled to a single concentrated tendril that stroked down my cheek, carrying away the tear that I hadn't realize had spilled out.

Then I was left in my prison, alone.

I woke with a sharp gasp, clutching a hand over my heart which beat a pounding rhythm against my ribcage. Outside, the sky groaned and rumbled, and brilliant arcs of light streaked above the tent.

Awe overtook the panic snapping its teeth at me in sleep. I glanced sidelong at Kai, his chest rising and falling slow and steady.

Crawling toward the flap, I slowly unzipped the panel and pulled it aside just as another dazzling bolt of white zipped by. It was beautiful and mesmerizing.

Small balls of ice began to shatter on the ground, bouncing off our tent. I braced for the acid to eat through the structure, or the size of the ice to become so large it tore through the top, but steadily the dark canvas let loose a deluge that glittered and made various clinking sounds that were almost melodic. I'd heard so much about acid rain—or in this case—hail, but when the sky just grumbled, I let my muscles relax, feeling the haltingly cold air outside mix with my breaths in visible plumes of white.

Softly, I let myself hum a tune—one that I'd listened to countless times. The music box was in my backpack, but if I pulled it out, the rustling would likely wake Kai.

It was the most peace I'd felt since we left Freeya, and it made my heart light.

"What are you doing?" Arlakai's voice had me whirling.

In a flash of light from outside, I could just make out his head propped up on an elbow.

"Watching the storm," I answered softly, loving the fresh scent and how everything felt still for just a moment. "I had a nightmare." If what I'd seen and felt had truly been a dream. Just recalling the Phantom's voice, his hot breath on my neck had my stomach falling into my toes once again.

"You'll get too cold. Close the flap and come lay down. You need the sleep to heal your wounds."

I nodded absently as the pelting bits of ice began to slow. Without thinking, I reached out, plucking a singular hailstone from the ground and held it in my palm.

"Fairs!" Kai sat upright in an instant, but I just held the little ball out, letting him see it begin to melt on my skin.

"No acid," I said by way of explanation.

He shook his head in the almost full-black before extending his arms to me. "Close that. I'll hold you until you fall back asleep."

Though I was loathe to stop watching the rare display outside, I zipped the tent shut and laid back, my side pressed against Kai's. His arm under my neck gave me a light squeeze.

In the silence, I listened to the last patters of hail hitting the tent while staring up at darkness, a sense of calm taking over my restless mind until eventually sleep claimed me once more.

Chapter 14

Raiden

The raiders and their crusade had gotten too close to Ferrah. I hadn't been able to save the two girls they slaughtered, but for now, at least, their bloodlust was sated. Plus, I'd created fake tracks to follow that led them in the opposite direction of Ferrah's current course.

Her companion made it difficult to stay with her the way I had hoped to. His keen tracking sense made it even more challenging to follow at a distance, unseen.

The wind howled across the flat expanse of stone, battering me the same way my mood was. Underneath the impending storm, however, I could hear the groans of Scottomb wandering the valley.

I hurried my pace to make certain I got to Ferrah before they did. They were as restless as the raiders set on ending Triste's race. All of Blood Valley, it seemed, was on the brink of a war that I alone couldn't prevent.

But maybe with her...

A brutal slash of white light arced across the sky, followed by a boom that rumbled the old bones of the valley.

Pressing on, I tried not to think about the irony of the storm beginning to unleash its fury on the valley when the valley itself was so filled with rage.

Just as the stones of hail began to pelt the ground, I arrived at the singular tent where two hearts beat; one faster than the other. Ferrah was awake, though I sensed it wasn't the storm that had roused her. She was unsettled. The flap was undone, fluttering gently in the breeze.

I sat as close to her tent as I dared, wishing that it was me taking shelter with her. We had so much still to discuss. A soft humming came from within, a melody that made my heart pick up its own pace. The tune my mother had created just for me sounded so much more beautiful in her voice than the gravelly rhythm I often used.

She'd not only kept the music box, but had clearly listened to its song enough that it soothed her as it did me.

For a brief moment I considered luring her out so I could have a chance to talk with her, but her companion would steal any chance for privacy. And I wanted nothing more than to stay here and listen to her hum the familiar song.

I hoped that sitting near her would settle her in some way, that she would sense my presence and know I would keep her safe. The boy's voice broke the silence, and I listened to their brief exchange with my body wound too tightly. I wanted to rip him out into the storm, or better yet, steal her away from his moody machinations that were meant to entice her. After they fell silent again, the storm's wrath softened to rain, and she stirred, her heart beating slower as she allowed herself to relax.

I smiled inwardly, telling myself that it was me that eased her worries. And when her breathing softened, I knew she was asleep. My back leaned against the weather-worn rock not far from her tent as I kept watch. It had been too long since I had slept.

The peacefulness of rain and darkness, along with the echoing melody of her voice in my mind soothed me. Drenched with icy droplets still kissing my hands and cheeks, I relished the cold. It was deadly, like fire, but the cold was more forgiving. Perhaps it had saved my life once, when my body was covered in burns. My musings faded, and before I could fight against the pull, sleep pulled me under.

By the time peak heat had rolled around, Ferrah and her annoying companion had made it to the gorge. It was faster to go through, but few did since it almost always meant certain death.

As far as the eye could see, shapes of rock towered high above, sloping and slanting into cliffs too treacherous to climb.

Part of me hoped they would turn back and go around instead. Colonies of Scottomb hid within the gorge, feeding on any animal foolish enough to try to brave the rocky slopes. Even the ruddy-color-haired boy voiced his protests loudly and frequently, but that didn't deter brave little Ferrah.

She hooked up her rock-climbing harness, a tightness about her lips and the shadows from lack of sleep smudged below her eyes the only indication that she'd woken last night. Relenting, her friend Kai followed suit with his harness, uttering a never-ending string of nonsense under his breath.

Perhaps he'd slip and fall to his death.

One could only be so lucky.

"Ready?" Ferrah asked him, her gaze snagging on the spot where I stood, though I knew I was hidden from view. Nevertheless, she always seemed to know when I was there.

"Yeah," Kai grumbled, snapping her attention back to him where she checked his harness for the third time.

"Okay." She released a long breath. "We can do this. Remember the mountains back home? We spent two weeks working on those in harnesses like these."

"Suspended from hovercraft!" Kai's protest sounded petulant, and I couldn't help but roll my eyes.

She snorted a laugh. "I know you're scared of heights, but we can walk through most of it, and if there's a threat or where it bottoms out, we can stay around the two-third's height and there won't be any significant gaps that we have to repel across. I studied maps of this place for weeks. It makes the way across seven light-rises faster."

"It won't matter if we're dead, Fairs."

I held back a growl that built in my throat. He was an idiot, even if I did agree that the gorge was too risky.

Luckily, they had me to guide them.

They lowered themselves into the valley where death waited in every shadow. In here, light couldn't quite reach every nook and cranny.

I went ahead of them, climbing down to scour for threats. An eerie sort of silence stretched over Ferrah and her companion, as though they too knew that the Scottomb would pick up on any sounds they made. Even their breathing was lighter.

During the light rotations, the monsters may not strike so readily, but once darkness descended, their blood would be a siren call from here until the Lufarium mines.

I just hoped that when the time came my skillset would be enough to keep Ferrah alive.

CHAPTER 15

Ferrah

From the moment we entered the gorge, I felt eyes on us. We kept a steady pace, but didn't run. I knew Scottomb liked to hunt in here. It was one of the reasons most runners went around.

Not even my jumpsuit could keep the sweat from beading on my back, but I refused to stop for long. The longer we stayed down here, the more likely we were to die.

Somehow, even the near-silent hover bot at my back sounded too loud. It took everything in me not to turn and slice through it with the echo blade I kept in my hand. Kai didn't make conversation like he usually did, most likely too terrified of what might hear us if he spoke. Our steps were light on the craggy stone, and even when we needed to pinch through tight spaces, we managed to keep almost soundless.

I know we needed to talk about the question of our bonding soon, but staying alive was higher on the to-do list. A few paces ahead of us, the light shimmered as it had done countless times. I narrowed my eyes, trying to decipher if a Scottomb was toying with us, but I didn't think it likely. They were mindless with bloodlust, and we were very much alone.

To test the theory, I kicked a rock at the blurred shape just as it vanished again. It sailed through the air before skipping over smooth stone.

Kai glanced sidelong at me. "What are you doing?" he whispered.

"I thought I saw something."

He stiffened, his hand going to his echo bolt as he assessed the area around us more thoroughly. "You of all people should know not to kick a rock at anything in Blood Valley."

My lips parted with a reply loaded on my tongue when a high-pitched, inhuman shriek reverberated between the stones.

"What do we do?" Arlakai asked, eyes wide.

I looked at the cliff face to my right, then the one on my left. "We climb. They can jump to the top of the gorge, but they can't appear inside solid stone." To punctuate my answer, I holstered my blade and ran for the steep wall of stone, grasping whatever grooves I could to propel myself up. Kai followed, muttering a string of curse words that I hoped Nona couldn't hear if she was watching.

My heart lodged itself firmly in my throat when the first Scottomb barreled around the corner, turning from translucent, ratty flesh, to invisible, then back again. It spotted us before tilting its head back and letting loose its horrid cry that made me want to cover my ears.

"Go, go, go!" Kai urged.

The next dip I found in the stone wasn't as deep as I'd hoped, and my nails scraped across it, breaking several of them. My hand slipped entirely, pulling a choked gasp from me.

Kai maneuvered up the cliff until we were side by side. "Follow behind me, okay?" he said.

"You're scared of heights!" I protested.

His Adam's apple bobbed. "I've got this. Just follow me."

I nodded, and Kai took off up the cliff. With a deep breath I shuffled over to where I had a better grip.

Below, the Scottomb clawed at the cliff, screeching. A few vanished and reappeared a few feet up, but over and over they fell back to the ground, almost as though some barrier prevented them from getting any higher.

I tried to just focus on the distance left to go. If my best friend could do this, then so could I.

The top loomed closer and relief began to bloom like the first bud of spring. Just as Kai turned to smile down at me, his hand so close to level ground, I felt the grip of cold, dead fingers around my ankle.

Then it pulled.

My grip slipped and a scream knotted with my terror, leaving me only with the view of Kai getting smaller and the wind rushing all around me.

Something dark and solid launched at me from the cliff. It was too dark to be a Scottomb, I knew, but when it wrapped itself around me, I fought against it.

"Ferrah!" Kai's shout only spurred my panic on further.

My elbow connected with something solid, earning a grunt of pain. I stilled, finally catching sight of the golden skinned hands and dark tunic that wrapped around muscular arms.

I didn't have time to confirm that Raiden was the one holding me before we rolled through the air, something slowing our descent before my feet gently touched the ground.

Panting, I whirled, finding Raiden's silvery eyes bright and his black hair windswept. Every angle of him as harsh as a blade that you need only graze your finger against to feel it split the skin.

"How…" I trailed off, shaking my head.

"Ferrah! I'm coming back down!" Kai called, pulling my attention away from the man in front of me.

"Be careful!" My words barely projected themselves loud enough to be heard, the strength of my voice vanishing altogether.

I glanced around at the scattered bodies of dead Scottomb. Most of them were missing limbs, some of them sliced in half.

"We better go, before they wake," Raiden said, his deep rasp sending a chill up my spine.

"Wake?" I asked. "How would they wake?"

A slight groove appeared between his brows. "Scottomb will not die unless you remove their heads. Surely you know that."

My mouth parted, but nothing came out. Internally I ran through everything I knew about the creatures that haunted our borders. *Stab or cut through a Scottomb in order to disable them. Any corpses left inside a border breach should be transported for disposal by the approved government vehicle immediately.*

I'd asked my officer why the bodies were transported to a facility to be disposed of, and she'd said they were burned, which was a much more dignified way to be put to rest than left at the border for creatures to pluck them apart.

But even in the brief training we'd received before the race began, I didn't recall anyone stating that a Scottomb's head had to be chopped off in order for them to actually die.

I frowned. "That's not possible. I've stabbed them and they've died. Just like a person would."

Raiden cocked his head ever so slightly to one side as his lips twitched with what could only be amusement. For some reason, it angered me that he thought my words funny.

With a huff, I demanded, "What?"

He shook his head, but that didn't wipe the hint of a smile that still played at the edges of his mouth. "I just forget that you know so little about my world."

My arms crossed over my chest in a defensive display that I didn't fully understand myself. "And that's funny? I've studied every book, every video clip, every audio file that pertains to Blood Valley. I'd say I know a fair bit."

Finally, his smile fled, and I instantly regretted chasing it away. "Not everything, *reickun freyr*."

The words were so close to the ones I'd heard in my dream that it made my stomach dip. "What does that mean?" I asked.

Just as his lips began to curve into a smile once again, Kai jumped the last little way down, landing with a huff. And just like that, Raiden's features hardened, shutting me out of whatever he was about to say.

"Are you okay, Fairs?" Arlakai asked, rushing toward me. He ignored Raiden in favor of patting my arms and turning my face side to side. I waved him off, slapping his hands away.

"I'm fine, Kai."

He took a step back, finally looking to the one who'd saved my life. "Care to explain how you lunged out of nowhere and practically floated down fifty feet without dying?"

"No," Raiden answered without inflection. "Now let's go before the Scottomb heal their bodies." He started walking through the gorge as though he were a natural part of this race.

"Were you following us?" I asked, unable to drop it.

"After dealing with some things, I doubled back to make sure you were okay and found you heading into the gorge, which I knew could only spell trouble. I followed to make sure you didn't get yourselves killed. Lucky I did." The muscles in his back moved in a way that held my gaze. There was something different about the sinewy movement, though I couldn't place it.

"Yeah, really lucky," Kai drawled. "But that doesn't explain how we didn't see you."

"You were climbing down a rock when I found you. It's not like you were really paying attention," Raiden answered, his tone darkening.

"Well thank you," I said, hurrying my pace to keep in step with Raiden's much longer strides.

He glanced my way before shaking his head. "Only you would be crazy enough to go through the gorge instead of around it."

"It's faster," I said by way of protest.

Raiden snorted. "I don't disagree. But most have a stronger desire to live than to save time."

I shrugged. "I'll do whatever it takes to win."

He didn't respond and the three of us walked in silence for several snaps before Arlakai cleared his throat. "While we're grateful for your help this far, you really don't have to stick around."

Raiden's shoulders rolled back. "I'm heading this way anyway. Besides, you'll need all the help you can get in the gorge."

"He's right, Kai," I said, looking to my best friend who pinched his lips together, but didn't say anything else.

The light began to fade from our path entirely, and I knew soon we'd have to set up camp down here. A shudder ran through me at the thought of being enclosed in a gorge this deep, but it was a calculated move I'd made when I chose this path.

Scanning the edges, I knew that climbing out to camp at the top wasn't an option. The rock was too smooth, looking like towering ripples that would mean instant doom should anyone attempt to scale it.

"Where do you bet is the safest place to set up camp?" I asked Raiden.

He pointed to a wide tower of rock. "Behind that. It'll offer a small bit of camouflage from wandering Scottomb, but your best bet is to sleep with your blade in hand."

I swallowed hard, suddenly wondering why I'd been so reckless.

Raiden's hand caught my empty one. The jolt of electricity that transferred between where our skin met felt stronger than a leftover Lufarium zap, raising the fine hairs on the back of my neck. He gave my hand a squeeze, clearly sensing my doubts, before releasing it. My stomach dipped with disappointment.

I shook myself mentally, reminding myself that I didn't need anyone to hold my hand.

"With your sleeping quarters, you'll be protected enough. There are tens of thousands of people who live in Blood Valley without the protection of your Lufarium." He spat the last word out like it was acidic, and my brows drew together.

"What's wrong with Lufarium?" I asked. "It powers our weapons, our cities, our borders. I'm shocked you don't use it too."

Raiden gave a humorless laugh. "Even if Triste allowed us access to it, we wouldn't touch it. Your nations do enough damage with Lufarium for the whole world."

"How is protecting ourselves damaging, blood-dweller?" Kai demanded.

I jerked my head in his direction, shocked by the derogatory term. It hadn't always been, but now it carried a connotation that inhabitants of Blood Valley dwelled in their own filth.

In all our birth-tides of friendship, I'd never heard him use that term.

Raiden halted, his eyes glinting like razor-sharp metal. "I recommend you don't use that term around me ever again, and all you need to do is look around to see how using Lufarium has hurt the rest of us.

"Each and every citizen in this valley is handed an early death sentence the moment they're born."

"Is your *king* not paid for the Lufarium we take?" Arlakai folded his arms over his chest defensively, but he was physically smaller than Raiden, so it did little to intimidate.

"There isn't enough money in the world that could save us," Raiden snarled, stepping closer. I tensed, preparing to jump between the two if necessary. "We were barred from trade, so what would money do anyway?"

Distant shrieks echoed through the gorge, dispelling the thick tension between the two guys.

"I'll set up my tent, Kai you can sleep in mine, and Raiden can use yours."

"No," they both said in unison. Then, Raiden said, "I don't sleep much. I'll keep watch outside your tents." He eyed Kai, making a point of him sleeping in his own tent.

"I'll stay with you, Fairs, but for someone so against Lufarium, it just doesn't seem right to make him use its protection." Kai unslung his backpack and took out his canteen and water tablets.

"What is your problem?" I hissed, getting closer to my best friend, though I knew that Raiden could hear us.

Kai handed me the full canteen. "I don't trust him, Fairs. And you shouldn't either."

I rolled my eyes. "Yes, you've said that already. He saved my life—twice—and he has more knowledge about this place than either of us do. It won't kill you to be nice if it means we can get home sooner."

He didn't look at me, but nodded, resigned. His jaw remained tight, even as he ate his rations. I offered some of mine to Raiden, but he said he'd hunt something later.

Just as I finished the last bite of my nutrition slab, my communicator chimed. Frowning, I opened the main screen and read the words projected there twice in stunned silence.

Do not collect Lufarium. Kill the Phantom to be declared winner of the 212th Blood Run.

"Fairy?" Kai leaned in to read the screen. I slapped a hand over the communicator, swiping away the message, but from how wide his eyes went, I knew he'd caught at least part of it. He glanced at Raiden who watched me with a careful expression, then Kai's eyes flicked back to me.

"That's your mission?" he whispered with a note of panic.

I shot him a warning look before jerking my head in the direction of the hover bot still active above us. Its camera looked as though it had focused on the gorge behind us instead, though I couldn't be sure.

Raiden got to his feet so suddenly, both mine and Kai's gaze snapped to him. "I'm going to go hunt before the chaos sets in."

I nodded before watching him walk back the way we'd come. Darkness was becoming complete, and with it came the cold.

We slipped inside the tent, settling in the small space with what little we had. I longed for the comfort of my bed back in Freeya, but above all, I missed Nona and Charle.

"Ferrah, please tell me that didn't say to kill the Phantom," Kai said, not wasting a moment of our relative privacy.

I sighed, making sure the hover bot had deactivated for the night before answering. "Yes, that was the mission I was assigned. For all I know, that's what everyone's mission is."

My best friend shook his head. "There's no way. You can't kill a ghost. No one has seen the guy since the end of the Ultimate War."

"I know, Kai," I replied with more anger than I'd meant to. But after the way he'd treated Raiden this light-rise, I could barely stop the floodgates of my anger once they opened. "I don't understand why after everything he's done for us, you insist on being such a jerk to Raiden. If I could just talk to him alone, then maybe I could get some answers. Because without them, I have no idea how I'll find the Phantom, let alone kill him."

Silence permeated the air, letting my words fall between us. I hoped he took them to heart, because whether or not he liked it, we needed Raiden.

After a long pause, he said, "If you really want to know why I don't like him, it's because I see the way you look at him." Kai glanced at me, and his deep green eyes were weighted with sadness.

"How do I look at him?" I asked, my voice barely above a whisper.

"Like he's the hero of your story. The one who carried you through your darkest nights, when *I* was the one who held you while you cried over Charle's declining health. I think you've fantasized so long about stepping over the barrier into the valley to meet the boy who sat on the other side wishing for the safety of Triste, that you've forgotten that it was you and I who grew up together. I'm the one who knows what your favorite things are, and that you can't stand the cold."

I reached for Kai, resting a hand on the forearm he'd balanced on his knee. He didn't look at me as I said, "I've never forgotten, Kai. And I loved every snap of our lives together."

He swallowed audibly, then turned his head, our eyes meeting. "Then agree to be bonded when we get back. You know it's the right choice."

My breath stalled in my lungs, even though I knew his proposal was coming again. I searched for the right words, but all that came out was, "I'm not even eighteen birth-tides yet."

"It doesn't have to be right away, but the Council won't say no. As long as you have someone like Nona to give her approval, that's all that matters to them."

A heavy weight dropped into the pit of my stomach, my lungs suddenly tight. Sure, I could probably keep the union from taking place for another two birth-tides, but law dictated when my freedom would end. I just hadn't thought it would be so soon.

Kai is the least offensive candidate for a union, I told myself. We loved each other in our own way, and that was more than most unions could boast. The mandatory two-child per union rule was something I'd face when the time came, but I knew Kai wouldn't force anything. That was perhaps the best future I could ask for.

"Sure," I said softly. "Assuming we make it home in one piece, that is."

Kai's smile felt like sealing the bargain we'd made. And that only made sleep harder to catch than the screeching of the monsters who sought their next meal.

The gorge felt as though it stretched on forever. Each light-rise was spent under the punishing light orb that Raiden told me was called "the sun". And the silvery ball that lit up the darkness was commonly referred to as "the moon." Apparently there were two moons, but we only ever saw one at any given time. When I'd asked how he knew these things, he answered with,

"In my numerous birth-tides of life, I've studied the world and everything that goes on around it. We have books on history, science, technology, and anything else you can think of. Tristé stamped out any information they couldn't control."

Kai had given a small scoff in disbelief, but didn't say anything to counter Raiden's words.

Raiden was a fountain of knowledge that I found myself absorbing to help pass the time. Kai had softened marginally toward our guide, but I suspected that had more to do with my promise to him than any feelings of friendship developing.

Somehow the Scottomb steered clear of us for the most part, though I couldn't speak for the night when Raiden stood guard outside. How he ever slept was beyond me.

"We're likely only a few rotations away from the end of the gorge," Raiden said, breaking the long silence that had settled on our group.

Excitement fluttered in my chest. Then crashed against my ribs like a ship blasted apart on the rocks. I was no closer to finding the Phantom, and after the gorge, the Lufarium mines were only another two light-rises' journey away.

But since I wasn't meant to collect Lufarium, what would I do when we reached the top of the gorge?

I cleared my throat, steeling my nerves. "Where did the Phantom—the king—live?"

Raiden's head jerked in my direction, surprise etched on his striking features. For a moment I didn't think he'd answer, but then he finally said, "If rumors are to be believed, then at the southernmost tip of Blood Valley."

My jaw fell open. "That would take, what, another thirteen light-rises past the mines?"

Raiden shrugged. "Depends on if you take any shortcuts. Why, are you going on a ghost hunt?" He smirked, the sensual tilt to his lips making my heart stutter.

I chuckled nervously. "Someone said the Phantom was looking for me."

The amusement fled from his face in an instant. "The Phantom doesn't 'look' for anyone. He just knows where they are. That's why his nickname is the Phantom."

Kai, who'd kept just behind us was suddenly at my side as though he could protect me from the monstrous king.

Tightening my grip on my backpack straps, I asked, "What do you know about him?"

Raiden released a heavy sigh, as though imparting such information was a burden he didn't wish to pass on. "I can tell you what people whisper, but if you're looking for the lies your Council told you in order to feel validated, you're looking in the wrong place. Despite the hardships our nation has faced, many are still loyal to him."

"Are you loyal to him?" I asked, my heart racing for reasons I didn't want to examine too closely.

He shrugged. "I'm loyal to my country."

"An admirable quality to have," Kai said on my other side. "But surely as someone who has suffered along with your nation, you can understand their frustrations and why your king is no longer relevant. Why hasn't anyone else stepped in to rule?"

A muscle feathered in Raiden's jaw, though he conceded a nod. "Many have tried," he answered. "I do understand their suffering, but after so long,

I finally have hope again. Things *will* change for the better." His gaze slid to me for a moment, lingering and making my heart do weird things.

"No one wants to see their people suffer," Arlakai said in a way that was meant to be the end of that particular conversation, but Raiden's next words sent a blanket of silence over us all.

"Not everyone can recognize that peaceful enslavement is sometimes worse than dealing with Scottomb."

The end of the gorge was far steeper than where we'd entered it, but it had large steps that would make climbing it far easier. I had to admit I wouldn't miss the shrieking and groaning of the Scottomb that had become like white noise on our journey.

"You two go first, I'll follow," Raiden said, and with a nod, Kai went first, eager to be past the fear of how high he had to climb.

I started after him, keeping a decent pace. With sweat coating my brow I saw the glint of a violet crystal splintering like a vein up the rock barely a thumb's width from my hand.

"Holy kwipai," I said, voice struck with awe. "It's Lufarium."

"Don't touch it raw!" Raiden called up to me.

I recalled that particular warning. Never touch Lufarium in its raw form, though no one could explain why. Only that it would require medical attention. "What will happen if I do?"

"Best not to find out," he answered.

I huffed in frustration, moving myself up with careful movements so as not to brush the exposed crystal. "I'm going to need a little more than that."

After climbing up onto the next platform, I panted with my hands on my hips. My gaze scanned the cliffside, following the lines of Lufarium. There was probably enough here to grab and take back without ever going to the mines.

But my message had been clear. I didn't need to harvest Lufarium, I needed to find the Phantom.

"I'm surprised no one in Triste ever told you," Raiden answered, looking to the energy source that was so close. "It contains raw energy within the crystal. One touch and the shock would stop your heart."

I blanched, taking a small step back. "After handling our weapons, we transfer a small bit of that energy through skin-to-skin contact. It's never killed anyone though."

Raiden's lips pressed into a disapproving line. "Yes, they'd never allow their own people to be harmed by it." I couldn't tell for sure, but I was fairly certain he'd sounded sarcastic.

"There's way more up here, so watch where you put your hands," Kai called.

"Okay!" My breathing had somewhat returned to normal as I began to climb again. Between the constant physical exertion and the heat, I wasn't sure I'd survive once I was back in Freeya. The cold had been unbearable before, but now I'd have to readjust all over again.

Sweat trickled over the bridge of my nose, stinging my eyes. I shuffled to the right slightly, noticing the step widened for better grip. A warm tingling shot through my fingers and up my right arm, making me suck in a breath. My heart jolted, adrenaline pouring through my veins.

"Ferrah, don't, there's Lufarium!" Kai called from above. He'd nearly made it to the top, and in his shock, his foot slipped, sending loose sand and stone raining down on me.

I pulled myself up enough to see that my hand was firmly on a vein of violet glowing stone. My eyes widened and my heart hammered hard, each thundering thump nearly painful.

"Move, now," Raiden snarled below me.

I shot up with a sudden burst of speed, practically sprinting up the cliff-side. The tingling spread through my entire body making me warmer than I already was.

Kai rolled over the top out of view only a moment before I clambered up as well, Raiden right behind me. He turned me so I was fully facing him before gently cupping my face in his hands. His eyes were so bright they practically shined as he searched my face—for what, I didn't know. The tingling eased, ebbing and flowing from me like a current until my heart stopped pounding against my ribs as though it might burst right out of me.

"What?" I asked.

Kai pulled me away from Raiden, wrapping his arms around me and burying his nose in the crook of my neck. "I thought you'd touched it," he murmured against my skin. "You scared the shit out of me."

"I'm sorry," I whispered back.

"It's okay." Kai's voice broke and when he pulled away, his eyes shone with unshed tears. "Just don't scare me like that again."

I didn't know how to tell him I *had* touched the Lufarium. Perhaps it just hadn't been enough to kill me, though I'd certainly felt the energy it zapped me with.

Glancing over at Raiden, I found his expression to be unreadable, though he watched me, probably expecting me to just keel over dead any moment.

Running my hands down the front of my jumpsuit, I said, "I'm fine."

"You moved so fast. I've never seen you climb so fast in my life," Kai said, looking to Raiden as though he would corroborate that statement.

I shrugged. "Probably the adrenaline."

"It'll make the impossible possible," Raiden confirmed. "How do you feel now?"

"Fine," I said. "We should keep going before we have to make camp for the night."

Kai nodded. "Then we can decide which direction we need to go in."

I shot him a look of exasperation which he realized a moment too late when Raiden asked, "Aren't you going to the mines?"

I tried my best not to look as sheepish as I felt. "Not exactly."

Chapter 16

Ferrah

When we stopped, Raiden pointed to a small pool of bluish green water.

"You can bathe here if you want. There's nothing in this pool due to the high mineral content."

"Isn't it toxic?" I asked, frowning.

Raiden's lips twitched, fighting off a smile. "No. Not to you, anyway."

I didn't know what that meant, but seeing as I hadn't bathed in far too long, I was eager to wash the dirt, sweat, and grime of the journey off.

"I'll stand watch," Kai offered. "For your safety."

Raiden snorted a derisive laugh. "Sure you will."

Kai shot him a glare, but I stepped in before the two males could find something so silly to threaten the fragile peace these past rotations had woven into place.

"I don't need a lookout," I said, meeting my best friend's hard stare. Pasting on a reassuring smile, I added, "Why don't you two hunt something to eat so we can save our rations?"

Raiden's smile was a slash of brilliant white and just a tad mischievous. He slapped a hand on Kai's back, making him jump. "Absolutely. Let's hunt."

He grumbled under his breath, following Raiden away from the pool, not that there was much to offer cover beyond some random ferns and cacti.

When they were far enough away, I stripped off my jumpsuit, thankful to have the skin-hugging fabric off. I stepped into the small pool, shocked by the coolness of the water. A groan escaped me as my battered feet were covered by the water.

Little by little I lowered myself into the water, crouching so that the water would cover my breasts and set to work scrubbing the dust and dirt from my hair. I had brought a soap pod with me from my bag and used it to scrub the dry, neglected strands, then my body.

As much as I wanted to linger in the refreshing water, I knew I needed to get dressed before the guys arrived back. I stood, looking down at the skin that been torn open by the beast the night Raiden saved my life for the first time. It was smooth, unblemished skin. Not even a hint of my previous wound remained.

I ran my fingers over the area in disbelief before checking my shoulder. It, too, had healed up perfectly. Clearly that herb Raiden had brought was a miracle worker.

A small kwipai only as tall as my forearm scuttled toward the pool hesitantly. Its eyes all blinked in my direction, both of us assessing the other.

"Hey little guy," I said, uncertain of why the creature had chosen to get close to me when they were notoriously shy.

It moved closer, the hairs on its elongated legs quivering. After a moment it tested the tip of one leg in the water before emitting a hiss and scurrying backwards.

I couldn't help the laugh that burst out of me at its surprise. If this young kwipai hadn't yet seen water, then it had likely traveled a great distance.

My smile fell when it hurried to my bag. The sound of fabric tearing had me running out of the pool. "No, no, no!"

Startled, the kwipai gave a small hiss and backed away from the bag. The front pocket was torn, several rations spilling out. My gut clenched as I glanced at the creature that had turned its body into a cage, protecting itself from the perceived threat.

I sighed, examining the ration that was partially torn open. Another click and it might have made off with several rotations of food. Plucking up the pack, I tore it open and tossed a chunk of the bar to the kwipai.

For a moment it didn't move. Then, slowly, it unfurled its legs and tentatively leaned toward the offering before snatching it up and running several paces away with happy clicking sounds that made me chuckle again.

I sat on sand-covered stone and watched it try to tear into the nutrition slab the way kwipai tore into carcasses for meat. While it ate, I slipped my jumpsuit back on.

"You must be pretty desperate for food to try to take it from a human."

The kwipai finished its portion then looked back across the pool at me, seeming to wonder if it could coax me out of more.

"Go find your family, little guy." I waved it away, but to no avail.

Instead it took a few steps around the pool, coming closer, then pausing to see how I'd react. Then it scuttled a few more paces and seemed to lose its nerve, going back into its defensive position.

"You better run along," I told the creature as though it could understand me. "The guys I came here with won't be as keen to share their food."

It peered at me from between two of its scrawny legs before unspooling itself again. Another tentative jaunt brought it so close I could almost touch it. With slow movements, I pushed my pack behind me, hoping to discourage it from trying to steal more food.

It flinched back a step, paused, then stopped. After eyeing me for another snap, it folded its legs to the ground, laying atop them—not in its fearful way—before its eyes blinked lazily.

Was this creature actually falling asleep near me? Had I won its trust so easily?

My gut clenched as I thought about what Kai would do when he saw it, but perhaps it would run off before they got back.

The kwipai was silent, but its eyes shut fully, and didn't blink back open, telling me it had in fact fallen asleep. I marveled at the scraggly hairs on its body that were covered in light dust, making it almost the same reddish orange color as the ground.

It seemed stupid to pity an animal that was just a part of the food chain. I may have given it the sustenance it needed for this light-rise, but when darkness set, who knew what sort of beast would hunt this kwipai.

Still, I couldn't help the flicker of fondness I felt at having earned its trust—and how it seemed so much more intelligent than I'd thought them to be. It was starting to feel like my education of Blood Valley was thrown out the moment I stepped out of the frozen tundra of Freeya, and each rotation I spent out here brought me a newfound knowledge that I'd cherish for the rest of my life.

Okay, maybe not every near-death experience so far, but this experience, no matter how miserable at times, was already beginning to alter me. And perhaps it was for the better.

"What in all the sacred tree is that?" Arlakai's voice woke the kwipai.

It jumped up to its feet with a terrified shriek before scurrying behind me.

"Stab it!" Kai called.

"You're scaring it!" I held up a hand, stopping Kai and Raiden who each carried one end of a heavy looking animal.

Turning, I saw the kwipai had curled itself into its cage, all of it trembling.

"I think it got separated from its family. It's so little." I spoke it loud enough for the two guys to hear me, but I knew that wouldn't change what their ultimatum would be.

To my surprise, Raiden said, "The younglings will often venture into a human village when they face starvation. Many have been known to keep them as companions."

"Are you serious?" Kai balked with a look of pure disgust. "You are *not* keeping that thing, Fairs. It's creepy. Besides, what are you going to do, carry it all the way back to Freeya?"

My stomach sank, though I wasn't sure why. I hadn't even considered keeping the creature, but Raiden's words gave me hope that it would find someone more suited to taking care of it.

"Can we drop it off in a nearby town?" I asked, looking pointedly at Raiden instead of Kai.

His usually sharp features seemed to have softened slightly. "There is one near the mines. It's a port village. Using ships to transport goods to the south is easier than trekking it by hovercraft."

Without thinking, I reached out and stroked the wiry hairs on the trembling creature's leg. It shifted, wide eyes blinked up at me with uncertainty, but it didn't move away.

"Don't the Scottomb attack your ships? Triste tried that for many birth-tides before giving up when too many vessels were sunk." The Scottomb always managed to stow away on the ships, even lined with Lufarium, and would attack once the ship set sail. Other times the ships were mysteriously compromised, though the Scottomb were still suspected of sabotage.

Raiden nodded. "Yes, it's not without its difficulties, but we manage to sail without incident around six out of ten boats."

My eyes widened. "How do you keep them out?"

His expression seemed to shutter off, turning impassive as he looked out over the vast desert wasteland. "They know who their enemies are. We don't show unnecessary cruelty, which means that unless they're desperate, they don't feed off the local villages."

"Are you saying that the Scottomb purposefully attack our borders? To feed from us?" Kai's voice was flinty.

Raiden's jaw flexed. "You would know if they concentrated their efforts. But with your tunnels being a weakness, they easily exploit it to feed. It doesn't help that you lot take any opportunity to fire at them. Hostility is bred when the land is a war zone."

"We only shoot them because they attack us for our blood! Do you know the level of massacre that would occur if we let down our barriers and tried to coexist with the vile creatures?"

Raiden scoffed, dropping the back legs of the creature he'd hauled back to camp. "Your kind forced my people to coexist with them, and we don't suffer terrible massacres. They are not as mindless as you may think."

My brows puckered together. "What do you mean?" I asked.

"How do you think they came to be?" Raiden demanded. When I gaped in stunned silence he nodded. "It figures that they wouldn't tell you that." He turned, storming back the way he came.

A lump rose in my throat. Who hadn't told us what? I looked to Kai, but he simply shook his head. "The guy is out of his mind. He's no ally, Fairs, no matter who he was to you when you were younger."

Anger choked out any other emotions that had risen to the surface. The kwipai seemed to sense the tumultuous turn in my demeanor, because it began to shake again.

I rose to my feet, hands clenched into fists. "Do you not think it's possible that we haven't had the whole story? That there's part of their lives we don't fully understand because we've been shut up in our protective bubbles for so long?"

My best friend reared back as though I'd suddenly grown a second head. "No, Ferrah, I don't. Do you know why? They let themselves be called Blood Valley instead of having a proper country name. Look around, is this any sort of civilized nation to you? They have no industry, no traditions or laws."

"That you know of," I countered. "You've been here all of, what, eight light-rises? How much of their culture have you seen for yourself?"

"We saw that village of starving, dying people. What more is there to see? These people live in worse conditions than they did before the Ultimate War."

I blinked back angry tears, refusing to let them fall. Kai and I rarely fought, but something about this time felt like a breach in our friendship that couldn't be smoothed over, even with time. If we didn't come to some form of agreement on the matter, that wound would only gape wider and wider until the very foundation split.

Glancing down at the kwipai who hadn't run off the moment things got heated like I'd expected, my heart swelled with resolution. Maybe the people and creatures of Blood Valley didn't need me to protect them, but I hoped they *did* find change soon. "And yet they've survived without everything we possess. If nothing else, I think that makes them far stronger than us."

Arlakai's shoulders drooped, looking exhausted from our small spat. "No one said they weren't strong. They've had to adapt to a harsh reality, and I commend them for that. But I also think they haven't helped themselves because they don't truly want to."

He stepped toward me, extending his arms for me to move into them the way I always did. I hesitated, making the tentative smile he offered, slip.

"I'm going to set up the tent. We need to make a fire if we're going to cook that." I nodded to the beast laying on the ground. "Plus, you should bathe while you have the chance. It's nice."

His arms fell to his sides, but I turned and crouched down in front of the kwipai so that I didn't have to see the rejection on Kai's face.

"Hey little buddy, I'm going to go find some non-threatening sticks. You can follow me, or stay here with him," I jerked a thumb over to where Kai was testing the water in the pool.

All eight of the blinking eyes looked from me to Kai, then back again. It unwrapped itself with cautious movements.

I smiled at it, then pulled the tent from my pack. The small, abandoned creature eyed my bag where it knew more food was hidden inside, before glancing at the dead animal.

With a laugh, I answered its questioning gaze. "Yes, there will be more food."

Once the tent was erected, I set off to find things to burn for a fire. The subtle scuttling behind me told me the kwipai had decided to follow.

We wandered to the ferns, looking for dead stalks to burn. I leaned into a particularly large one with my echo blade glowing bright. Trying to not disturb any of the pods beneath the leaves, I worked to saw one of the stalks free.

It crackled, the woody appendage nearly freed when a voice spoke from behind me.

"You touched the Lufarium, didn't you?"

I choked on a scream before whipping around. The kwipai hissed at my feet, causing me to lose my footing. I fell backwards, into the fern.

The *pop, pop, pop* of pods exploding had me scrambling from the bush, but it was already too late. A foul odor eeked into the air, seeping into my skin.

Raiden laughed, pulling me to my feet. "I can help you get that smell out." In his other arm, was a large bundle of wood. Still not enough to keep a fire going long enough to roast the entire creature they'd killed, but it would be enough to cook strips of the meat.

I grimaced. "Great."

His hand didn't release my forearm, and if anything, his grip tightened when I moved to pull away. The laughter hadn't fully died from his metallic eyes, but his expression morphed into one of seriousness before he asked the question again. "You touched it, didn't you?"

I sucked in a long breath, then gagged on the smell, my eyes watering. "No. I mean, I would have died right?"

Raiden didn't respond, though he stared at me with such intensity that my cheeks began to heat.

"I felt something. A zap of some sort, so maybe I just brushed against it—"

He shook his head. "If your little friend had *brushed* any part of his skin against even the smallest fleck of Lufarium, his heart would have exploded."

Frustration took root, blooming in my chest at the expectant look on his face. When I tugged my arm away, he let me go, allowing me to place my hands on my hips. "What are you trying to say?"

Raiden stepped closer, not seeming at all bothered by the rotting stench clinging to me. "I'm saying there are few people who can touch Lufarium without dying."

"I thought you said it killed everyone." I answered, but my curiosity was piqued.

"Back before the Ultimate War there was a race of people called the Béchua who could not only withstand its touch, they could harness its power to fertilize the ground, create power for entire cities, and even use it as a weapon if needed." That muscle that ticked in his jaw whenever he was agitated about something pulsed. "During the war, the Triste Council enslaved the Béchua and forced them to act as a conduit for their energy source."

My own mouth fell open. "What? If they were so powerful, how did they enslave them? Couldn't they have fought them off?"

Raiden shook his head, a flash of sadness filling his eyes for a moment. "They used torture and drugs that essentially rid them of all brain power until they were just husks that turned raw Lufarium into an energy source. They eventually died. All but one."

It took a moment to click the puzzle pieces into place. "The Phantom."

Raiden nodded. "That's part of why he hides away in the shadows. If he were to be caught by Triste, they could use his power for all sorts of heinous things."

"Why doesn't he use his power to fertilize the ground, like you said? Nearly everyone is starving or going thirsty."

To my surprise, Raiden rolled his eyes. "They're not starving, or going thirsty. Their stores of food and water are underground."

"What? No." I recalled my encounter with the boy in the village, how he was coughing and hoarse. Raiden sighed heavily.

"They knew the runners would go near them so they got you to feel bad for a little kid and then tried to attack you to steal all of your goods. Most likely, they're a radical bunch that were looking to kill anyone belonging to the empire.

My jaw dropped in shock. "The boy had water? What did they do, deprive him long enough to make him sound like that?"

Raiden nodded. "Not everyone in Blood Valley cares for peace. Some of them are so sick of Triste coming in and upsetting the natural order of things that they'd rather see them all dead."

I sat, unable to speak for several clicks. I'd known that Triste was hated. But I hadn't known they were likely to kill us for being on their land.

Raiden leaned a little closer despite my acrid scent. "Don't worry, I'm not going to let anything happen to you. Now, we have enough burnables to cook what we need. I'll bring the rest to the nearest village."

I nodded, ignoring the pleasant warmth that coated my cheeks. The man was so intense. "Can I come?"

Raiden hesitated, looking to my kwipai friend who still hadn't departed. "I'll be running all through the night. You need your sleep."

I frowned. "So do you."

He lifted a single shoulder in nonchalance. "I get it when I can, but I've mostly learned to go without. Let's get you back so I can find dombur berries for the smell." The smirk he shot in my direction sent a tingle through my limbs that I tried to ignore.

"Yeah, yeah, yeah," I grumbled. "Maybe don't sneak up on someone when they're leaning into a fern."

"We call them dung bushes because of the smell," Raiden chuckled.

I joined him, laughing at the fact that I smelled so bad.

"Do you know what kwipai means in the old language?" he asked, looking at the furry creature scampering along at my side like a loyal companion.

I wracked my brain before finally shaking my head.

His grin widened as he answered. "Dung rat. Rats were a different kind of creature back in ancient times from a different planet; they're extinct now. The kwipai got their name because they're scavengers, just like rats were."

Pursing my lips together, I tried to hold back my laughter at the name but failed miserably. "Poor little kwipai. It makes sense though since they hide in the ferns." It was fascinating to hear about his knowledge of the old world. "Wasn't most of the old-world history destroyed, even the stuff in Blood Valley?"

Raiden nodded. "By wars, the Council, and just through time. But my family kept a collection of records and books that I've memorized over time."

I couldn't stop my curiosity from peeking through. "You're what, nineteen or twenty birth-tides?"

He shrugged. "Time is kept by the Council. Out here, we follow a different way of passing time, but even that has changed during my life."

I hummed thoughtfully. "Has it been a hard life? Do you ever wish you could have grown up on the other side of the borders?"

Raiden made a sound of disgust. "Never. I'd not trade a thousand lifetimes out here for one miserable one behind the bars of a cage that is for your supposed protection. But for my people, I wish they had the option. The opportunity to do something more than what is offered out here."

After a long moment, I released a gust of breath. "You sound so much wiser than your age."

He chuckled at that. "You'd be surprised."

After successfully washing the horrid smell from my jumpsuit, we sat around the fire with our hunks of charred meat.

Raiden managed to wrangle a broody Kai into a conversation about hovercraft, allowing me to feed bits of meat to Alvy—which is the name I decided to give to the kwipai. When we were done, Raiden hefted the rest of the slaughtered beast over his broad shoulders.

"I'll be back before you wake. You won't be as likely to draw Scottomb attention, just make sure you put out the fire before the light is completely gone."

I nodded, getting to my feet.

Alvy cracked open one of his eyes, tracking me as I grabbed my canteen and filled it with water from the pond to dump on the fire.

"That thing is not sleeping in the tent," Kai said with a shudder.

"If you sleep in yours, then you won't even notice." I winced at the bite in my own voice, then turned to face him. "I didn't mean for that to sound so harsh."

Kai had gotten to his feet too and toed loose rock on the ground. "I'm sorry we fought earlier."

I nodded. "Me too."

His gaze lifted to meet mine. "I love you, Ferrah. It was dumb of me to wait so long to say it, but you're the only girl I want to be bonded to."

"I know," I said softly. When his expression pinched, I realized that my answer hadn't been the one he was expecting. Stepping toward him, I laid a hand on his shoulder. "I'll always love you, Kai. I'm not quite ready for a union, but we have time."

"I have one birth-tide left. It just has to be before then."

I nodded, hating the twisting in my gut that felt like an animal burrowing inside me. Why did every mention of us being bonded make me feel like a caged beast? "It will be," I assured him, then tried to assure myself that this was for the best. I did love Kai, that wasn't a lie. But he loved me in a different way than I loved him. I wasn't sure how I hadn't seen it, but it felt cruel to reject his affection when so many were bonded to people they didn't even know.

No, this was a good thing.

"I'll sleep in my tent tonight if you want. But if we get attacked, I'm blaming the kwipai."

A small smile pulled at the corners of my lips. I stood up on the tips of my toes and pressed my lips to his cheek in thanks.

To be honest, I had no idea if Alvy would want to sleep in the tent. It had probably never been in an enclosure like that before, and I didn't want him to get spooked and end up tearing the thing apart. Still, I was grateful for the space that Kai provided. I needed a night to myself to be alone with my thoughts.

When Kai's tent was set up and darkness had blanketed the valley, we said goodnight. He disappeared into his quarters, while I held open the flap for mine.

"Want to sleep in here, Alvy?" I asked the kwipai. It peered into the tent before backing away. I sighed. "Okay then, stay safe, buddy."

I climbed into the tent, but just before I secured the flap, Alvy barreled in with a fearful squeak. Smiling, I made sure the tent was secure, then laid down on my bedroll.

"Don't you even think about stealing food while I'm sleeping. Got it?" I gave him a stern look, but the kwipai had already settled its body atop its legs and closed its eyes.

With a smile, I reached out and stroked the strangely coarse-haired creature and let my eyes fall closed.

No sooner had sleep claimed me did I jerk awake to chaos. A knife pierced the thick, metal lining of my tent. I heard Kai shouting along with a bunch of other voices and howls.

Again, and again, blades stabbed through the material with a horrid screeching sound. Alvy shook and hissed in the far corner. I scooped up his body in one arm and used the other to pull my blade from its holster.

In one clean cut, I sliced through the flap and leapt through it, curling my body so I rolled against the stone and rose to my feet.

I barely had a snap to take in the mania of what was taking place outside when a man in tattered clothes barreled into me. A familiar screeching rent the air, coming from the guy's elongated mouth. His skin was far too dark to be that of a Scottomb, and his head wasn't quite as oblong as it should have been, yet he clawed at my body with too-sharp nails. Jaws with razor sharp teeth snapped for my neck before I jammed my blade into the man's temple.

The thrust sent him tumbling off me, though he writhed and choked.

I bent down to retrieve my blade when I heard the whispered words coming from the man's mouth. "Must... destroy... the mines."

My skin went colder than the icy wind that buffeted my body. I didn't have time to stop and ponder his words though. Yanking my blade free with a sickening sound I'd never get used to, I scanned the melee.

Arlakai blasted through three men with his echo bolt before whirling on his heel and landing a swinging kick to another guy's jaw.

It didn't knock the now-groaning man out, however, and I sprinted for him. Just as I got close enough to strike, the man howled an animalistic cry, eyes crazed and milky. He swung claws in my direction, snarling incoherent words.

I backed away, hesitating for the first time to kill a monster. Something like humanity flashed across his face before his features twisted into rage once again.

"Ferrah, kill it!" Arlakai screamed.

"Yes," the man rasped, shuffling to its feet again. Then it charged.

I let my indecision go as my survival instincts kicked in. My blade left my hand, meeting its mark, sinking through the man's throat. He made a gurgling sound, dark blood bubbling from his mouth and oozing down his chin.

His hands wrapped around the hilt of the blade before he pulled it free. When he collapsed, I lunged for the blade, picking it up just in time for someone to swipe at me. The whisper of sharp metal played through a loose lock of my hair, severing it.

I rolled, sending my blade sailing again and wishing I'd grabbed the other two from my bag before coming out here. It hit the man in the chest, but it didn't so much as slow him. He had two longer blades that he crisscrossed in front of my face.

Driving my knee up, I dislodged one knife from his hand, catching it before it hit the ground. I spun out before plunging the weapon in his throat, the broadest part of the blade nearly taking his head clean off.

Before he even hit the ground, I pulled my echo blade free, as well as his own well-crafted knife. Panting, I looked around at the carnage strewn over the stony ground.

The blinding blast of the echo bolt crackled again before silence fell. Arlakai met my gaze over it all, his chest rising and falling as heavily as mine.

"What were those things?" My voice sounded hollow and strange to my ears.

"I don't know. They looked human."

"But they acted like..."

He shook his head. "It doesn't make sense. Scottomb are their own species, aren't they?"

"I thought they were," I said, wishing Raiden were here to explain it.

A whimper sounded from behind me, and I turned, finding Alvy approaching me slowly, as though he wasn't sure he wanted to get close to me. I crouched down, letting the weapons fall at my sides.

"Hey, buddy, it's okay," I cooed. "You're safe now."

Kai gave an exasperated sigh. "You and that kwipai. He's lucky he didn't get trampled in the chaos."

I nodded without taking my eyes off Alvy. "Very lucky. You were very brave."

The kwipai scuttled the rest of the way to me, climbing into my arms. It was awkward to hold a ten-legged creature, but Alvy situated himself without issue.

"Your tent sustained the most damage," Kai said, drawing my attention back to him.

"Is it still useable?" I got to my feet and strode toward him where he examined the damaged structure.

A few of the internal rods that contained the Lufarium were bent at odd angles, and a faint sizzling came from one of the larger holes.

Kai grimaced. "I don't think so."

I groaned. "What about yours?" Structurally it still appeared to be intact, but a Lufarium leak could be lethal.

"It should be fine," he confirmed, stalking around it to look for damage. "I was about to come to your tent to tell you I heard something weird when the guys ambushed me outside."

"It's lucky you're such a light sleeper," I said, with a strained chuckle.

He didn't return my attempt at a smile. "I am when I'm alone. When we share a bed, it relaxes me. Maybe a little too much." The idea looked as though it bothered him, though his words warmed me.

When we were in early guard training, he had horrid nightmares that would wake everyone in the barracks. The first time I crawled into his bed with him was the first night he hadn't woken screaming.

Everyone had teased us mercilessly when they found us asleep together, but I didn't care as long as I could take away the terrors he faced in his sleep.

"Well I guess we'll camp in your tent then." I yawned.

Kai nodded. "You go ahead, I'll join you in a snap."

When I didn't immediately leave his side, his hand reached for mine, our fingers entwining. I gave him a gentle squeeze while examining the inky black canvas above us dotted with tiny blooms of light.

Out here, the sky was filled with them, and I found myself wishing I had a view as magnificent as this every light-rise. Alvy stayed asleep on my other arm, obviously worn out from watching me fight.

The three of us stayed like that until the cold made my teeth chatter. Arlakai nudged me toward the tent and sleepily, I obeyed. He didn't protest when I laid Alvy in the corner by my feet, which made me smile to myself.

And when Kai laid beside me, I didn't recoil at what it meant to him. Because just maybe it meant something more to me, too.

CHAPTER 17

Ferrah

I wasn't sure what I'd expected from Raiden when we told him about the attack. He'd clearly seen the bodies because when we'd emerged from Kai's tent the next morning, they were all gone.

Only the dark smears of blood left any proof that the fight had taken place at all.

However, I certainly hadn't expected him to confirm that they were Scottomb.

"How is that possible?" Arlakai looked stunned by that fact, even though we'd already suspected that's what they were.

"They spoke human words, well, some of them anyway. Not the whole time. It was like they would switch back and forth between human and not." My confession drew Kai's gaze to me.

Raiden's lips thinned before he spoke. He wasn't as light-hearted as usual, and I wondered if it was the journey he'd taken last night, or because he hadn't been there for the attack, or perhaps something else entirely. I knew he wouldn't tell me if I asked, so I let it go. "They were mid-change. For some, it's a slow process, taking up to ten birth-tides to be complete. In that time, they lose their mind. Their memories of those they loved, the capacity for basic human emotions, all of it. For others, the change is faster."

"How are people changed?" I asked. "From Scottomb bites?"

Raiden shook his head. "Remember when I said that everyone in Blood Valley is given an early death sentence the moment they're born?"

I nodded.

"That's because, eventually, they all turn."

A sharp gasp slipped from me before I halted, clapping a hand over my mouth. My mind went to the little boy in the village, along with the older woman who cared for him. Despite their plot to steal from us and probably kill us, I felt a pang of sadness for them all. Would that little boy lose her before he was fully grown?

How old would he be when he turned? I'd never seen a child-sized Scottomb, but with how little I knew about everything, that didn't mean much.

"Why?" It was all I could think to ask with the storm of questions bombarding my mind.

"They're poisoned." He spoke the words as though they were the most obvious ones, as he continued to walk ahead.

I hurried to keep stride with him again, trying to process this new information. "One of them whispered, 'Must destroy the mines' before he died." It was too painful to think about the fact that I'd murdered men. *Men who would have become fully fledged Scottomb if you hadn't put them out of their misery,* I reminded myself.

"How are they poisoned?" I asked.

This time he stopped, looking from me to Kai, then back again. "I don't think you're ready to hear that information, little flower."

His nickname for me made my stomach dip, but I didn't have time to dwell on that.

"I can handle it," I vowed.

"It's not whether or not you can handle the information," he replied. "It's what you do with it once I give it to you."

I stepped closer to him, imploring. "Please."

His eyes searched mine before he relented, running a hand through his dark hair. "The electrified Lufarium that surrounds the nations' borders emits a toxic gas. That gas has saturated the air that people breathe, and once a person has consumed enough of it, the change begins."

"But that's..." I paused. "If that's true, how does no one inside the borders ever change?"

Raiden's eyes slid to the communicator on my wrist. "Besides purifying the air, they also created an antidote that they inject into their people."

I turned wide eyes on Kai who looked ready to argue. "That's why every time there's a border collapse, we get another injection."

"So why didn't the Phantom just bargain for doses of the antidote for his people in exchange for the Lufarium we take?" Kai asked, sounding defensive.

Raiden's features darkened. "Why don't you ask your bloody Council?" he snarled.

The rage that radiated from him felt like heavy waves of electricity. I stepped between him and Kai before they could come to blows.

Alvy must have sensed the tension too, because he coiled his legs around himself for protection.

"We should keep moving," I reminded them.

"To where?" Kai asked. "We still don't know where the Phantom is, and all *Raiden* is good for is filling your head with lies about Triste. It's clear that the people out here are delusional."

"Kai!" I stared at him with a mixture of horror and anger that he would think Raiden was lying about any of it. "What would he stand to gain by lying?"

"You!" he bellowed, gripping my arms and giving me a hard shake. But the click the word was out, he froze, expression morphing to panic. Wordlessly, I broke his hold and took a step away.

"Why are you being like this?" I asked. "I told you I would be bonded to you. I'm literally giving you the rest of my life, but you can't seem to accept that fact."

Kai's face fell, and his head dropped to look at the ground. After a moment he said, "Because it's your heart I want, Ferrah. But I have a feeling it's leaning in a different direction. Every light-rise that we're out here, you act like I'm not even here. Only in the dark do I get some small part of you."

"What small part?" Raiden ground out.

I opened my mouth to respond, to refute Kai's claims. But the words wouldn't come. My heart didn't belong to anyone but me. I couldn't tell him that eventually I'd probably come to love him in that way. Tears burned my eyes, from shame, or embarrassment, or sadness I didn't know.

Eventually, I managed to say, "You're my friend, Kai. So is Raiden. That's all."

Arlakai stared at me a snap longer before the chirp of a communicator sounded, but it wasn't mine. He sighed before opening the message, his expression turning to stone.

"What does it say?" I whispered.

His gaze flicked so briefly to Raiden that I almost missed it before he dismissed the blurred screen and said, "Nothing." He marched past me, carrying on the way we'd been heading.

I stared after him, knowing that my fear had finally come true. Kai's feelings for me had begun to change our friendship. His expectations tore down the comfort I'd found in his presence for the past seven birth-tides.

"Why do you want to find the Phantom so badly?" Raiden asked in a gentler tone than I'd heard him use so far.

I turned to him, letting all pretenses fall away. Maybe if Raiden hated me then Kai would see I wasn't trying to fall in love with the boy from the desert. "Because I have to kill him."

His silvery eyes flashed with a look I couldn't decipher. Then with long, purposeful strides, he ate up the distance between us until we were almost chest-to-chest. My breath caught in my throat and the rapid beating of my heart betrayed my involuntary reaction whenever he got close.

He towered over me, leaning close so I could feel the heat of his breath on my lips. With a whisper, he said, "You might be the girl I've been waiting for, but if you seek to harm my people, I will stop you, flower. Do you understand?"

I steeled my spine despite the current of fear his promise elicited. "My duty is to Freeya first. Just as yours is to Blood Valley."

He shook his head, "Call it by its name. Krovaya."

"Krovaya," I repeated, my head fuzzy from the smell of ash and something warmer on him.

"It's the name your people gave it when they slaughtered most of my country and abandoned the rest to this hell. It means 'Land of Blood'." The cruel hatred in his voice made something in my heart crack.

"I'm sorry," I whispered.

"Don't be," he answered flatly, straightening and creating enough space between us for me to suck in a lungful of air. "Just be prepared to choose between your duty and what is right when the time comes."

And with that, he stalked away, following the small, blurred shape that was Kai and leaving me to wonder what in the sacred tree had just happened.

CHAPTER 18

Ferrah

We made it to the mines in two light-rises, and despite having to share a tent with Kai, he didn't speak more than a handful of words to me. And neither of us did anything to try to patch what was fractured between us.

It made the rotations long and the dark even longer. Unsurprisingly, we were the first ones to arrive in the mines. It looked a lot like the gorge, but instead of stone, it was all a gleaming cavern of jagged violet crystal. The closer we got, the steadier I felt the thrumming of its energy—like a god split the earth and what bled from it was a power so potent you could feel its heart beating.

I glanced at Raiden, wondering if he felt it too. His answering look told me he did. I didn't bother to ask Kai, because the only response I'd get was some form of a grunt, and I was getting tired of him freezing me out.

As a child I'd desperately wanted to run this race with Kai by my side, but never would I have dreamed that it would tear us apart.

"Obviously, don't let any of the Lufarium touch your skin," Raiden called, his raspy, damaged voice echoing off the expanse of crystals.

"How far is the town from here?" I asked.

"Less than a light-rise's walk." Raiden gestured to the kwipai who'd somehow convinced me to carry him so he could nap. "Are you still wanting to get rid of him?"

I glanced down at the strangely endearing creature who'd wrapped his spindly legs around my arm as though ensuring he wouldn't be put down anytime soon. "Well, it's not like I can take him with me," I answered, echoing Kai's words. "It's dangerous. He'll be safer with someone else."

Raiden tilted his head, observing us. I imagined we looked like an odd pair. Most Freejians were either creeped out or scared of kwipai. But none of them knew that these creatures were loyal, and had the ability of forming bonds with humans.

"You underestimate Alvy. Besides, if you decided to stay here, you wouldn't have to give him up."

I tripped over my own feet, startled by that suggestion. "I could never—Nona and Charle need me—and besides, I would turn into a Scottomb too, wouldn't I?"

The realization that Raiden would turn made my gut clench painfully. "You should come back with me," I suggested.

He shrugged. "Nothing is impossible."

I smelled the brine misting from the sea just before we crested the top of a sandy hill. The air left me in a rush as I took in the sprawling city stretching across the valley that met with an endless, glittering ocean.

This wasn't a derelict village like the one we'd seen on our journey. There were tall, proud buildings, pathways that bustled with sound, though we were too far away to see the finer details.

Raiden chuckled at my stunned silence. Even Kai stood, motionless on my other side.

Part of me wanted to rush into those lapping white waves and let the waters carry me away. Away from the weight of commitments, and a future looming ever closer.

"I have many acquaintances here. We can stay here for a night or two. If you wish to board a ship and journey to the south, then I'll help arrange it." Raiden didn't look away from the ocean, just as enthralled with its majesty as I was, though there was a tinge of sadness in his tone.

"Is this where you live?" I asked.

"I did once," was his only response before he began the trek down the dune. He slid with far more grace and skill than me or Kai could manage.

The air was less stifling here, a breeze winding through the town that carried the faint aroma of spices and fruit. Muddy-faced kids played in the ocean, laughing and carefree while the adults bustled around with their duties.

As we made our way deeper through the streets, faces turned toward us. Many of them recognized Raiden, waving and calling out words I didn't understand. Raiden responded in kind.

The people here looked a little healthier, their faces less drawn from the heat and stress of having to find their next meal. I wanted to ask why they didn't share their food with the other villages that were admittedly a great distance away, but after seeing two older, faded hovercraft passing through the crowds, I knew they weren't entirely without transportation.

However, after everything I'd learned so far, I decided not to pass judgement. I always ended up looking a fool when I did.

"Raiden!" Someone called his name over and over. I turned, spying a girl roughly my age with long black hair and delicate features weaving through the throng of people to run toward us, her lovely face split in a broad grin.

He smiled at the girl, and when she launched herself at him, wrapping her arms around his neck, he returned the embrace. They were clearly very familiar with each other, which for some reason made my chest ache.

When they pulled apart, his gaze landed on mine. "Ferrah, this is Zaary. And Zaary, this is Arlakai."

I nodded at the girl. "Nice to meet you."

Zaary took in my clothes and the Triste insignia on my shoulder before looking to Alvy, then Kai. Her gaze lingered on him, a subtle blush coloring her golden cheeks. "Nice to meet you," she answered, though her attention still hadn't moved away from Kai.

I fought the urge to snort a laugh. Kai was definitely handsome, but I secretly wondered how she could have such an immediate infatuation with him when Raiden and his imposing form stood so close.

Where Kai was boyishly handsome, Raiden was intimidating in his strikingly dark features.

"Is your mother at home?" Raiden asked, pulling the girl's gaze to him.

She nodded. "Poppy too. He'll be pleased to see you."

"And I him," Raiden said. "I was hoping your family might provide a place to sleep for a few nights."

Her face lit up with excitement, stealing a look at Kai again before nodding eagerly. "Yes, absolutely."

She beckoned us to follow her down the lane between what looked like shop fronts. There was something about the way everyone lived that felt free. No regimented schedules, no rations or meals calculated to each individual.

As part of the guard, I was granted certain freedoms that others in Freeya didn't have, but for all people to choose where they went and when felt like a wild sort of existence that bred contentedness.

Zaary slowed her pace to match Kai's, making conversation with him. Or mostly, she talked *at* him, and he answered in his moody fashion.

Raiden leaned toward me and said, "Zaary's father, Ferris, is the ship master of Golunfield. It'll be up to him to get you a ship to the south."

I glanced at him through my lashes. "Why are you helping me get to your king if you know I will kill him?"

One side of his full lips quirked up in the barest of smiles. "Let's just say that I think you're on a fool's errand."

"You don't think I can do it." The words hit like a slap to the face.

Instead of looking remorseful, Raiden's smile only grew. "That's not what I said."

"We're here!" Zaary announced, stopping in front of a small stone house with a roof covered in what looked like sand. It looked primitive compared to some of the places we'd passed, but quaint and endearing.

She led Kai up to the door which opened a moment before they reached it. A man with silver hair sat in a chair similar to Charle's. His thin face sported a long, bushy beard of salt-and-pepper hair. Kai stepped away from Zaary as the man scrutinized him through narrowed eyes.

"Poppy, look who I found!" She turned, letting him catch sight of Raiden.

The man's eyes widened, his lips trembling as they parted.

Before he could speak, Raiden strode up the steps. "Good to see you again, Ferris." He bent at the waist, pressing his forehead to the other man's for a moment. I wasn't sure if that was a custom in Krovaya, but at least for them, it appeared to be the norm.

"What brings you here?" Ferris asked, though his gaze strayed to me and Kai as he spoke the words.

"My friends and I require a place to rest for the night, possibly longer. You can put us to work to earn a few meals—"

The older man shook his head. "I won't say no to a little extra help, but you're always welcome. As are your... friends." The hesitation at the word nearly made me laugh. Raiden had been quick to say the word, but it was clear from looking at us that we were outsiders, and they had to know why we were here in the first place.

Ferris welcomed us inside, the space was small as I would have guessed, but lovingly furnished with hand-sewn pillows that could seat an entire person, and blankets stitched an interesting flowery pattern. It was all mismatched, but it breathed of sentiment and care.

Alvy was awake now, perching on my arm, but looking timid.

A woman bustled out from an adjoining room, wearing a stained apron like Nona donned when she used the meal-prep quarters. "Oh, Ferris, we have guests!" Her voice was cheerful and young, though fine lines creased her face that had likely been as beautiful as Zaary's.

"Reya, I hope you are well." Raiden inclined his head to the woman, and she did the same.

"Raiden, ever a pleasure, dearie. Are you staying?"

"If it's okay with you, my friends and I would like a warmer space to lay our heads for the night. We may seek to board one of the vessels heading to Terrikult," he answered with a respect for the woman that I found all too endearing.

Her mouth pinched. "Of course you can stay, but I thought the runners went no further than the mines? That's the deal, right?" she asked, an edge of disapproval coloring her words.

"Reya," Ferris chastised gently, though he cast Raiden an apologetic look.

Raiden merely shook his head. "The rules are different this time. For both sides."

The ominous words hung in the air, feeling like walls dividing us.

"Well," she cleared her throat. "Let's get you three settled in the underground. Eh?"

I looked to Raiden, wondering what that meant, but he offered no explanation. It became clear what she'd meant, however, when she led us through her meal-time area to a set of stairs that led down, under the house. Zaary didn't follow us as I'd expected her to, though I was sure we'd be seeing plenty of her during our stay.

The walls and floor remained stone, but down here, the area was at least five times the size of the upstairs. It had two enclosed rooms with metal doors that Reya explained was hers and Ferris' room, and the other belonged to Zaary.

"When our Tawlin is home from sea, he stays out here." She pushed a button on the wall and a large shelf slid out. Only when she tossed a blanket atop the mattress that sat on it, did I realize it was a cot.

For a nation with so little technology at their fingertips, the hideaway bed almost reminded me of Freeya.

"Ferrah, you take that, and you two boys can sleep on the foldout cots in the storage area." Reya opened a free-standing closet that was made from the most beautiful dark wood. Inside were spare pillows and handmade blankets that she pulled from, passing them into Raiden's waiting arms. Kai stepped forward to grab a set as well before Reya showed them to their space.

I stayed put, sitting on the mattress with a groan. It had felt like an eternity had passed since I'd sat on anything so comfortable. When I flopped back, letting my boots hang off the side so as not to get any dirt on the linens, I felt myself melt into the soft material. Alvy raced back and forth at the top of the mattress, as though he were trying to make sense of its foamy texture.

I laughed. "Don't you even think about hogging the bed or I'll make you sleep on the floor."

Reya and the guys reemerged from around the corner, and Raiden hugged the woman who was almost as tall as him.

"Thank you, Reya, your kindness will not soon be forgotten."

She waved his words away. "You're a good man, Raiden. I trust you."

He pressed a fist to his chest. "That means more than the all the grains of sand in Krovaya."

A smile chased away the flash of worry I caught in her expression. "I suppose I'll need to fetch some more fish for dinner tonight. You lot clean up and then you can help with whatever is left to be done."

"Thank you," I said, and Reya nodded before disappearing back up the stairs.

"You can wash first, Ferrah. I'll show you where everything is." Raiden gestured to a door near the stairs that opened into a washroom with a toilet set just off from the tiled bathing area. Kai followed us silently, listening to Raiden explain where everything was and how it operated.

When he was done, they both left me to get clean. The water wasn't hot, and it smelled a little fishy, but proper soaps and cleansers helped me feel as though I'd finally achieved a normal level of cleanliness that I wouldn't again experience outside of Freeya. I let myself enjoy it for the fleeting moments that it lasted before wrapping a long cloth around my body to dry.

A knock sounded just before the door cracked open and Zaary's head poked around it. "If you want to wear something other than your uniform to wash it or something, you can borrow this."

She held out a blue floral dress that looked light and airy to suit the hot climate. I took it, fingering the woven material.

"Thank you," I said with genuine sincerity. She smiled, dipping her head in acknowledgment before the door clicked closed again.

Once I dressed in the borrowed garment and ran my fingers through my hair to detangle it, I opened the door and stepped out.

Raiden was nowhere in sight, but Kai sat on the pull-out cot, as far from Alvy as possible. He looked up the moment the door opened, and his eyes went wide.

For a long, tense moment, neither of us spoke.

Finally, he cleared his throat, "I don't think I've ever seen you wear a dress."

"Well they're hardly in fashion in Freeya," I said with a small smile.

His lips twitched, but the smile I longed to see didn't come. We stood like that for another painfully awkward breath before Zaary came barreling down the stairs, shoving away the opportunity to speak whatever words neither of us were brave enough to put voice to.

"Oh my skies!" she squealed. "You look fantastic! That color matches your eyes! It's why I chose the fabric, because we have similar eyes. Doesn't she look fantastic?" Zaary nudged Kai with her shoulder.

He nodded. "I'm going to go see if anyone needs help with anything."

"Raiden's up there, don't worry. He can do no wrong. Mother *adores* him." Zaary followed him up the stairs, continuing to speak so fast all the words blurred together.

I started my ascent last, a nervous twist in my gut holding me in place a beat longer. My hands smoothed the skirt of the dress that fell just above my knees. Never had I worn something like this, and I wasn't sure exactly how to walk in it, let alone do any sort of work for Reya and Ferris.

Voices came from the dining area, all of them happy and unburdened. It felt like a luxury I didn't deserve, this reprieve, while others remained in the wicked clutches of the desert, using every snap to ensure another rotation's survival.

When I entered the room, it went silent. Raiden's gaze snapped to me, his eyes heating to molten silver. I forced myself to look away, both to hide the heat that flooded my cheeks, but also to look around.

"You look lovely, Ferrah," Reya said with all the sweetness of a mother. Not that I knew what that sounded like firsthand.

"Thank you." I smiled. "What can I help with?"

"Do you know how to use a knife?" she asked, and Raiden snorted a laugh.

When Reya turned to him with a brow lifted in question, he said, "She broke the record for almost every knife-training skill Triste has to offer."

"I've since been beaten," I clarified, but Raiden scoffed.

"Your skills are second-to-none."

My blush deepened, and Reya sighed, "Yes, but can she chop a vegetable?"

I looked at the familiar purple bulbs I'd seen in the prepared meals and tried to recall if Nona had ever chopped them before.

Embarrassment curdled my insides as I said, "Sorry, I don't even know what that's called, but I'm willing to learn."

Reya gestured me closer. "These will stain your hands for light-rises, so try to hold them like so." She pinched the vegetable with her thumb and forefinger before demonstrating how to chunk the hard, woody thing that I was certain was softer after it was cooked. "Now you try, but don't cut off a finger if you please. And wear one of these."

She slipped the apron from over her head before passing it to me. I tied it around my middle to protect the dress and set to work. Though Raiden made conversation with Ferris and Reya, I could feel his gaze slip to me every so often, but I kept my focus on the task at hand.

I didn't need any more reason to hurt Kai, who I could also feel watching me, even once the meal was cooked, served and we ate around a large table.

If Zaary's family noticed the discord between me and Kai, they never let on, and Zaary nattered away enough to keep the attention off me as much as possible, though I answered simple questions about Freeya—most of them pertaining to my dislike of winter.

When it was over, we helped clean up and thanked Reya and Ferris for their hospitality once more.

"We have an early morning at the docks tomorrow, so you'll have to forgive us going to bed so early. The four of you are welcome to stay awake and talk some more if you like," Ferris offered.

Raiden smiled. "We'll be up with you to help with whatever you need. You know I like to earn my keep."

Ferris clapped him on the back with a laugh. "That you always do," he said. With a wave to the rest of us, he wheeled himself to the stairs that groaned and clacked before turning into a ramp.

Once he was gone and the stairs returned to their original shape, Zaary said to Kai, "Have a cup of tea with me, won't you? It's far too early to sleep."

He shook his head. "I haven't slept well in light-rises, I'm just going to turn in." Rising from his chair, he left down the stairs without so much as a backward glance.

My chest constricted, the chasm between us stretching ever wider. Those that said time healed all wounds of the heart had never met Kai. He was the type to let things fester and eat away at him until it plagued his dreams like the abuse his father inflicted on him and Daria before his death.

Raiden glanced to me, before bidding Zaary goodnight for us both.

"You're so dull," Zaary complained. "I think I'll go for a nighttime swim."

"Don't you work with your parents?" Raiden asked, not the least bit offended that she'd insulted him.

"Of course," she answered, already heading for the front door.

Raiden's mouth tightened. "Be careful, Zaary. There are a lot of things to fear out there, especially as an untrained woman."

Rolling her eyes, she sighed, "Whatever. Sometimes you act like you're my parents' age, not mine."

She didn't wait for his response before heading out the door, closing it with a small *snick.*

I looked to him, wondering if I should go with her to keep her from getting hurt. It was true that Raiden seemed older than his birth-tides, but Zaary seemed so much younger and more carefree than even I did.

Perhaps that was the difference between living without rules and regulations instead of being drafted into the Freejian Guard at eight birth-tides old. Or maybe it was being raised without parents and a sick brother who relied on me for everything.

"Should I go after her?" I asked.

He shook his head. "I'll follow her from a distance to make sure she doesn't get herself into any trouble."

"Right, you know her better than I do." I paused when he looked as though he wanted to say something.

He glided around the table, graceful as ever. When he stopped in front of me, his eyes looked like they were trying to memorize my features, and I did the same, tracing every sharp angle, the color of his eyes, the fullness of his lips.

"You look absolutely beautiful, little flower." His hand came up, tucking a lock of hair behind my ear.

A shiver tingled up my spine at his nearness and the intimate way his fingers lingered on my jaw. My heart jumped, pounding faster.

"Why did you stop coming to the border?" I asked, my voice thicker.

His fingers stroked up and down my jaw slowly. "I didn't. It was hard to let you see me when the watchers might have perceived me as a threat. But I saw you more times than you know. I watched you stand there and search beyond the wall for a glimpse of me. And I was there."

His words sent a rush through my chest that made me dizzy with its implications. He'd been there. Waiting for me.

How many times had I looked out and saw a glimmer that I thought to just be the charged Lufarium?

I swallowed down the lump climbing up my throat. There was nothing I could say to that. *Thank you* didn't seem sufficient.

His lips hitched to one side, the smirk setting off a flurry of flutters in my stomach. "Why did you promise yourself to him?" The question was filled with loathing and longing.

It snapped me out of the haze of my own desire. *Arlakai*. He knew I'd agreed to be bonded to him. And here I was, standing alone with a strange boy hoping he would kiss me.

"I..." The reasons that Kai had listed piled up on my tongue and I nearly choked on them as I read them out. "Because my brother is sick. He'll be taken away if his condition becomes too much of a drain on the Council and I know they're considering it. I just need to get him the surgery he needs and better mobility equipment. Even as a guard I don't make enough to—"

Raiden bent closer, his lips hovering tantalizingly close to mine. "Do you *want* him, flower?"

It took me a moment to remember how to breathe before I could answer. "I want..." My throat worked, the lump expanding and making it hard to breathe. "I—we—we've been friends for so long..."

My words trailed off as his thumb slid over my lower lip.

He hummed. "That's what I thought." Leaning in, he pressed his lips to the corner of my mouth, so close to where I wanted them that a noise of indignation escaped me.

Then I remembered that Kai was just below us, no doubt fully aware that the two of us were upstairs, alone. My heart constricted with guilt.

Raiden took a step back, his eyes somehow brighter in the dim light. "Your sense of duty is admirable, but if you ignore the duty you have to your own heart, you'll bleed yourself dry for everyone with nothing left to sustain yourself."

"Freeya requires unions to be formed before nineteen birth-tides. At best, I have two left and then they'll decide for me."

Raiden shook his head. "Yet another disgusting law set forth by the Council of Corruption."

A pang went through my chest. "It's not as bad as you think," I said, but the words sounded weak, even to me.

"No, little flower," he answered, "it's far worse."

Then he slipped out of the main door to make good on his promise to protect Zaary.

Chapter 19

Raiden

Following Zaary was the perfect distraction to keep me from going back to Ferrah and pulling her slender body to mine to finally slake the hunger for a taste of her. It gnawed at my bones.

It was unhealthy, really, this need to be near her. To touch her. To watch her. I knew it before she stepped over the border into my lands. So much so that I offered to take her to Terrikult, which was a death sentence for anyone associated with Triste.

But if I was with her, then at least I could assure her safety. For how long, I didn't know. Already my protection of her meant that I was spending less time making sure raiders didn't screw up the plans set in motion to finally end Krovaya's suffering.

Word was sure to get around that a blood-dweller was aiding two Freejian runners, and that alone had the power to undo everything this nation had worked for.

Zaary sat on the beach with the chill of the night stirring her hair, but she'd sooner freeze to death out of spite for what she thought was a small, confined existence. If only the foolish girl knew what Krovaya was really like. The major cities were not unlike the way the old world existed, but for someone like

Zaary, who wanted adventure, she wouldn't be happy until she packed up and set off on her own.

I was just going to make sure tonight was not that night.

Sure enough, the chill started her teeth chattering, she got to her feet, dusted the sand from her dress and walked back to her house. I kept to the shadows, my steps as silent as the dead. At the doorway she paused.

"Thanks for looking out for me, Raiden," she said, glancing in my general direction, though I knew she couldn't see me.

I didn't answer, and after a moment, she slipped inside the house.

Before I could follow, the sound of footsteps approaching from behind made me turn.

A handful of men and women stopped at the streets edge.

"The hawk carries the flower," one of the men said. He was a tall, burly man in a thick coat made from animal fur.

Now? I thought with irritation. The insurgence was a large group, but sometimes it was hard to weed out the radicals from the ones who wanted freedom over bloodshed. Gritting my teeth, I nodded. "When the hawk lands, the flower will bloom."

The man that had spoken gestured me back into the shadows. I followed, finding Isak and a few more people waiting on the narrow side street.

"What is it?" I asked, still feeling distracted by Ferrah and the fact that I'd almost kissed her. Only her angry, Triste-loving friend stood in the way, though I suspected he wouldn't be an issue much longer.

"The runners will be arriving soon. It's time," Isak said as though proclaiming himself leader of the group. The kid had lofty ambitions that I didn't quite like. He was one of the ones to watch.

"We set sail in the eve tomorrow. Wait until then," I said. It wasn't like I had much authority with these people, but I'd sooner slaughter them all than let Ferrah get caught in the crossfire.

"What does it matter if the Freejian girl is nearby?" Isak spat.

I narrowed my eyes, the deep gravelly rasp of my next words swirling through the alley like a cruel assassin choosing its prey, "You will wait until she is gone. She seeks the Phantom, and he stalks her even now. Imagine how he'd punish you for harming his mark."

My words hit their intended target, an uneasy air stirring among those gathered.

"What is he waiting for?" Isak pushed. "If he's been following her this whole time, why doesn't he just kill her? Or have you do it?"

"I won't act until I know for certain what he has planned. There's a far greater plan at work here than just each of us."

That finally shut the Kondez boy up. "Fine," he agreed. "We wait until sundown."

I nodded. "After that, the stones will topple, and Triste will finally get what they deserve." A few excited murmurs spread, but another voice cut them off.

"What if some of the other runners get here before sundown?"

A woman near the back nodded. "Are we to spare the Triste-bred scum?"

Isak snarled in her direction, but she ignored him.

"The only blood that needs to be spilled is those of the Council, as well as the Empress. Do not harm the runners." I let my gaze fall on Isak to make sure he understood. The little bastard was thirsting for a full-on war. But if we did this right, the fall of Triste would be swift and silent.

Once I was sure he got the message, I spun on my heel and stalked back for the house, letting myself inside, then securing the lock.

I stepped lightly, fully expecting to find Ferrah still awake, but her soft, even breaths told me she was asleep. Despite my better judgement, I snuck closer, wanting a peek of her at rest. Alvy didn't so much as move, and if a timid kwipai didn't sense my approach, then neither would she.

Once I stood next to her bed, I couldn't help but gaze at the way her hair fell over the pillow, or the way her face was free of the guilt and pressure she placed on her shoulders. To save her brother, to bind herself to a boy who knew nothing about caring for a woman, and to stay alive in a race that was about to become the bloodiest yet.

She would soon walk in the city that I called home, marching toward a fate that she would never escape.

Not even I could protect her from the king of Blood Valley, even if I wanted to. And as I bent close, breathing the same air as her, I found that I *didn't* want to.

Heaving the net up the rest of the way, fish flopped and slapped against the side of the boat before being dumped into the large container.

Between the six of us, we'd nearly filled it and the sun had barely crested the horizon.

"I've secure the three of ya passage on tonight's barge," Ferris said. "It'll leave at last light."

My stomach dropped. "Last light? Is there not a sooner ship leaving?"

Ferris shook his head. "None that could comfortably hold the three of you."

I swore low, earning a sharp look from Reya.

"What's the matter, I thought you weren't in a hurry?" Ferris asked, a deep groove settling between his thick, graying brows.

I glanced at Ferrah who stood beside Kai, straining to pull up another net. They worked in absolute silence while Zaary's lips never stopped moving. Without the necessary communication, they each pulled on their end of the net, not caring when it slipped or rose too high on one end.

What a fine partnership they would make, I thought with a barely audible snort of laughter. It was almost comical to see the hover bot floating around the two of them, capturing them doing the most mundane of tasks.

"I wasn't," I told Ferris, keeping quiet enough to not be overheard. "But the insurgence met last night and they're going to act this eve. At last light. I wanted to get my companions away from the area before chaos broke out."

His eyes widened. "Tonight, eh? I reckon the walls will go up then. That way nothing unsavory gets in."

"And no one escapes." I offered a pointed look at Zaary and Ferris nodded sagely.

"I don't know how much longer we can keep our flighty girl here. But it's too bloody dangerous to let her out on her own now. She has no interest in sailing. Truth be told, the life she wants doesn't exist anymore. Maybe it did once, but not for hundreds of birth-tides."

I nodded my agreement. "Yes." Clapping him on the shoulder, I added, "Hopefully that sort of life will come again. Now much longer now."

Ferris didn't answer, watching his daughter before he sighed and went back to shoveling fish up into the hold.

We made it back to the shore in time to help Reya cook lunch. It was impossible not to sneak glances at Ferrah while she learned how to fillet fish for cooking. Her cheeks were flushed from the heat, and a few errant strands of hair had escaped her braid, blowing about her perfect face in the breeze. When she laughed at something Zaary said, even her eyes that reminded me of deadly cold waters glittered.

Her appearance was non-threatening, but I'd seen her work with a blade through means I wasn't at all ashamed of, and when she held a knife, another part of her came alive. A part of her that was made for survival.

She'd need that for what came next.

Her companion caught me watching her on several occasions, but I didn't care. If the boy couldn't handle another man's attention, then he didn't deserve the girl in the first place.

Slowly the sun began to sink back into the waters beyond, and my nerves frayed with every click that drew closer to the maelstrom about to take place.

"Why don't you get cleaned up?" Reya suggested to all three of us, though she bumped her hip against mine to get my attention. "You'll be boarding soon."

I nodded, wordlessly slipping back into the house.

With my thoughts a jumbled mess, I stepped under the spray of water just to keep my thoughts from straying to whether or not Isak would betray us all.

I'd just wrapped the cloth around my midsection when the first tremor shook the ground, followed closely by a faint *boom!*

A string of curses fell from my lips as I dressed in a hurry. Reya called out to someone, and I raced up the stairs, strands of damp hair falling over my eyes.

I shoved them back, looking around for Ferrah. "Where is she?" I demanded.

Reya's eyes were wide, panic filling them. "She and the boy took off the moment they heard the explosion."

Snarling, I swept from the house, running through the side streets that would lead me to the edge of the city fastest. They hadn't made it far, not even to the edge of the city when I caught sight of their dark shapes. The siren wailed, belatedly, before another explosion rocked the ground.

Ferrah and Kai stumbled, barely keeping on their feet. I pushed my body harder, my skill of running through sand aiding me in speed.

"Ferrah!"

She whirled, blade in hand. As I expected, there was no fear in her eyes, only determination. It was the exact reason why I wanted her away from here, because she would run head-first toward humanity's last act in hopes of saving as many people as possible.

If everything went to plan, there would be no one she needed to save.

"The mines!" she called, then started running again.

"There's nothing you can do, it's too late!"

Either she didn't hear or didn't care. She ran like the wind itself carried her over the sand while Kai barely kept up with her.

We made it past the city's border just as the sand vibrated beneath our feet. One by one the wall panels rose up from their hiding place. Large metal spikes decorated their surfaces, ensuring that anything that tried to throw itself against the wall would be impaled.

When the last panel shut into place, our way back to the coast was gone. Our way to Terrikult was gone.

I resisted the urge to growl at how badly the insurgence had messed up. I'd deal with it later.

The next explosion threatened to knock me off my feet, but I managed to right myself. Ferrah wasn't as lucky. I grabbed her hand, pulling her against me to steady her.

"What are you doing? You're running right into danger for no reason!"

She struggled in my hold, but I only squeezed her tighter, forcing her to focus. "There might be runners down there." Her voice was pleading.

"Even if there were, they're dead, Ferrah. Let it go."

Her features turned menacing as she fought against me, the blade coming dangerously close to burning my flesh.

"Ferrah!" The boy's scream was jarring.

She spun as much as my tight grip would allow, a gasp audibly spearing through her chest.

When I caught sight of the sand swirling, funneling down, my stomach dropped.

"Great, this is just what we need," I snarled.

"Kai!" Ferrah's cry was what made me release her. The gut-wrenching terror as she followed her friend to where he clawed at the sand, fighting his way back up, only for the current to pull him back, set me in motion.

"Ferrah, don't! It'll pull you both under!" I was behind her in an instant, dragging her away.

Her screams were guttural, nails gouging my skin, while her blade sliced into me in her panic. I hissed out a breath.

"Kai!" she screamed again. Then at me, "Let me go to him!"

"I can't," I growled. "I'm not going to lose you, Ferrah."

She stilled for only a breath. Arlakai thrashed like a man possessed, his eyes filled with wild desperation. Part of me wanted to let her try to save him. She would hate me for keeping her away.

I couldn't let her leave me, though.

It took me this long to have her, and even if she hated me for a few birth-tides, it would be worth it.

"Arlakai, hold your breath when you go under," I called, unsure if he could hear me over his own bellowing. "The whirlpools usually lead to open tunnels under the ground. Don't fight against it too much or it'll sink you without any hope of ever getting out."

"Kai," Ferrah said, her voice breaking. I had to commend her on how well she kept it together when the rapid storm of sand pulled him lower and lower into the eye of the whirlpool. "Did you hear him?"

"I love you, Fairy," he called, going still. The sand claimed his shoulders. Then his neck. "I'm sorry for everything." He choked against the grains and Ferrah let out a sob.

When his head vanished completely, she went slack in my arms, her head falling back on my shoulder. Every inch of her shook with grief.

"He may live." I wasn't sure why I offered her hope. Maybe it was to assuage the guilt I didn't feel.

"I could have saved him," She whispered, her voice hoarse.

I shook my head, a familiar dull ache blooming anew in my chest. "Many have tried to pull a loved one from the sand funnels, but it almost always claims them both."

"You sound like you speak from experience."

Slowly, I nodded. "My little sister. She fought against it, and it trapped her. I knew the legends and didn't fight. It dumped me out in an underground hole that was connected to a tunnel system underground. I followed it until it led me to the surface after many rotations. When I made it out, I was half-starved and almost too weak to move. We never found her body, though I looked for several lunar shifts."

She swallowed loud enough for me to hear, no doubt trying to soothe the raw ache in her throat. "I have to find Kai." Her head fell forward into her hands, the blade long since dropped. "I owe him that, if nothing else. Daria" – Ferrah sniffled — "She deserves to know."

A sigh built in my chest until I released it in a slow exhalation. "Ferrah, if he lives, he'll find his way out. But you'll die out here trying to find him."

She got to her feet, smoothing her hair from her face. "I don't care."

Holding her gaze, I said, "Charle will."

She cast a guilty look over her shoulder at the floating drone before seeming to come to a decision. Her expression went blank. "Did you know the mines were going to be destroyed? It's what the guy said before I killed him. 'Destroy the mines.' He knew it was going to happen too, didn't he? That was the plan the whole time. The runners were never coming to collect Lufarium were they? They were being sent to their death."

I shook my head. "No one is meant to kill the runners. Only destroy the thing that's killing our people. We should have done it ages ago, instead of letting generations of people live half-lives, knowing they wouldn't get to see their grandchildren. Most of them don't even get to live to see their children to adulthood. Triste makes orphans of my people."

She shut her eyes, probably unsure of how to process my role in all of this. When they snapped open, her spine straightened. "I'm going to Terrikult. Don't follow me."

Before she could march more than a few footsteps away from me, I said, "The walls are erected around Golunfield. I'm not sure when they'll come down, and we've likely already missed the ship we were meant to board."

"Then I'll walk," she insisted.

I shook my head. "It'll be faster to take the ship. Two rotations beats a ten light-rise walk, does it not? The sooner you complete your mission, the sooner you can get back to Freeya."

A frown pulled at her luscious lips that I wanted to claim with my teeth but refrained. For now. "I don't understand why you are so calm about me going on an assassination mission."

I shrugged. "I'm interested to see how this plays out. Now let's see if we can catch a boat."

CHAPTER 20

Ferrah

F erris met us at the wall and told us the ship would stop further down the coastline to pick us up, so we ran.

When we caught sight of the ship with lights flashing docked along the rocky shore, a small sound of relief escaped me, unbidden. Raiden must have heard it though, because he glanced back at me for a breath. I could see the question in his eyes. If I boarded this boat, I would end up in Terrikult if everything went according to plan.

The weight of guilt at leaving Kai behind gnawed at me, yet still I nodded. I had to hope that he'd taken Raiden's advice and was alive. Alvy was safely back in Golunfield, and hopefully Zaary, or one of the other townspeople, would care for him in my absence.

A board slid down from the main deck of the ship and Raiden's hand took mine as we climbed up it. The moment we made it aboard and the ship set into motion again, I pulled my hand free, wrapping my arms around myself.

"Ferris said to show you where you'll be able to sleep," a man with a heavy, unfamiliar accent said. He sported a large, bushy mustache that hid his entire top lip, but not the long beard most of the other men had.

"Thank you," Raiden answered, following the man who led us below board without preamble.

From the stacked metal crates that took up nearly the entire lower deck, I knew we weren't going to have comfy beds and carefully prepared meals like Reya's. The man who I guessed was the captain or something similar gestured to a lump of tattered insect-eaten blankets and old, stained pillows.

"You'll sleep there. Sorry it's not the comfort you're used to, but it's all we got."

"It'll be fine, thank you," Raiden said.

My lips didn't seem to want to move to offer up my thanks, but the man was rushing back up the stairs before I had the time to make myself speak.

"You should get some sleep," Raiden said, gesturing to the unsavory bed of sorts. "There will be little else to do until we arrive in Terrikult."

I nodded, feeling as though an escape from my own mind was exactly what I needed. Kneeling, I rearranged what was probably the excess linens to make the sleeping space big enough for the both of us.

I opened my pack and filled my canteen with water, but I couldn't bring myself to eat any of the rations. Instead, I held the bar out to Raiden, who came to sit at the edge of the covered floor.

He shook his head. "You need those. I'll bug the cook for something later."

"Okay." I put the bar away and laid the pack against the wall. With my head resting on a questionably bumpy pillow, I stared at the ceiling, letting the gentle rocking of the ship carry my thoughts away. I tried to think of Charle and Nona and not about my best friend who was possibly dead in the desert, or what I was soon to do.

Instead, they twisted to flashes of the dream I'd had, and my imagination conjured wretched images of the monster who had abandoned his people for so long.

"You're not sleeping," Raiden commented after a long stretch of silence.

The boat gave a sudden jolt, the crash of a deafening wave reaching down to where we were tucked away.

I rolled onto my side, facing him, and observed the casual curve of his back. "How many siblings do you have?" I asked, pausing, because I knew at least one was dead.

"I had five siblings. Four brothers and one sister. They've all... passed on."

My chest gave a violent ache for the grief he must feel, even now. "I'm sorry. I shouldn't have brought it up."

Raiden turned, letting me see the muted pain in his eyes. With his knees bent and his arms resting atop them, he looked so much more his age. "I don't mind telling you about my past," he answered. "I lost my parents too, when I was twelve or so. It's hard to remember now."

"How...How did they die?" I asked.

"From thoughtless violence."

I wanted to press, to ask what that meant, but I'd lost mine to Scottomb during a border breach, and even though I never knew them, the pain of their absence in my life was a weight that I carried with me everywhere I went. If he wanted to tell me the story, he would.

And just as I'd thought it, he began to speak. "They lived in Golunfield. It's where I was born. I can't remember why now, or if there was even a reason, but the trade bargain between our city and Maudeer was already unraveling, so they set fire to the town, stole the ships at port and killed almost everyone they came across. But before they took the ships, they loaded up the few living people who'd tried to flee and fed them to the ocean with heavy stones tied to their ankles."

Horror twisted my features. "But, the treaty between Triste and Blood—Krovaya—"

He shrugged. "Violence between our worlds has always been a reality. It's why radicals exist for nothing more than the thrill of slitting a few Triste throats."

My hand went to mine automatically as though I could protect it from a wayward blade. Raiden's gaze followed the action lingering there before he blinked. Then his attention went to the hover bot floating at my shoulder and his expression shuttered closed.

"Get some sleep," he said in a tone that was more demand than suggestion.

I hesitated for a moment, then rolled onto my other side, away from Raiden. Not that it mattered, because he got to his feet and stalked away, up the stairs to the main deck.

Time passed with nothing more than the slapping of waves against the hull, the rocking to and fro, and the muffled voices from above. But eventually, sleep weighted my lids, forcing me to succumb.

When I woke, I found myself curled into the solid, warm body beside me. For a few breaths, I thought it was Kai.

Then the memories of the past light rise cut through my chest, stealing my breath. My lashes fluttered, and slowly I peered up, finding Raiden's eyes closed. His chest rose and fell in the slow steady rhythm of sleep.

He looked almost peaceful, save for the crease that appeared between his brows. His arm, draped over my waist, tightened when I tried to slowly extricate myself from him. I knew that he needed the sleep, so I stayed put, despite the dryness in my throat and the need to relieve myself.

It was impossible to know how much time had passed, but judging by the light bathing the steps across the space, I knew I'd slept through the night.

I tried again to move, my fingers wrapping around his wrist to move his arm when his breath halted, and his body went rigid.

My lips parted to say his name when he lunged, pushing me to my back with my hands pinned on either side of my head. His eyes were wild and unseeing.

Every inch of him was pressed against me, our mouths dangerously close. I licked my lips before saying, "I'm sorry I woke you."

Whatever madness had clouded his mind began to filter away. He blinked, taking in our current position, though he didn't move.

"Lucky I didn't have a knife," he rasped.

I let loose a nervous chuckle. "Yeah, definitely lucky. Do you plan on getting off me?"

His lips twitched. "If you insist." He withdrew his heat and his scent of ashes and smoke.

With a deep breath, I sat up, wondering if I should ask what he was dreaming about, but thought it best to leave it alone. He was haunted enough by his memories without my dredging them all up for him to relive with his eyes open.

"I'm going to go see if I can scrounge up a decent breakfast. Meet me on the top deck when you're ready."

I nodded, waiting for him to vanish entirely up the stairs before I found the toilet—which was more of an open bucket that fell through to who knew where—for me to do my business and use as much of the hygiene products as I could spare to make myself more presentable.

Through it all, I couldn't help but think of Raiden's smirk and the way that all his hard edges fit against my lean body so perfectly. I'd never been so flustered after sleeping against Kai before, nor had any of his quirky little smiles sent the beating of a thousand wings loose in my belly. I squashed all fantasies of Raiden when Kai's face entered my mind.

Kai, who was either dead or fighting for his life, while I was curled up on ship thinking about a boy I couldn't have.

I headed up the steps, hearing the crew of the ship shouting back and forth to each other. Looking around the wide ship moving at a decent pace, dozens of faces glanced in my direction. A few lingered until Raiden called my name.

My head snapped back, a hand raised to block the bright sun. Sitting high up on the edge of the bridge, with one foot dangling, was Raiden. He grinned down at me.

"Come up here."

"How?" I asked.

He pointed to the side. "Ladder."

I rushed around to where he'd pointed and found the ladder meant for maintenance. Blood rushing with excitement, I climbed up, fully expecting someone to yell at me, but no one did.

At the top, I stood, taking in the view all around me. The coastline was nothing but a dark shape on the right, but everywhere else I looked, the ocean, dark and unending, reflected the golden light from above. It looked like the surface was made of moving crystals.

My eyes stung with the majesty of what I got to experience. No one in Freeya ever saw the ocean, or anything beyond the icy master that was winter.

Time stood still as I watched a large, blue creature break the surface not far from the ship before diving back down into the dark depths. Raiden's form was suddenly at my side. Or maybe he'd been standing there for as long as I'd been lost in the beauty of the world this far from monsters, Lufarium, and politics.

His fingers stroked down my forearm, a soothing gesture that instead made my heart jump.

"If I could live out here, away from it all, I would," he said, his voice gravelly.

I turned my head, our gazes colliding. "Why can't you? I bet Ferris would let you."

The beginnings of a sad smile touched his lips. "My life belongs to the land."

"Your life belongs to you," I replied, turning to face him fully. "Weren't you the one who told me not to give all of myself to everyone else?"

He shook his head. "That had to do with matters of the heart, not leaving an entire nation of people to fend for themselves."

"It's not your job. The king is the one that should be helping his people, not you." My hand came to rest on his shoulder without thinking, and his eyes snapped to that personal touch.

Before I could remove my hand, he placed his over mine and moved it across his chest. I could feel the hard-earned muscles beneath his shirt before he stopped above his heart.

The beating was steady, and I could do nothing but stand there, wondering where this was going.

"As long as this beats, I'll fight for a better life for my people. And for you."

My mouth opened, but no response came. Heat bloomed in my cheeks, earning me a small smile. I had to admit that without it, he was stunningly handsome, but in the moments when he *did* smile, I was certain that kingdoms could be toppled from such a glorious sight.

The intensity of his stare sent liquid heat through my limbs. If desire could burn so hot it looked like hunger, then Raiden was a man starved. I felt the pull toward him so strongly in my middle that I leaned into him without meaning to.

The boat rocked suddenly, sending me careening into Raiden who hadn't moved an inch. His hands grabbed my arms to steady me, though he didn't force me away from him as I expected.

Embarrassment flared hotter when I breathed in his smoky scent instead of immediately righting myself.

I jerked away, smoothing my hands over my hair and cleared my throat. "Sorry," I mumbled.

"Never apologize to me, flower," he said so lowly I almost missed it.

My stomach answered for me in a loud gurgle, causing him to turn, peering over his shoulder. "I have breakfast for us."

His hand took mine as though it was the most natural thing to do, and led me to where he'd been sitting. When he released me, I tried to dismiss the pang of disappointment. We sat on either side of a platter piled with foods that I mostly didn't recognize. I could point out the bread since Nona made her own with illicit ingredients, as well as a few fresh fruits that I'd seen a handful of times, but the rest of the items were foreign.

"Where did you get all these exotic ingredients?" I asked in an awed whisper.

Raiden tilted his head as though unsure if I was being serious or not. "They make and grow it back in Golunfield as well as in Terrikult."

"I wonder if that's where Nona gets her ingredients," I mused softly before popping a rounded berry into my mouth. The moment the words were out, my eyes went wide, and I whipped around, searching the air behind me for my bot. It bobbed slightly, turning this way and that. I hoped that it didn't hear what I'd said. The sacred tree only knew how much trouble that would get Nona into.

A groan of ecstasy burst from me as the sweet juice coated my tongue. It had been several birth-tides since I'd last had fruit. I knew these grew in the warmer climates of Triste, but Nona never said where she'd gotten them, or how. Only that they were incredibly hard to come by and usually on the verge of decomposing after traveling such a long distance before ending up with Nona.

He watched me eat another, his throat working. "Well I did trade this for the promise to help with clean up later," Raiden admitted, his voice somehow rougher than usual.

"I'd do just about anything for berries," I said unabashedly.

He leaned forward, snagging a solid white cube. "Try it with this."

I opened my mouth on instinct, letting Raiden place the strange food on my tongue. The moment I began to chew its salty, creamy goodness with the sweetness of the fruit, I let out another appreciative sound that made Raiden shift, though he looked pleased.

"Good?" he asked.

I nodded. "What is that stuff called?"

"Khor."

"Okay, well I'd do pretty much anything for berries and khor."

He laughed, the sound vibrating in his chest. "I'm glad you approve. And I'll be sure to trade for them both as often as I can."

When I'd eaten most of what was on the platter while Raiden ate only bits and pieces like someone who was familiar with each item. He grabbed the platter and we both went back down to the main deck to help with whatever was needed.

One of the surly looking sailors had handed me a long rail with a bunch of frayed rope at one end, and a bucket of foamy water with the instructions to "mop the deck", I got to work slopping the water around. No one commented to tell me I was doing it wrong, so I carried on until my hands ached.

Raiden had been sent somewhere to the back of the ship and hadn't returned, even when a female sailor with one green eye and a sagging hole where the other should have been handed me a tray with more fruit, khor, and bread.

I smiled down at the delights, knowing it was Raiden who had sent them. After leaning the cleaning tool against the side of the bridge where I was sure it wouldn't fall, my feet carried me to the front of the ship where I sat at the rail, my feet dangling over the edge.

I ate in silence, catching sight of several large creatures along with a smaller one leaping from the water, their glittering green bodies dazzling in the light. From here, it looked like they tried to keep up with the ship.

"Hey, Triste filth!" A voice bellowed from behind me. "Why don't you try leaning *over* the rail?"

A few laughs echoed the sentiment. I turned with a roll of my eyes.

"I'm not hurting anyone, and not everyone from Triste is filth," I shot back.

The guy that spoke was shirtless, his belly protruding and the skin on his arms flappy. His wide grin revealed the lack of teeth remaining in his mouth, but as I got to my feet, I decided to relieve him of a few more.

"Yeah, we should feed her to the sea beasts," a younger guy with a crooked nose and greasy blond hair barked, laughing at his own cleverness.

Another two men gathered with them while others on the deck stopped to look on. I took a step toward them, readying myself for a fight that I didn't really want to get into. Fighting at the first hurled insult would only prove what people thought about the northern nations, but from the way the four guys approached, I had a feeling they fully planned to make good on their threats to toss me over.

"Grab her," the pot-bellied man told the others.

They rushed forward, and I pulled out my knife, spreading my legs in a defensive stance. A figure leapt from the bridge, landing between me and the men in a crouch before rising to his full height.

"If you touch her," Raiden snarled, sounding so terrifying that even my heart stuttered, "I will slice open your bellies and string your entrails into the ocean for the creatures of the deep to feast on. And believe me, it takes a while before you die from such a fate."

Whatever they saw in Raiden's expression had the men backing up.

Only the one in charge kept any of his earlier bravado, though it slipped when he retreated a step.

"Fine. But if that bitch steps out of line, then don't be surprised if the captain himself puts a blade in her—"

In a blur of motion Raiden moved and the guy screamed, the sound blood-curdling. His hands grasped at the reddish, fleshy cords that began to spill from his oversized middle.

I turned away, my lunch rising up my throat at the gruesome sight.

"The captain would sooner keel-haul you the rest of the way to Terrikult than blame the only person on this ship with even a shred of decency," Raiden answered with cruel detachment for what he'd just done.

The man whimpered before groaning something that I couldn't hear.

"Best you not open your mouth again. You'll live until we make berth, though you'll probably develop a nasty infection." He turned, addressing the rest of the ship. "If anyone else has a problem with a Triste runner being on board, I suggest you keep it to yourself. If I hear so much as a sideways whisper threatening violence toward her, you'll answer to me, then your captain."

When only a few unsettled murmurs answered him, he turned to face me. I still didn't look at the half-gutted sailor struggling to get all of himself to the bridge where he likely lived, but I heard his grunts and moans of pain.

"I'm sorry I wasn't here," Raiden said, standing in front of me in the space of a blink.

"I would have taken care of it," I replied, sounding as shaken as I felt. "You didn't have to cut him open."

Raiden glanced around, likely to see if anyone was paying attention to us. Then he wrapped an arm around me and guided me down to the hold.

Once we were completely alone, he bent down to force my eyes to meet his. They reminded me of a storm in the dim lighting, but everything else about him was calm. I had to wonder how often he sliced into people who made him angry.

"His type of people are how hatred grows, flower. He had to be dealt with in a way that would discourage anyone else from causing trouble."

"I understand that," I said, my feet pacing the little walking room there was down here. The stacked crates creaked as the boat tilted to the left, then the right. "But I would have dealt with it. Maybe not as graphically, but I had it handled."

Raiden gave a soft laugh before lowering his eyes to the floor and shaking his head. "I have no doubt, flower, but if you'd been the one to mete out justice, they might have banded together to toss you overboard, whereas I am one of them. It's unfortunate, but my status grants me more liberties."

I stopped to stare at him incredulously, but I couldn't argue that he had a point. "Well next time could you not gut someone after I've just eaten? Then I wouldn't have had to clean the floor again."

He inclined his head once, looking as though he battled the urge to smirk. "I have to go back and finish my dealings with the captain, but no one will likely bother you again." Stalking toward the stairs, he paused before me, leaned in, and placed a kiss atop my head. "I'm glad you're safe. Had you been hurt in any way, there might not have been a crew left to get us to shore."

And with those cheerful words, he disappeared up the stairs, leaving me in stunned silence.

I didn't receive a plate of berries and khor when the sun began to slip away, though I didn't expect it. My nutrition bar was lackluster at best after the delights of fresh fruit and khor, but I had no room to complain.

I kept to myself at the back of the ship, watching the sun set the top of the water ablaze with color and light. No one so much as looked in my direction after the earlier incident, but it suited me just fine.

A thread of nervous energy began to unspool the lower closer nightfall came. Tomorrow we'd be in Terrikult, and now that it was so close, I found myself jittery. I wanted Raiden here to put my nerves at ease, but also to tell me about the city I'd never heard of.

The maps I'd studied of Blood Valley had only a few noted towns and villages, but none of them had names. It didn't seem likely that the Council simply didn't know the names, but was more to do with a disinterest in anything other than the mines.

The mines that now no longer existed.

Would Triste retaliate with war? Had they already struck?

Slowly the colors painted above turned darker, bleeding to black while stars studded the inky expanse above.

"I thought I might find you out here." Raiden's voice was light as he sat beside me.

"I want to look at the stars for as many nights as I'm able before I go back." The words sounded more melancholic than I'd intended.

Above all else, I despised the idea of returning to the cold.

Raiden remained silent, staring up at them too.

Slowly I reached into one of my inside pockets and pulled out the music box I'd kept. "This is yours."

He stared down at the worn wooden carving as I passed it into his hand. His thumb caressed the wood.

"Did you make it?" I asked.

"The eagle and the flower? Yes. My mother was an engineer and made the musical machinery for me. The original box... burned... in a fire. So I made a new one."

My lips parted on a sharp breath. "And your mother is, uh, gone?" I tried to be gentle, but the reverence with which he spoke of his mother and the way he'd mentioned her in the past-tense made me think she was possibly dead.

"Yes," he rasped before passing the music box back to me. "But I want you to have this. It's why I gave it to you in the first place. So that when you heard the music you wouldn't feel quite so alone."

My chest squeezed with the desire to comfort him, but I wasn't sure how he'd react if I did. Silence stretched out between us like a heavy garment.

When at last he spoke, his words were quiet, as if they were meant to be a thought instead of said aloud. "If I could command the moon and the stars, I'd tell them to paint the sky for you whenever you wished to see it."

For several heart beats that thumped harder than before, I thought about his words. Then I said, "I like them better wild and free to burn as they do. Being caged would only snuff out their light."

"And that's why I want so desperately to lock you away with me, keeping you to myself, but I know you'd refuse to shine as brightly as you do. I'm just not sure how to let you go."

My heart and lungs froze, forgetting how to work. I forced myself to look at him, a million words rising to the forefront of my mind, but none of them able to form a response befitting his confession.

"I don't want to spend any more light-rises waiting on the other side of a wall, hoping you'll walk by and know that I'm there too." His breath tickled my lips, our faces suddenly so close. "I want to keep you, Ferrah. And I want to be yours in return."

Before the word, "yes" could slip past my lips, he swallowed any response I could have given, this soft, drugging kiss stealing all rational thought.

I leaned into him, tasting him the way I'd wanted to for too long. He was smoke and fire and destruction with the way he claimed my mouth, his tongue parting my lips and demanding entry.

I tangled my fingers into his long, soft strands, pulling him closer as if that could take away the fact that I would return to Freeya, and he would remain in Blood Valley. His chest rumbled with a sound of pleasure that I felt all the way down in my toes.

I was vaguely aware of the bot somewhere at my back watching and listening to everything, but I couldn't bring myself to stop.

"You were made for me, flower, and I for you," he said against my lips.

Each breath we shared wasn't enough. The bruising force in which we sought to claim the other couldn't tear down the barrier that would always keep us apart.

I was drowning in him, losing myself in the boy that I barely knew, but felt as though I'd known all my life, but I couldn't bring myself to care. I'd die a thousand times over just to have this moment. Feel his teeth nip at my bottom lip and drag out a breathy sound I had no idea I was capable of making.

Before I knew it, Raiden yanked himself away, both of us panting. My lids fluttered open, feeling dazed by the intensity of my first kiss. It had been more epic than I'd ever imagined it would be.

And already I wanted more.

I must have made that evident, leaning back in for round two, but Raiden simply clasped my face between his large hands, holding me still to rest his forehead against mine.

"You are going to be the death of me, little flower," he rasped.

A shaky laugh bubbled up from my throat. "I hope not." *Because I want that to happen again and again until I forget who I am or where I come from.*

"You should rest, and I should… take a walk," he said, getting to his feet and pulling me up along with him.

I wanted to pout, or offer to walk around the ship with him, but even though I didn't think I could sleep for all the pryani in the world, I knew I needed to try. Once we landed in Terrikult, sleep would likely be something I couldn't afford until the mission was complete.

Raiden seemed to be thinking the same thing as me, because whatever softness had been in his gaze fell away, replaced by the mask of cold indifference he projected to the world.

Suddenly the realization hit me. If I killed his king, he would hate me.

It would be more than a wall that separated us if I succeeded. I'd been foolish to think that was all there was to begin with.

He would always choose Krovaya first, and I chose whatever was best for Charle and Nona.

I wouldn't let my duty spoil what we'd shared, though, however briefly. Not even the Empress herself could make me regret the most magical moment of my existence. Lifting up on tip-toes, I placed a chaste kiss to his jaw where the scrape of early stubble pricked my skin.

Then I spun on my heel and headed for the hold, content to let myself enjoy tonight. Tomorrow I'd worry about making an enemy of the boy that I would never have.

And when that moment happened, I'd let myself feel the chasm of pain that threatened to split apart my being at the unfairness of having to choose.

Chapter 21

Ferrah

I saw the approaching landmass before the lookout called it out.

Beyond the obvious port, where a few people milled around, I saw nothing but sand and trees.

"That's Terrikult?" I asked. "There's nothing there."

Raiden allowed a rare smile to pull his lips up. "You'll see."

When the ship docked, and the ramp slid down, we followed the first group of sailors to the beach. They all seemed to know exactly where they were going, Raiden included, so I let myself be guided along in silence.

The tree line was thick, their trunks decorated with rows of diamond shapes and topped with long fronds that fluttered in the breeze. We stalked through the buzz of insects growing into a deafening drone the further we went.

Finally, the first sailor came to a boulder set in the sand and several others helped to shift it.

"What are they—"

"Just watch," Raiden whispered against the shell of my ear.

I waited a way away, and when a hole in the ground grew as they shifted the boulder to one side, I gasped.

Then again when all three of them jumped down into it.

I started forward, and Raiden strode to my side before taking my hand. "Ready?" he asked.

Leaning forward, I tried to peer into the utter darkness within the hole, but I couldn't glean a single bit about what lay in wait for us below.

Yet without knowing why, I trusted Raiden.

"Yes."

No sooner had I breathed the word did Raiden wind an arm around my waist, shaping my body to his. Then he stepped into the darkness.

The sensation of falling sent my heart up into my throat. All around us the darkness seemed to glitter like constellations, growing brighter and brighter until we slid against smooth stone. Every click the blistering heat began to cool.

It curled like a tunnel, then opened up all at once.

We came to a stop and Raiden set me on my feet, facing away from him. My jaw dropped at the sight spread out before me.

It didn't look real, a towering city laid within what looked like an entire ecosystem of greenery. There was no light down here, but the buildings provided enough light to make it look like natural.

Ropes of green and brown hung high above while creatures swung around on them. It was wild and strange, but I found myself smiling.

Raiden watched the expression grow. "Isn't it amazing?" he asked.

I nodded, unable to form words. He took my hand and we trekked over dirt and grass until we reached the edge of the city.

"Is that the only way into Terrikult?" I asked as we entered the fray. Thousands of people hurried in every direction. Bots of varying sizes walked—or hovered—down the streets with things to offer.

"No, there are shoots all over." He pointed to tunnel-like things that I had thought to be pillars at first, spiraling down and vanishing among the vast city.

When I spotted a stationary bot like Bernard back at the compound selling pryani, I nearly squealed with delight, rushing to where it stood. "Does it take drekels?"

Raiden pulled a card that looked like an ID from somewhere and swiped it over the display on the bot's middle. It chimed merrily before it began to dispense a cup of steaming, sweet pryani. It extended a soft cup that tasted sweet itself.

"You can eat it," he explained. "It's a cookie."

I nibbled the edge of the treat, the sugary delight crumbling in my mouth. "My Nona made something like this once." I said before sipping the warm, cinnamon spiced drink which was sweetened by the cookie. "Charle could still hold a spoon back then, so the three of us baked them together and then decorated them during a snowstorm." The memory brought a smile to my face, and Raiden reacted in kind.

"And pryani is your favorite drink, I presume?" he asked. "Given the way you nearly attacked that bot to get it." His rough voice was teasing.

"I did not almost *attack* it," I retorted before taking a bigger bite from the dissolving cookie. "I had no idea that you guys served pryani too."

Raiden chuckled. "I should hope so, it originated here."

My eyes widened. "Really? In education lessons, they say it came from Werea-Hoat."

"I'm not surprised," he answered dryly. "It's a better story than allowing anything the nations enjoy to come from a place they hate."

The last swallow caught in my throat at the disgust in his voice. I forced it down, then held out the crystalized cookie. "Do you want some?"

Raiden shook his head. "I didn't mean to spoil your treat. You have it."

What I'd consumed already sat heavily in my stomach, but I made myself take a few more nibbles before I discarded it in a receptacle bot. Raiden didn't comment, for which I was grateful.

We passed towering buildings, some of them with insignias I didn't recognize, others, just sleek metal with lots of windows.

"What are all of these?" I tipped my head back to gaze up at one that seemed like it might touch the domed cavern high above.

"Various things. Places for people to live, places for people to work. It operates much like your nation. This is the technology centre for all of Krovaya. Not that it has much use for it, with the other villages being too remote to keep tabs on."

I hummed thoughtfully. Everyone seemed to have somewhere they were going, but it didn't possess a stagnant air of duty. It didn't feel lifeless. If anything, it was exhilarating.

Where Golunfield was calm and open, Terrikult was teeming with life and ideas. The people here all had a purpose, even if I had no idea what those purposes were.

A man working on the open panel of a bot waved to Raiden, and he inclined his head politely.

After a while longer of walking, watching the people in their brightly colored clothes and intricately styled hair, I glanced at Raiden. "Which building is the Phantom in?" I made sure to keep my voice low, but still several heads snapped in our direction.

Raiden led us down a different pathway before leaning in close to say, "It has to reveal itself to you. That's why many leaders and military have tried to find it and been unsuccessful."

My shoulders dropped slightly. "And how long do I have to wait for that?"

He glanced over his shoulder, and I wondered if he sensed the Phantom here with us now, watching.

When I glanced behind us too, I noticed several men following in matching ashen grey uniforms, though they didn't actively watch us. Raiden's pace increased and a spike of nervous energy jolted through me.

"Where's the hover bot?" I asked, suddenly noticing the absence of its soft whirs and clicks. Had it been unable to follow us down here for some reason? Though I hadn't remembered it on the ship...

After I fell asleep. When I woke, I couldn't recall hearing or seeing it.

"I... disabled it," he answered.

"What—?" An almost imperceptible shimmer in the air appeared in front of us. But before I could warn Raiden, he grabbed my waist and yanked me through the split.

I tumbled, Raiden's grip on me harsh as he yanked me back up to my feet. Shock warred with an inherent instinct to fight, but when I reached for my echo blade, it was gone.

I whirled on Raiden, a snarl curling my lip. "You stole my blade!"

The echo of my voice and the musty smell had me spinning, taking in the dirt floor, stone walls on every side except one. Where there were thick metal bars caging me in.

"You tricked me." The realization hit like a punch to the gut.

"I didn't," Raiden said firmly. I turned to glare into his eyes, not trusting his words so easily. "I just knew what to look for. And your blade must have fallen out somewhere. Check your pack."

"It's never in my bag," I said through gritted teeth. "You knew we'd end up in a cell!"

Raiden sighed with a shake of his head. "I told you, this place reveals itself to you. Clearly it saw you as a threat."

My anger fizzled out when I saw no trace of deception in his cool metal eyes. Still, he didn't seem surprised that we'd ended up in a prison.

"How am I supposed to get out of here?" I hissed.

Raiden tsked. "You're resourceful, flower. I told you I could get you in, not deliver the Phantom to you. Although this is as good as it gets. He'll know you're here."

A shiver ran up my spine as those words. If Isak was correct, then he'd known where I was every moment from the when my boot stepped into Blood Valley.

I lowered myself to the cool dirt against the wall facing the only exit. Now I'd wait and hope that the king came soon.

To occupy my time, I went through my bag, not entirely surprised when my echo blade wasn't in there. Nor were the two backups that had been stashed in a hidden pocket.

"All of my blades are gone," I announced, suspicion returning.

Raiden glanced over at me from where he casually leaned against the bars by the door. He shrugged. "Maybe they were confiscated when you stepped through the illusion."

"The illusion?" I asked.

"The king's castle is cloaked and always moving around. Terrikult is so large that you could fly a hover craft up and down it all light-rise long and never encounter the entrance if it was meant to reveal itself to you. We were barely there a rotation before the doorway appeared. Since it put us in the cells instead of at the castle's gate, it's possible that it also stripped you of your weapons." He paused. "Or the Phantom himself did."

I didn't want to consider that theory too hard, so I refilled my canteen. "Why did you destroy the hover bot?"

He turned so his back was against the bars, looking up at the ceiling. "No one can know how to enter this place, or where it exists, though I suspect the Council knows already."

"Well if they do, they didn't tell me when they gave me my mission," I grumbled.

"Such a good girl, doing as you're told. Going blindly into a situation you can't possibly understand, and even after you learn some of the truth, you still want to fulfill the mission." A mocking grin pulled at his lips, revealing perfectly white teeth.

I scoffed. "For my brother. If I don't win this race, then they'll…" My voice trailed off. I couldn't speak the words aloud. It was too awful to even consider.

Raiden quirked a brow. "How do you know you haven't already lost? Not all the runners were tasked with killing the elusive Phantom, were they?"

"I don't know," I answered honestly. "I think Kai was given a mission before the sand took him. He didn't tell me what it was, though."

He hummed in contemplation. "The Council could stand to cause a lot of damage here to weaken us so we can't counterattack. There were rumblings of a village near Werea-Hoat under attack, but targeting small clusters of the population isn't exactly strategic."

"Maybe that's the point," I countered. "They might make it look like they're striking randomly, but who better to hurt than the innocents? It would incense the king, wouldn't it? Provoke him from his hiding place?"

A slow, more mischievous smile played on his sensual lips, reminding me of the way they felt against mine.

"My little flower is certainly a clever one," he mused, resuming his nonchalant stance against the bars. "Let's hope the king doesn't hear you or he might try to keep you for himself."

I couldn't deny the dip of my stomach at being called *his*, but it was overshadowed by the fear that the Phantom would keep me here. "That's not funny."

His lips curled again, seeming entirely too at ease with being held captive in the Phantom's prison.

Rotations passed with only the muffled clang of a door somewhere too far away to see. The hall outside was dark, but from what I could tell, we were in one of many cells.

"What were your parents' names?" Raiden asked. He'd moved to sit next to me, twirling a rock between his fingers so fast I could barely keep up.

I opened my mouth to answer, then paused. "Nona called my mother Yresim. I'm not sure she ever mentioned my father's name."

A slight crease appeared between his brows as he nodded. "Misery." The word was said almost under his breath.

"What?" I jerked my head toward him.

His shoulder lifted in a shrug. With a flick of his wrist, he tossed the rock into the air. I watched the small stone fall back into his palm, that then curled into a fist.

After a breath, he peeled his fingers back open, but his hand was empty. My eyes widened.

"Cool trick."

His mouth began to pull up in a self-satisfied smirk. Our gazes clashed, and all amusement fled in the wake of an instant burst of scorching heat. Leaning in close, he whispered against my cheek, "I'm full of tricks, little flower."

I shivered, the pulse of heat dipping low in my belly. "Got any that will get me out of this cell?"

He gave a non-committal hum. "It's only a matter of time before someone comes down here to see the new prisoners."

"I could try shouting again?" I suggested, though I had a feeling it would get me about as far as his approach.

"They know we're here. It's just a waiting game for now."

"I don't understand what the Phantom is waiting for." Irritation flared anew, forcing me to my feet again. I paced the floor once more, determined to carve a path so deep that I could tunnel my way out if all else failed. "Isak said he wants me dead, but if he's been following us and knows I'm here, then why is he hesitating?"

"Observation is a powerful tool," Raiden answered, though he sounded bored.

"Or he's not really here!" I let my voice grow louder. "Maybe the cowardly Phantom never existed to begin with!"

Raiden shot to his feet, pressing a hand over my mouth, moving us until my back hit the wall. "You can't say such dangerous things here," he growled, lips brushing the side of my throat as he spoke. "Even if the Phantom *isn't* watching you right now, there are a thousand others who would die to preserve his name. Never forget that while you dwell in his lair."

I couldn't speak under the press of his hand, but I rolled my eyes to convey what I thought of his warning. Until I finally saw proof—a glimpse of this Phantom—I wouldn't tremble in fear the way everyone else did at the very mention of his name.

Raiden's fingers slowly pulled back, gliding over my lips. His molten metal gaze fixed on them like he was fighting the urge to kiss me again. I both wanted him to give in to the desire, and to slip away from the heat his body gave off. That, combined with his scent was a heady combination. Not to mention I'd already gotten to experience his intoxicating kiss.

And I couldn't even begin to suppress the disastrous way in which my body became pliant against his whenever he was this close.

"Don't go getting yourself killed, little flower," Raiden rasped. It was hard not to imagine closing that small distance between us when he sounded as delicious as he tasted.

I tried to act less affected than I truly was by releasing a laugh, though it sounded strained. "If Blood Valley hasn't killed me yet, then I just might be immune to it."

He didn't smile back, but he didn't move away either. When a bang sounded from closer down the hall, I jumped.

Footsteps pounded over stone, getting louder and louder until a large man in the dusky grey uniform stood outside our cage. Raiden turned lazily.

"Can we help you?" he asked.

The man was bulky and intimidating. His dark, beady eyes flicked from me to Raiden, then back.

"You're free to go."

My heart leapt until he said, "Not you, girlie. Just the boy."

"What? Why?" I asked.

"I don't give the orders, I just follow them," he answered in a bored tone.

Raiden blocked most of me where he stood, so I pushed past him. "Who gave these orders?" I demanded. "I want to talk to them."

The soldier laughed before sliding a key into the lock. "I bet you do, kid."

I launched forward, ready to show him what I thought about being called a kid when I was one of the youngest Lieutenants in the Freejian Guard. A hand gripped my shoulder, jerking me to a stop.

I whirled, fist clenched and ready to meet its mark when Raiden's perfect face was there before me. He grabbed my head in his hands, forcing me to focus on him. Not that I ever had much trouble with that. "It's going to be okay, Ferrah. I'll get this sorted out, okay?"

A sense of panic gripped me that I didn't understand. "You weren't sup- posed to leave me." The words were out before I could stop them, and just as quickly I wished I could pluck them from the air and shove them back where they'd come from.

I was not some weak, pathetic girl who needed any guy to save her. But the little orphan girl who sat at the border missing her parents and talking to the outline of a boy who couldn't hear her, nor respond, had surfaced the moment she realized that her mission was hers alone.

Raiden was not an outsider trying to assassinate the ruler of this nation. I was.

His eyes closed on a sharp breath that pinched his features in what briefly looked like pain. "I'm not leaving you, flower," he said at last. "I'll be back for you."

I had to believe those words, or the worry that I'd never see him again would eat me alive. This wasn't supposed to be where we said goodbye.

Then again, I didn't think he'd just stand by and let me attempt to kill his king. No. This is where it was always supposed to end.

Taking a deep breath, I forced down the ache of grief that wrapped around my heart like a noose. I nodded. "Okay."

Raiden scanned my face as though looking for cracks in my suddenly calm demeanor. Then he pried his fingers from my face and backed away. He saw what this was too, I could read it in the hurt etched beneath the cold gray of his eyes.

The door swung open, and Raiden walked out, pausing when the door clanged shut again. Our gazes locked for what felt like would be the last time.

A small smile played on my lips until they began to tremble, and I forced them into a tight line.

"I'll see you soon," he lied.

"See you soon," I replied, knowing full well this was goodbye.

But it was too late for any last-snap confessions or declarations. I wanted to tell him that I appreciated his help, but he turned to follow the guard down the hall.

My ears strained to count the footsteps, to at least gauge how far he had to walk before he was gone forever.

Nineteen, twenty, twenty-one. A door creaked open, then closed again.

Then it was silent.

Chapter 22

Ferrah

There was no outside light to tell me how long I'd been locked up. Only that when my lids grew heavy did I guess it was now dark.

A cool shift in the air stirred my hair and made my eyes snap open. Shadows formed in front of me, taking the shape of... a man?

I scrambled upright, preparing to defend myself when the darkness retreated through the bars like mist. My heart thrashed in its cage as realization centered itself in my mind.

"You're the Phantom," I whispered to the darkness. Only a slight illumination came from out in the hall, but where the shadows congregated, I could still feel his presence.

He didn't answer or so much as utter a sound. I stood there watching him, knowing somehow the creature he was watched me in return.

"I want my weapons back." The demand was delivered with far more conviction than I felt.

The shadows laughed.

A deep, gravelly chuckle that reeked of violence.

"I don't see how this is funny." Folding my arms over my chest, I waited for him to speak. To form a solid shape again. Slowly I approached the bars, the blood rushing in my ears. He was here. The king of Blood Valley.

And I had to kill him.

How did one murder a shadow? Perhaps his power was like that of a Scottomb, where he could appear solid one moment and then nothing but air the next.

If they could be killed, then so could this monster.

But standing this close I was acutely aware of the fact that I had no weapon. And no way of defending myself against a creature who could walk through solid objects.

"Why haven't you killed me?" I asked, standing at the edge of my bravery. At least if I were armed, I could trust my own skill. But right now, it was just me against the cruel, immortal ghost that haunted Blood Valley.

The shadows writhed in agitation before stretching out. I could just make out the outline of a man, his features indistinguishable, and skeletal appendages that shot out from his back. After a moment I realized what they were.

Wings.

I stared in horror for several clicks before they retracted. Then a guttural hiss filled the air around me.

"Sleep."

There were a number of things I wanted to do right now, but none of them involved sleeping. The Phantom melted out of view, his dark presence vanishing just as suddenly as he'd come.

To what, though? Get a better look at the foolish girl who thought she could do the impossible?

I wanted to laugh at myself, and then rail at whoever had assigned me the task of murdering the Phantom. Why hadn't they made it a group mission to ensure the deed was done?

Because now I needed not only to get myself out of here; I had to find my blades and remove the head of the most dangerous and elusive creature in all the world.

Sleep didn't come so easily again. Each time I dozed, I felt certain the air had moved the way it had before and my eyes shot open, only to find everything exactly as it had been.

Maybe the Phantom's game was to make me question my sanity before he struck.

Being alone with my thoughts only brought Kai and Raiden to mind. I wasn't sure I'd see either of them again, and it made my heart mourn.

A guard brought me a meal at some point, but with no way to tell time, it was up to when I felt hungry. My wrist communicator was nothing more than a cuff on my wrist since arriving in this cell. If I had to guess, I'd say that something was messing with outside technology.

I slept again, dreaming of the shadows that transformed into a monstrous, deformed creature who watched me without speaking. He kept his face hidden, leaving me to conjure up horrid images of a scarred, hideous man.

When the second meal was brought, I eyed the keys on the guard's belt. It was a different guy, but the uniform was the same.

I screamed for him to bring me to the Phantom and when I was alone, I tried to taunt him out of hiding until my throat was raw.

A third guard came, holding a steaming mug that contained a sweet, spiced scent that made my mouth water. I scooted toward the bars, hoping it was an offering.

"Oh, you want this?" he taunted. "Triste trash!"

The hot liquid splashed over me, and I shouted with rage, shaking the bars. I sat there long after the guard had gone, wet and sticky; shocked at what had transpired. Part of me wondered how Raiden would have reacted, had he been here.

Then I realized I didn't want to know.

I poured a full canteen of water over my hair to wash the pryani out, but also because it was getting to be in need of a wash.

I'd just sunk back against the bars when a door down the hall was thrown open. A man screamed.

Pressing my head into the bars, I tried to see down the hall. The shadows were all encompassing, but for a softly glowing light on the wall that showed a cluster of writhing darkness, and one of the guards.

"No! Please! It was just a joke!" the man's voice was familiar, causing my stomach to bottom out.

Something snarled in a purely animalistic way until I heard the sickening sounds of fabric tearing, the man's blood-curdling screams, and a blade sinking into flesh over and over.

I put a hand over my mouth, listening as the last echoes of the soldier's struggles lingered in the hall. Then descended.

Had the Phantom just killed that guard? And what for? For dumping hot pryani on me? The shadows writhed against the wall across from me, flickering in and out of view.

I held still, feeling as though my time had finally come. The Phantom was here to stop me from what I planned to do.

An inky black swirl appeared in the cell with me before something was tossed to the floor at my feet. It landed with a wet *thud*.

The guard's head rolled slightly, stopping his unblinking eyes wide in horror. I tried not to react—and definitely not to throw up, even though my stomach clenched against the rising nausea.

"Why did you kill him?" I asked the creature that continued to hide from me.

It was foolish to think I'd get an answer.

"Do you want me to thank you for killing him?" I demanded, a surge of anger and frustration bubbling to the surface. "He didn't deserve to die for anything he did to me."

The stroke of cool air on my cheek was followed by the hiss of something *other*. "You're mine to break. Not his."

His words made my mouth go dry. "I'm no one's, and you'll find I don't break so easily."

"We shall see," the wicked voice rasped. All at once the shadows vanished, leaving the unblinking face staring up at me.

With a shudder, I replayed the words over and over in my head. Each time I did, the eerie sensation that I would not get out of this mess unscathed settled deeper in my bones. If I didn't get out of here soon, there would be no making it out of here at all.

My sleep was interrupted by voices. I sat up abruptly then put a hand to my head to try to stop the cell from spinning.

"Get off me!" The voice that shouted the words made everything in me soar.

"Kai!" I rushed to the bars, trying to catch a glimpse of him.

"Fairs?" he asked, sounding uncertain at first. Boots squealed against stone, several grunts followed, then, "Ferrah!"

A sob rose unbidden, my eyes stinging with tears. "I can't believe you're alive!"

"Me either—let go of me!"

A body hit stone, then footsteps pounded toward me. Kai came into view, his eyes finding mine before he came to a halt.

"Are you okay?" he asked, searching my body for any wounds. "Where is Raiden?"

I nodded. "They let him go. Can you get me out?"

He swore. "I didn't get his keys. Where is your echo blade?"

"He took them."

"Who?" Kai asked only a split click before shadows formed behind him, the monster with ruined wings grabbed Kai's jumpsuit, then launched him down the hall.

The walls and floor shook with a violent tremor.

"Kai!" My scream halted the figure, but it didn't matter. Dozens of guards poured down the hall from the other direction, past my cell and hauled an unconscious Kai away from me.

I called his name, pounding my fists on the bars and rattling the door.

The Phantom took a step toward me, looking more human with that single action. His arms raised allowing me to make out the outline of what he wore. A black, trim-fitting jacket with buttons that ran up the sides of his forearms, and pants that matched. Around him was a longer jacket that may have been a cloak of some sort.

His face became more pronounced as well. Ivory bone caught in the low lighting. No skin nor eyes were visible. Just a skull to match his skeletal wings.

Wispy fingers curled around the bars on either side of my face before they turned to bone. Then his voice echoed into the cell, a cross between a rasp and a hiss. "Your freedom will come when you pledge your loyalty to me."

Without thinking, I spat at the monster's face, repulsed. "You have done nothing to earn it!"

His hands of bone snapped out wrapping around my wrists and yanking me forward until my face was sandwiched between two of the bars. He was so tall I had to crane my neck to look at him. This close, the cloying scent of death and fire filled my nostrils. "Haven't I, *reickunteel*?"

"I'm a prisoner here and you just knocked my friend out, so no, you haven't."

Another deep chuckle rattled in his chest. "You've seen the desolation wrought on my people, have you not? You've seen firsthand the corruption of Triste, yet still you stand before me ready to sink a blade into a heart I don't possess? The *only* way I'll let you out of your cage is if you agree to serve my army."

I couldn't pull away, the grip of ice-cold bone around my wrists feeling more confining than the cell I'd been locked in for however long. Gritting my teeth I spat, "Then I guess I'll rot here."

The Phantom laughed, the sound utterly haunting. He released my wrists, letting me stumble back before he dissolved into shadows and vanished once again.

For our first proper interaction, I was shaken, but also confused. Why would the Phantom have gone to such lengths to lock me up and get me to vow my loyalty to him?

I was just a single Freejian guard. Death made more sense. Yet he didn't seem inclined to mete it out on me.

At least now I understood why he hadn't taken his bodily form before now. A walking corpse was a terrifying sight.

And as far as I knew, unkillable.

Wonderful.

Chapter 23

Ferrah

The meal delivered to my cell was a slab of bread with butter. And a knife.

It wasn't sharp, nor did it harness Lufarium, but it was a weapon. I made sure to tuck it away so no one could realize their mistake and confiscate it.

The only other problem I had was that the Phantom hadn't returned, though it had only likely been a few rotations.

"Fairs?" Kai croaked.

"You're awake!" Rushing to the corner closest to him, I waited for his response.

With a groan of acknowledgement, I heard him shift around. If I had to guess, I would imagine he was only two or three cells down.

"How long have I been out?" he asked.

"Too long, how's your head?"

"Throbbing," he answered, then paused. "So that was the Phantom."

My throat suddenly felt thick. "Yeah. What are you doing here?"

"Besides looking for you, you mean?" His tone almost sounded hurt.

"I'm sorry," I whispered, letting those words encompass it all. "I wanted to look for you, but Raiden said you might end up in the tunnels."

"I did. I'm not sure how long I walked through them, but it led to a creepy looking castle where a bunch of guards jumped on me."

"You saw the outside?" I asked, amazed.

"Briefly."

A thought occurred to me, and I spoke the question aloud before I'd truly thought it through. "Do you think you could find the tunnels again? To get us back home, I mean."

"I'm not sure. The Scottomb got my supply bag though. Everything is gone."

"Everything?" That could only mean that he had no water and no food as well.

"I had my canteen out already, so I kept that, but the water tablets and rations as well as everything else is gone."

I worried my bottom lip before asking, "What about your echo bolt?"

"The guards took it."

"Figured," I muttered, letting my head rest on the cool stone wall. "But if I'm lucky I can get us out of here. If we conserve food and water as much as possible, I'll have enough to get us both back."

I could practically hear how dry his throat was when he rasped, "And how are we ever going to get out of here?"

Though I couldn't sense the Phantom's presence near, I still kept my voice down, afraid that he would hear. "I have a plan." All I needed was the right moment.

And that moment came when a guard appeared outside my cell, holding a tray.

"Mealtime. Then you're going to bathe and join the king at his table." His bushy moustache twitched as he slid the tray under the cell door. It scraped across the floor with a metallic rumble.

"Bathe?" I queried, ignoring the stale bread, and rotting plum. The food had been progressively getting more disgusting with each passing light-rise. How many that had been, I wasn't sure.

However, I was sure the worsening selection of foods was a tactic meant to weaken my resolve to destroy the king. And somehow being allowed to bathe was part of the plan too. Giving me food I was sure to decline would mean I'd be more likely to eat with the king.

The guard didn't answer, his eyes carefully avoiding me. In fact, he hadn't looked at me once since visiting my cell.

"I'm not going to eat with the king unless I'm given back my blades."

He chortled, his entire body jiggling with the action. "Reckon the master will seat you at his table whether you like it or not, little lady." His gaze moved from over my shoulder to my feet, never ever crossing over my face.

I frowned. "Then he can come drag me there."

The guard's amusement lingered, but a nervousness crept into his eyes that shot back and forth both down the hall. "You'll not get a chance to get cleaned up if you refuse. It's best you do as he's requested."

I had to tamp down on the urge to argue further, offering a jerky nod of ascent.

"No, Ferrah, it's not worth it," Kai called. I'd thought he'd gone to sleep, from how silent he'd been.

"I'm ready to wash now." I stood.

The guard bowed his head. "I'll send one of the female soldiers to fetch you." He swiveled on the ball of his boot and marched back the way he'd come, leaving the tray he'd brought.

"Ferrah, no matter what he promises, if you betray Triste, you'll never see Charle again. He'll die without you." The desperation in his voice made my chest ache, but I ignored the feeling.

"I have a plan, Kai," I assured him. Or maybe it was me that needed the reassurance.

I rushed to my bag and plucked out the knife I'd stowed away, shoving it in a hidden pocket inside my jumpsuit just as another set of footsteps approached.

I hadn't seen a female guard during my time here—whether because the Phantom didn't want me trying to appeal to her softer side in order to escape, or for some other reason—but when the tall, dark-skinned female stopped outside my door, her expression cold, though not directly focused on me, I had to admit I was glad.

She was built more solidly than half the men who'd passed by and had to stand more than a head taller than me.

"You will follow me to the prisoners' bathing chambers and then you will make yourself presentable to stand in our lord's presence." Her tone was unyielding, but the term "our lord" made me snort aloud.

Finally, she looked directly at me, a rage igniting in her crystalline blue eyes. "Want to come out of that cage and tell me what you think is so amusing?" she challenged.

"Only if I get my weapons back."

She smirked. "Don't they train you in hand-to-hand combat in Freeya?"

I folded my arms over my chest, cocking a hip to one side. "Of course they do, but I think you'll find that I really shine with a blade."

She laughed, the sound reverberating around the cell and in the hall. "I like you. It'll be a shame if the master kills you."

"Won't it just." I nodded my agreement as though it would keep that very thing from happening.

Pulling a set of keys from her uniform pocket, she warned, "If you attack or attempt to flee, I may have to use lethal force. Which would be a shame, because you would be fun to have around."

"Well I can't exactly stay, but I appreciate the sentiment. What's your name?"

The lock on the door clicked open and the guard stood to one side, ushering me down the hall. Toward Kai's cell.

"Jasmynth, and you?"

I was shocked that she gave me her name, but even more surprised that she didn't already know mine. "Ferrah."

"Head straight down the hall, Ferrah. No touching anything or stopping."

And we were back to guard and prisoner. I sighed, peering into each cell we passed.

Kai sat against the bars of the third one down, waiting for me. His face was mottled with bruises of varying colors.

"Fairs!" He reached for me, but I gave a sharp shake of my head, recalling Jasmynth's warning.

"It'll be okay, Kai, I'll come back for you." I didn't stop, but I let him see the sincerity in my eyes. He watched me pass, and I hoped he saw how much I wanted to treat his injuries, but I couldn't stop.

The hall stretched on for another ten cells before we came to a room at the end that opened into a wide space with nothing but stone walls, intermittently spaced shower spouts, and a single drain where all the water went.

"Strip," Jasmynth said, and I obeyed with my back to her, carefully peeling my jumpsuit down, and rolling it so my blunt knife was concealed. When I kicked it to the side and turned a set of knobs to get the water flowing, I almost didn't notice Jasmynth pick my suit up.

"What are you doing?" Panic flared and I stepped out from under the spray of cool water to grab my clothing back, but stopped when she held up a hand.

"These need to be washed."

My eyes bugged. I was standing completely in the nude, but it didn't bother me the way it probably should have. After many birth-tides of sharing training quarters with other female guard members, I was less inclined to feel embarrassed. "Then what am I supposed to wear?"

"Someone else is bringing you the garments the king has requested you wear," Jasmynth answered.

I fumbled for an excuse to snag the suit back. "It doesn't have to be properly cleaned, I can just rinse it," I suggested.

She pursed her lips, seeing right through my excuse. Her hands felt around the bunched-up material, stopping abruptly when she encountered the long bulge that I knew was the knife.

Suddenly a girl not in the guards' uniform appeared in the entrance, holding a folded piece of blue fabric with a pair of strappy gold shoes on top. Jasmynth handed her my jumpsuit in exchange for what I hoped was not a dress.

"Make sure you remove the knife before it's washed," she told the girl, whose eyes widened, before nodding.

To me, she said, "The king said to deliver a message for the girl. If she does not wear the chosen attire, she will attend the dinner in flesh alone." The poor girl's face turned a deep shade of crimson as she delivered the message despite my already being naked.

I blew out a gust of air. "Well at least your ruler isn't rash or dramatic."

"He's effective," Jasmynth replied automatically.

"Tell that to the people with no water, or food." My quip was delivered harsher than I'd intended, but it was no less true.

"They are provided for." Her response wasn't wholly unexpected. "They've all been offered shelter here, far enough away from the poison that's killing us all. Our king is called many things, absent being the most common. But when he's not here, do you know where he is? Making sure the people who can't make the journey south, or those that simply refuse to live underground as we do, are cared for."

I frowned. "If that were true, why is it people think he's either dead or never existed? Most of Triste believes he's merely a tale told to unruly children."

"They don't always see him," came the other girl's answer. "He may be cruel when he needs to be, but he deeply cares for his people."

"As a corpse?" I scoffed.

The soldier and the servant girl exchanged a sideways glance that I couldn't decipher. Without another word, the girl turned and rushed away with my jumpsuit in hand. I clenched my jaw against my frustration. The object that my plot for escape revolved around was gone.

"Finish up," Jasmynth said. "You need to get ready."

Once I had scrubbed myself clean with a singular bar of soap that smelled faintly of something sweet and wild, I shut off the water, disappointed that the luxury was over. Jasmynth had barely let me dry when she tossed the deep blue garment to me.

I caught it, holding it up so I could examine what was confirmed to be a dress. It was long, but when I slid the smooth fabric over my curves, it just barely brushed against the tops of my toes that were partially exposed in the shoes provided.

None of my outfit was fit for combat or running. Both of which I'd need to accomplish in order to get out of this prison.

"Let's do something with your hair," Jasmynth said.

I waved her off. "A braid will be fine. It's not like I'm trying to be bonded with a corpse."

Her lips pressed tightly together, but she didn't object. Instead of a full guard-style braid, I wove the strands around the sides of my head, letting most of it fall around my shoulders. Even damp as it was, it began to form gentle waves that I knew would turn into a frizzy mess if not properly tamed.

"Do you have any hair-hold?" I asked, looking at her slicked back hair and knowing the answer was yes.

"I do, but I'm not leaving you here. You'll have to wait in your cell while I go get it."

"Can't I just come with you?" I asked.

Her bark of laughter was no doubt heard by Kai, but at least I'd tried. "Not a chance, girl. Let's go back to your cell so I can get it."

I followed behind her, gauging how much movement the hem of the dress would allow. Then I increased my pace until I was right behind Jasmynth.

I kicked the back of her leg and she started forward before swiftly pivoting into a crouch.

"Dammit, Ferrah," she hissed. "You'll ruin everything."

I didn't know what she meant, but it was too late now. My fist struck fast and hard, colliding with her cheek before I leapt onto her, one hand going to the keys, the other raised to strike again.

A coalescence of shadow descended on me, wrapping around me and squeezing my windpipe. I gasped, clawing at the intangible shapes.

They lifted me off Jasmynth and pinned to the stone wall. In a breath they took shape, and the hand that squeezed my throat was nothing but bone and darkness.

"Calm down, *Reickunteel*," he said against my face, but his words held no breath. The bone that would have been his cheek brushed against mine in what might have been a caress. "Why do you test me in these ways? I let you bathe, and you attack my soldier. Give you clothes and offer a meal to fill your stomach, yet you betray gifts with an act of violence." Despite the horrid sound of his voice, his words were sad.

I thrashed and kicked against the monster holding me. Every area I struck that would have weakened a human into releasing me was entirely ineffective on the Phantom. A scream built in my throat, rising but never releasing when he tightened his grip on my throat.

Kai rattled his cage, bellowing my name and adding to the chaos.

"If you think any of that is a kindness after keeping me locked up in a cell with no bed, no comforts of any kind, then you're just as vile as I imagined you to be," I choked out.

It was hard to read an expression on a skull, yet, the subtle tilt of his head made me shudder.

A tongue flicked out of the darkness of his seemingly empty jaw, the rough pad running up my cheek. I squirmed harder, desperate to get away. "Will you still drive a blade into my chest the moment your weapons are returned?" he asked.

"Yes," I snarled.

He loosed a small sigh that was riddled with disappointment. "Then you will not have your freedom, my *reickunteel*."

"What does that mean?" I asked, wondering if it was a foul word in his old language.

A hum sounded in his chest. "You'll have to earn that answer. Now shall we have dinner together?"

"Does a corpse eat?" My sneer was involuntary.

Leaning into me again, the slow swipe of cold bone ran along my jaw, stopping tauntingly close to my lips that I pressed tight to keep from giving him access to them. "Only the blood of his enemies," he answered, then laughed as though he'd imparted some great joke.

Yet I couldn't tell if he was actually joking or not. I'd heard several accounts of a *kind, generous, benevolent king*, yet all I saw was a monster who liked to torment me.

"Just kill me and get it over with," I spat out, moving my head as much as I could to gain space between me and the king.

"Ah, but you have so much use yet. Besides, you and I have so much potential."

I didn't bother hiding my disgust, but I didn't need to voice it, because I knew he saw it. Sensed it in me.

He pulled back, his hand leaving my throat at last before snagging my wrist instead. It might as well have been a manacle for all the give it allowed.

"Ferrah!" Kai called out to me once more.

"I'll be okay," I answered, hoping that it was true.

The Phantom marched us down the hall to where a large door was shut tight. It was likely the one I heard every time a guard came to feed me.

He thrust it open as though the heavy slab of wood and metal didn't weigh a thing. His pace was relentless as he practically dragged me up the stairs, choosing halls to turn down so many times I couldn't keep track of them all. Not that it mattered. I doubted that wherever we were going was the same way one took to get out of this castle.

Finally, we made it to a corridor that felt more intimate than the others. The stones underfoot were veined with threads of gold, and the double doors shut before us were carved into faces, some frozen in shock, others in fear. A select few looked simply at rest. The sight was haunting, and I felt myself digging my heels in.

The Phantom tugged me hard to his side, wrapped an arm around my waist that didn't feel as unforgiving as bone. I could have sworn I felt the flex of muscle, the dip and curve of corded biceps, but when I looked at the offending appendage, it looked to simply be bones draped in a black cloak. In the better lighting, I could see silver stitches that ran throughout the cloak, but the details of the design evaded me, no matter how long I tried to make sense of them.

The doors opened without either of us touching them, and the king guided me inside. But almost as soon as I saw the private area, I wanted to turn around.

A fire crackled in a reddish stone arch on one side of the room. The table in the middle was big enough for at least six, but only two places were set. Furniture that looked ancient sat throughout the room, shelves filled with books lined two of the other walls from floor to ceiling. On the wall spanning from the door to the corner were old and new maps, some browned and torn from time.

I recognized one of the older maps as the old world. Whole land masses that once existed before the people obliterated them with weapons so powerful, they broke the world apart. Now all that remained was Triste.

It was beautiful and captivating. Under any other circumstances I would have been eager to explore every inch of the room, but as the Phantom ushered me to one of the chairs, I had to fight down every instinct in me that told me to run.

There were no guards. No one to witness my death if the wicked ruler decided to detach my head from my body.

But when I caught sight of the gleam of familiarly detailed metal, I dropped into my seat without a fight.

Seeming pleased, the Phantom rounded the table to sit at the other end, facing me. We were still too close for my liking, but my gaze stayed on the echo blade lying beside his hand.

Somehow, I sensed the smile that warped the corpse's face. "I have a bargain for you, *reickunteel*."

My throat was impossibly dry. "And what's that?"

"All in good time," he said. "Water?" His ivory fingers wrapped around a crystal jug filled with clear liquid. He poured some into the glass in front of me. Every dish on the table was stunning and glittered in the firelight.

Even once the cup was filled though, I didn't reach for it. He lifted a plate covered with the same cookies I'd drunk my pryani from. "I have it on good authority that you like these." The arrogant way in which he said the words soured my stomach.

"Don't poison the few things I enjoy for your own gain," I snapped. "Or I'll refuse to play whatever game it is you're trying to trap me in."

He chuckled. "I don't wish to poison the things you love, nor am I trying to trap you. Your loyalty is easily given to those you know so little about, but you've assumed that I am a monster off nothing more than the lies told throughout all of Triste."

I folded my arms across my chest and leaned into the high-back chair. "That's funny, I have yet to see where the lies are."

The corpse morphed his face until his eyes narrowed. "Don't play the fool, Ferrah. It doesn't suit you. You've seen my people; they fear me, yes, but those that know me respect me. They trust me. And I do all that I can for them."

"I didn't encounter a single one that trusted or respected you," I countered.

"That's because you only see what you want to see." His words were flat and even, not letting himself rise to anger that I knew I provoked within him.

The doors reopened, and several men dressed in straight, grey jackets similar to the guards strode in. These uniforms bore a higher collar, looking dressier rather than practical. The men carried platters of food that still sizzled and steamed, the aromas wafting in with them, making my stomach growl.

Never had I smelled food so divine.

Another embarrassing gurgle rumbled loudly from my stomach when the food was set in the middle of the table, nearly everything unidentifiable. There were mashes of various colors, stews and soups of some sorts—those things I knew from Nona—but everything else would be an education.

The Phantom watched me, clearly pleased with himself. "I forget how little you know of culture and the finer things a land not ruled by the greedy and corrupt has to offer."

I ignored his patronizing comment, waiting to see if the Phantom would touch any of it himself. He clearly didn't need to eat food.

"When was the last time you tasted any of this?" I asked.

"I'm not dead, *reickunteel*, though I may look it right now." His answer made me curious to know more, but I didn't feel like giving him the satisfaction of my curiosity.

He scooted his chair around the side, close to mine, and I froze. "May I?" His eerie hands picked up a fork and speared a dark, aromatic slice of meat that glistened with spices and oil.

Lifting the piece, he brought it to my lips and waited.

The scent was the closest thing I imagined divinity to be. When my stomach gave another loud protest, I relented and parted my lips.

"I believe you've had the meat of a wild boask before, though I'd wager not prepared like this."

The groan that escaped me was completely involuntary, but it was too late to stop it. I put my fingers over my mouth, like that could stop anymore embarrassment.

"You don't need to hide your enjoyment, Ferrah. I've seen the way you enjoy pryani. It's why I had some sent to your cell, though regrettably the guard didn't deliver it in the way I'd ordered."

I recalled the boiling hot drink dumped on me, but that wasn't the memory that filled my mind. It was his scream and the shadows that had sliced through his neck. The wet slap of his head hitting the stone in my cell as well as his hazy, unseeing eyes.

Disgust coiled through me, making the meat I'd just eaten feel like a stone in my stomach.

"Why did you kill him?" I asked. "For disliking me? *You* don't like me."

He laughed, though the sound was hollow. "How little you know, Ferrah Zunnock. I wish to tell you all of it, but you would only mistrust my words because of what I am." Before I could offer any response to that curious statement, he continued, "When I give my soldiers an order, I expect them to follow through to the letter. Any betrayal is met with swift and unavoidable death. No trial, no excuses. If anyone that serves me is not completely loyal, I have no use for them. There is enough chaos with the raiders killing without cause, and I won't stand for it in my home."

Though I couldn't exactly begrudge him his reasons, I still couldn't fathom killing someone over something so insignificant.

My gaze roamed over the array of food spread over the table, landing instead on my blade yet again. I licked my lips, considering briefly the chances of me reaching it before the Phantom had me by the throat again, or worse, sliced in two for daring to make a move against him. "You said you have a bargain for me."

He stabbed the fork into a chunk of something red. "Try this next."

"Only if you tell me," I retorted.

His sigh turned into a laugh, one that momentarily felt familiar. I told myself it was just because it was gentler—doubtlessly another attempt at his false civility. "Open your mouth, Ferrah."

For some strange reason, I did.

The flavor was sweet and tangy, so bursting with flavor that it rendered me momentarily silent.

"That's a kerrybaya. They're not grown in Triste because they don't offer enough health benefits to dry them into one of the powders that goes into your balanced nutrition slabs." His lip curled as though the idea of turning something so delicious into something so simple and plain was a travesty.

And to be honest, I had to agree.

He put the fork down and cleared his throat. "Now for our bargain."

I straightened, eager to hear what he had to offer.

"I will give you one of your blades, if you can hold this for thirty clicks." He stood and walked over to a small wooden chest near the fire and opened it. A hunk of raw, glowing Lufarium sat inside before he picked it up and walked back to his chair.

I stared at the crystal, feeling its energy the same way I had in the gorge. My throat threatened to close with panic. "It could kill me," I said.

The Phantom inclined his head. "If you are human, it will. But if you are not…" He let his words trail off, and I knew that he'd somehow seen what had happened in the gorge. I remember Raiden saying that only the Phantom could touch it—not only that, but harness it to fulfill his every command. He'd also said that all the other Béchua were wiped out by the Council.

"It's possible that I brushed only a tiny amount of Lufarium, and that's why I didn't die," I began to explain, but the Phantom held a hand up to silence my protests.

"This task in exchange for your blade. You may survive. If not, then you will be released from my hold by death."

"That's hardly a fair exchange," I said. Yet the thrum of the Lufarium urged me to touch it. I felt my body leaning closer before I jerked upright. "Why would you give me back my blade?" I asked, suspicion pinching my brows together.

"A worthy experiment," the king replied, extending the stone closer.

My hand lifted before I knew what I was doing, reaching to take it. The closer my hand got, the more the *need* itched under my skin. It pulsed in my chest and my resistance grew too painful.

The first brush of my fingertip made me gasp. Pure adrenaline—or maybe it was the power of the Lufarium—shot through my veins. My heart ricocheted between my lungs. I took the heavy crystal fully in my palm, wanting to hug it to my chest.

The Phantom watched with rapt attention, leaning forward as though he too were attracted to the crystal's presence.

I sucked in a deep breath, the air crackling in my lungs. When I let it out, the electricity arced off my skin in visible bolts of jagged white light.

"Magnificent," the king praised with awe. "You're exactly what I had hoped."

The words barely registered. My blood was too warm; rushing too fast. I suddenly felt like *I* was going to explode.

"Well done," the Phantom said, stealing the stone from my grasp. I hissed, preparing to lunge for it, but the moment it was gone, the fizzing in my veins began to settle. He walked back to the trunk where he placed the crystal gently, and shut the lid. "Young Béchua can only handle small amounts of Lufarium at a time. If they overwhelm themselves, they run the risk of creating an electric storm and burning themselves to death as well as everyone around them." He lingered by the fire, staring into the wild, unpredictable flames that sought to devour. The light played off the morbid display of bone on his face, making the sight even creepier.

I had no idea what an electric storm was, nor did I intend to find out. "How is this possible? Aren't all the Béchua supposed to be dead?"

A slow, imperceptible nod. "The last two on record fled once they knew they were being hunted, taking with them their offspring."

I froze, unsure of where this was going, but somehow, I knew it had to do with me... and Charle.

"During a border breach they used the opportunity to place their children inside the barrier of Triste, where a woman agreed to care for them. You know her as Nona, but her name is Oma Honee."

CHAPTER 24

Ferrah

The room spun and I gripped the table for support. My head shook violently back and forth. "Nona had a daughter who was my mother, Yresim..." I trailed off. Nona had always been secretive about my parents, but what if that was because she knew so little about them?

"I didn't know Yresim or Tsol all that well, but I did know they had two children," the Phantom said, stalking across the rug colored in whorls of maroon, a burnt orange, and flecks of golden yellow. My mind spun. "A daughter, and a son born three birth-tides apart. The two Béchua parents were captured after the border breach, and as far as I know, are dead at the hands of the Council."

I didn't want to believe what he was saying. I couldn't. Nona wouldn't lie about where we'd come from, and whether we were even blood.

Unless it was to keep us safe.

"Records would have had to been faked, Triste doesn't let a single citizen exist without a communicator band and—"

"Do you think I don't have people in each of the eleven nations?" the Phantom asked. "It's how I know what the Council is planning. It's how I got you into the Blood Run, to ensure you'd be assigned the task of killing me. All I had to do was show you the way to me and you fell right through my door."

A ringing began in my ears as I rose on shaky legs. "Please tell me you didn't send Raiden to me, that you didn't make me... *care* for him just to have him deliver me to you." I spat the words, disgust tearing up my insides.

The Phantom's head cocked to one side, watching me fall apart over the news. "Raiden is simply a man with no family, and no friends. You two bonded over that commonality when you were young. His job was to watch over you, to protect you and ensure that you were the Freejian runner for the Blood Run. And he did it. Once you were in the race, I had him continue to see to your safety, bringing you to here to my castle. Everything more than that is something that cannot be fabricated or faked. He might have grown a little too obsessed with you, but he knew the truth of who and what you are. To him, you are a beacon of light in suffocating, unending darkness."

I caught sight of my blade out of the corner of my eye. Rage and humiliation mingled together as a flame too hot to quench. I lunged for the blade at the same time the Phantom leapt for me.

My hand wrapped around the hilt of the blade just before I was knocked to the ground. Platters and dishes followed, shattering. The shards nicked my exposed skin, a hundred tiny cuts that couldn't compare to the one slashed across my heart.

Raiden had lied and manipulated me into giving him a part of myself. I'd believed him to be honest with me despite his obligations to his king.

I swung the blade in a powerful arc, but the Phantom's skeletal hand caught my arm. He positioned himself over me, capturing my other arm and holding them to the rug now soaked with water. For a corpse he felt entirely too solid. It felt like an illusion of some kind, but I didn't have time to examine it.

"He cares for you without my say-so," the Phantom hissed. "Do not let yourself be so easily wounded by an act of duty. After all, yours would have brought you here eventually. And it still would have ended like this. You beneath me with a blade in your hand, yet I'm still the one with all the power. Surrender to me, *reickunteel*. Triste will bow to me, and you with it. So give in now. You're too valuable to the future. You and your brother are the only remaining Béchua besides myself. In order to keep the bloodline alive, I need *you*."

Sudden realization hit me. Bucking my hips, I set the king off balance just enough to toss my blade from one hand to the other. The one I pulled free before I brought it down, hard. It sank through what felt like flesh and bone.

He looked down at the echo blade protruding from his chest like it was a mere inconvenience before he slowly pulled it out. Sitting back on his heels, he held the knife that was stained with blood.

Still reeling from the implication of what he said, mixed with the horror at seeing a man stabbed but unaffected, I heaved. Bile and what little food I'd consumed worked their way up. He let me twist to one side, expelling the contents of my stomach before I gasped, "I am *not* helping you save your people. All you'll do is create more slaves to be abused by Triste or any other corrupted kingdoms."

A sneer entered his expression. "It's so flattering that the idea of bonding with me makes you throw up what immaculate creations I had made for you, but alas, Ferrah, I'm not going to force myself on you. You can think on it. But know that what your brother needs to save his life is the raw Lufarium that can heal his body." Ever so slowly he released me, getting to his feet before I could lodge my blade between his ribs.

I sat up, watching him with so much hatred it burned in my chest, though my fire had banked. For now. "What do you mean?" I asked. "How will it save him?"

"Béchua are, for all intents and purposes, immortal when they have enough contact with Lufarium. It is their life source. Only they can use its power in a clean way that doesn't poison humans. And when their body is weakened with a mortal affliction, they can be healed with enough contact from the crystal's energy." He stared down at me, wisely seeming wary of the blade I still held in my hand. But he didn't go back on his promise by taking it away.

"How do I know that this—any of this—is true?" I demanded, waving my arms around to encompass everything he'd told me.

"If Raiden had told you, you wouldn't have questioned him. So why me?" The question bore a note of genuine curiosity, as though his admission of his other manipulations and lies weren't reason enough to mistrust him.

"You're the king of a ruined nation full of dying people. Why did you wait two centuries before you acted?" I didn't expect an answer, and he didn't offer one. "I'm going to save my friend and we're leaving. If you try to stop us, I'll cut your head from your ghostly shoulders."

He hummed thoughtfully. "I've never had a complaint about my shoulders before. Or any part of my anatomy, to be honest."

I turned, stalking for the door as fast as my legs would carry me.

"Ferrah?"

I halted, glancing back at the corpse-like king. In one swift motion he tossed my blade through the air, and I caught it easily. The Lufarium had burned away the blood that had coated the metal, leaving just specks of it on the handle that my hand was wrapped around. "You may run from me now, flee back to the wicked rulers you think you're safe with, but remember what I said about Charle. When we see each other again, I'll expect your answer in exchange for saving your brother."

I ground my teeth together until it hurt. "You know, if you didn't bargain for my fealty, maybe I'd be willing to give it freely." I knew it was a lie the moment I spoke the words.

The Phantom laughed, the eerie, dead sound wrapping around me like his embrace. "I'll see you soon, *reickunteel*."

I fled before he had time to change his mind, but the entire way back down to the dungeons I felt certain a horde of angry soldiers would converge at any snap to toss me back in my cage.

But they never came.

And just like everything else the Phantom said and did, this moment of freedom felt like just another calculated move in his game. One that I was trying desperately to figure out in order to win.

It was possible that he thought granting me and Arlakai the ability to leave would convince me to help him create new Béchua, but I would never agree to such a fate. The winding twists and turns finally came to an end when I reached the closed door that led to the cells.

Guards stood outside it, turning to face me with shock written on their expressions. I didn't give them time to react to my sudden appearance, driving my fist into the soldier on the left's temple, then ramming an elbow into the other's throat.

The first guard's eyes fluttered, and he staggered back before dropping like a bag of stones. Wheezing, the second, taller one with long, mousy brown hair knotted neatly atop his head lunged.

"I don't think so," he snarled.

My knee came up, cracking against his ribs. He howled in pain, rolling to the stone floor. I climbed on top of him and held the blade to his throat.

"Your king let me go. Sorry you didn't get the message, but I'm taking my friend and we're leaving. You will not stop us." I kept my voice firm, hoping he would leave to nurse his bruised ego.

"Oh he let you go, did he?" the guard sneered.

"If you don't believe me, go ask him," I snapped, pressing the blade in just enough to draw blood. "Really, I'll wait."

Indecision warred in his dull brown eyes before he said, "I'm not letting you get me killed." His hands came up, one of them wrapping around my neck and rolling us so I was on my back. Then he attempted to pry the echo blade from my hand.

I strained to move him off me. "The one time your stalker king doesn't follow me…" My mutterings were choked off as the guard's pressure on my throat increased.

With one final thrust of my knees into his back, his grip slipped from my blade, and I stabbed him through the side. Then again in the back, making sure I hit his heart this time.

Blood, thick and warm coated my hand. Nausea roiled in my gut as I shoved him off. The dress was splattered with crimson, and the scent of it tingled my nostrils.

Getting to my feet, still panting, I fished the keys from the pocket of the dead guard, refusing to look at what I'd just done.

It took multiple tries to find the lock that unlatched the door, but once I got it open, I could just make out the outline of Kai, straining to see who was coming down the hall.

"Fairs?" he called to the eerie silence.

"Yeah," I answered, stopping in front of my old cell where my pack still sat, along with the folded-up jumpsuit I would need to get back home.

The next lock took less time to open, but with my shaking hands, it might as well have been an eternity. I threw the ruined dress to the floor and pulled my jumpsuit back on, finding comfort in the snug fabric.

"Are you okay?" Kai rasped.

"Yeah," I answered, though my voice quavered. I'd killed a man simply for standing in my way. Yes, he was a danger to me, but he hadn't been half-feral like the partially-turned Scottomb. He was wholly man, and I'd ended his life without thought of who would miss him.

I forced myself not to linger on those thoughts, shouldering my bag and rushing to Kai's cage next.

My hands were steadier as I undid the lock. Kai stumbled out, pulling me into his arms. I sank into him for just a moment, allowing myself a breath of relief that he was here, alive, and free.

"We have to go," I said, grabbing his hand and leading him toward the exit.

"I think I remember the way out." He took the lead in the hall, limping slightly from whatever wounds he'd sustained. Something I'd have to ask him about later.

For now, we needed to get as far from the Phantom's reach as possible.

As if the Phantom had given orders to let us pass, none of the guards we passed stopped us, though they tracked us through the castle. A sense of foreboding settled in my gut. This was too easy.

"Why aren't they trying to stop us?" Kai whispered. "Do they know that the Phantom is dead? Why aren't they leaving, or at the very least, panicking?"

I cast a sheepish look at my best friend, trying to figure out how to tell him what had transpired between me and the king. "He's not dead." My simple answer was met with Kai halting in a wide corridor, his eyes wide. I shoved him forward, "Don't stop, I'll tell you everything once we get out of here."

When we found the main entrance, the walls lined with still, watchful sentinels, we slowed our pace. My body hummed with the anticipation of a fight.

But none of them engaged.

Just as we reached the impressive double doors, a chilling caress of air slithered around me, carrying a whisper with it, "I'll see you soon, *reickunteel*."

I fought against a shiver before shoving against the door and running out into an elaborate garden filled with morose-colored blooms. Burgundy, crimson, and black married together with deep green foliage.

Dark purple fruit dangled from a nearby tree, swollen with what I imagined would be the sweetest juice.

I didn't know how the Phantom made all of this grow without true light, and now, I never would. We sprinted down a cobblestone path before Kai jerked me to a stop.

"Over there!"

I squinted to see what he was pointing at, but the dark, dramatic architecture was so similar to the castle we skirted around that I couldn't be sure what we were running toward.

Soldiers marched down a sloping hill that vanished deeper underground. There had to be hundreds, if not thousands of soldiers that milled about with purpose. Each one a cog in an epic piece of machinery that I was beginning to understand had been grossly underestimated.

Kai crouched behind a row of perfectly square bushes with small drooping flowers that were so similar in color to Raiden's eyes that my heart couldn't help the renewed pang of sadness.

"What are we doing?" I asked, confused.

"You may not have completed your mission, but I can't leave until I've fulfilled mine." He leapt up and sprinted to the next offering of cover, a tree with tall yellow flowers surrounding it.

"Kai," I whisper-shouted, following after him. "We're free, we have to go."

He turned, finally meeting my incredulous stare. "I have to see this through. One of us has to earn the money. Daria needs me to try."

I hesitated for a breath before answering, "What is your mission?"

He turned back to the compound we were approaching. "Blow up the military air fleet."

My jaw dropped, but any protest I might have come up with died in my throat when Kai ran full speed toward the hovercraft base. I chased after him, waiting for the Phantom to drop in front of me and stop us from what we were about to do.

"You don't have your echo bolt, so what are you going to do, throw rocks?" I called, certain this was a very bad idea.

"We're going to steal a ship," he answered when we made it to the side of the building. I expected sirens and for the full force of the Phantom's army to discover where we were.

"And then?" I asked, my heart beating erratically.

His answering grin was one I'd seen countless times before, but since stepping into Blood Valley, he'd worn it less. The longer I took in the expression, however, the more I noticed the tightness around his mouth, or how his eyes had dulled slightly. "Then we crash it."

He peered around the corner, taking longer than I could stand before whipping back out of view. "There are three hovercraft right at the entrance. Similar design to the ones we're used to. We should be able to snag one before anyone can stop us."

His plan was utterly mad, but I knew there was no talking him out of this. If it were my sister's life on the line, wouldn't I do the same? The Phantom had handed me the information I needed to not only help Charle but cure him.

And as far as I knew, Béchua could only heal their own bodies, not that of a human. If they could, I imagined the Phantom would have healed at least some of his people by now to prevent them from turning into Scottomb.

His head poked around the solid stone wall again before he whispered, "You fly it, or I might lose my nerve."

Though a bead of sweat had appeared above his brow, the determined set of his jaw told me he wasn't likely to be as affected by being in the air as he would have been a lunar shift ago.

"I can't, Kai. Besides, it's your mission."

He nodded in agreement. "We run for the closest one in three... two... *go!*"

We sprinted into the wide mouth of the hovercraft bay, a silver and blue tactical ship sitting close to the edge.

At least a dozen soldiers caught sight of us before shouts rang out. We dove into the open windows, pulling the doors shut in record time. Kai flipped switches until the ship whirred to life. It lifted up, just off the ground and trembled.

I gripped the safety strap above and held on as he maneuvered the hover pod higher, then angled it toward the exit.

Blasts of red light shot toward us, pinging off my side where the soldiers attempted to pull their ship back. Whatever straps they'd roped around the resting gear snapped, and the pod hurtled forward.

Kai whooped as we soared out of the compound. "I cannot believe that worked," he said, sounding as disbelieving as I felt.

One by one, ships spilled out after us, and his smile faded.

"Now how exactly do we crash this without dying and without being shot down?" I asked, my knuckles white from how tightly I gripped the overhead strap.

"Autopilot." The word quavered, betraying Kai's fear. I felt it too, a deep sort of panic that shredded my insides.

The other ships blasted at ours relentlessly, the tremors threatening to bring our hovercraft down.

"Do it now!"

Kai spun us back toward the bay and jetted forward. "Get ready to jump!"

I gripped the handle in one hand, bracing myself on the dash with the other. Everything around us passed too fast, and before I knew it, Kai bellowed, "Now!"

The door flung open, and I leapt blindly. Air rushed around me, the ground zooming up to my feet too fast. A shriek of fear escaped me.

Our ship impacted with a staggering *boom!* My body was sent sideways, face cracking against the wall and my vision darkened for a moment. The blast sent a wave of electricity lashing over me, singeing my skin. My feet hit the ground next. Pain ricocheted up my legs, knocking the breath from my lungs.

Smoke built in the tunnel while feet pounded all around me. My vision swam as I tried to make out Kai in the wreckage, but I couldn't see him anywhere. When I tried to part my lips to call for him, all that came out was a whimper that fell on deaf ears.

Hands wrapped under my arms and then I was being dragged back. I fought to stay conscious, to see who had me, but the world was hazy. Unable to hold my head up any longer, it fell back, and a blurred face came in and out of focus.

I blinked over and over, sure I was imagining things.

"Raiden?"

Steely gray eyes snapped down to mine, filled with an anger so potent, I flinched.

"What were you thinking?" His beautiful, broken voice made my chest swell with joy.

He was real. He was *here*.

"Kai had to," I tried to explain, "save his sister."

"By getting both of you killed?" he growled.

I reached for his perfect face which had doubled. A huff of frustration escaped me. "You're so pretty, there's two of you."

Raiden halted to gaze down at me with a mixture of amusement and worry. "Exactly how hard did you hit your head?"

The pain was everywhere, including my face. I lifted a hand that slowly found my head. My cheek was tacky, and when I pulled my fingers away, they were smeared red. Already, away from the blazing ship bay, my head was clearing, though its throbbing became more pronounced.

"Where is Kai?" I asked.

Raiden's jaw flexed as he crouched beside me to examine the wound on my face. His fingers were gentle, turning my head ever so slightly to get a better look. "Someone pulled him out of the wreckage while I was getting you out."

I leaned forward, trying to get myself to my feet when a wave of dizziness crashed into me. Raiden steadied me, leaning me back until I laid on the cool dirt.

"You escaped just to nearly get yourself killed." He shook his head. "I knew your heart longed to create peace, but to what end? If lover boy had told you to steer the ship while only he jumped, would you have done it?"

I could barely muster up the strength to be angry. "Of course not. But he risked everything to follow me into Blood Valley, so I figured I owed him." It was true, but even more than that was the guilt over what I might do to save Charle while he had only one option.

"You owe nothing to anyone, flower," he whispered, stroking a knuckle down my uninjured cheek.

I shook my head. "What is the point of existence if I live it only for me? You said I'd bleed myself dry for everyone else, and it's true, but I'd rather empty my veins to fill another's than watch those around me perish from my own selfishness."

A small smile cracked his lips, giving me a glimpse of blindingly white teeth. "You misunderstood me. I love that you're so willing to help others, it's what drew me to you so long ago, but I won't ever let you empty yourself completely because nothing and no one in this world breathes air into my lungs like you do. None of *them* force my heart to go on beating with just a smile. You might wish to save the world, but you *are* my world, Ferrah Zunnock."

His words made my heart trip and tumble while my mouth worked, seeking the right response.

I shook my head as gently as I could to keep the nausea away. "You can't mean that."

He leaned down, pressing a kiss to my forehead. "You have no idea how much I mean it. But I know you need a little more time to feel the same."

In truth, I wanted Raiden like I'd never wanted anything before, and hearing his confession made me feel lighter than I had in too long. But I didn't know where things stood with Kai and if our arrangement still stood. I hadn't told him that Raiden and I had kissed, or that I had feelings for him. Once I did, would he still want a union with me, or would he choose someone else?

He deserved happiness, and for someone to feel as strongly for him as I did toward Raiden.

I sat up fully, ignoring the way the world swayed. "I need to find Kai."

Raiden released a long breath that I knew was disappointment. But I couldn't keep hurting Kai. Plus, there was the possibility that I would be forced to join with the Phantom for my brother's life.

The devastation I felt in that moment must have shown on my face, because Raiden cupped the side of me that wasn't still pulsing with pain.

"Don't think on it now, flower. Let's get you to your friend." He helped me to my feet, keeping me balanced as we walked through the chaos of soldiers. We may as well have been invisible for all the attention they paid us.

Suddenly my gaze went to his attire.

To the uniform he donned that looked too much like everyone else's. I paused, shrugging his arm off.

"You're a soldier?"

He looked around, seeming uncomfortable. When I didn't recant my need for an answer, he sighed. "Yes."

Maybe it was the knock to my head or just the untainted joy I'd felt at seeing him again when I'd thought him gone forever.

Memories that had been carefully tucked away inside my heart resurfaced. The Phantom's words playing over and over in my head.

They sounded aloud from my lips. "You work for him."

He ran a hand through his dark hair. "You already knew that. It wasn't that much of a stretch to guess."

"You brought me here. To him." Anger kindled hotter in my veins the more I spoke. "Do you know why he wanted me, Raiden? You know who I am, don't you? *What* I am to him?"

His gaze held mine without an ounce of remorse. "Yes."

The pain at his betrayal fled as calm suffused my heart. I'd been stupid.

"All those pretty words..." I gave a humorless laugh. The hurt was gone, replaced with something far more dangerous. I was numb. "You lied the whole time."

He shook his head. "I couldn't tell you. And I didn't keep an eye on you from the other side of the border in order to trick you. You know that. Our interactions have always been authentic, Ferrah."

"Except when you pretended not to know what I am. And when you pretended you didn't quite know where the king lives. Or when you *kissed me* knowing that I could never be yours!"

He stepped into my space, invading all of my senses with the powerful way he moved and the intensity of his stare. "I did what I had to," he snapped, a low rumble vibrating in his chest. "The fact that you were born in Krovaya isn't relevant to me. What you are, doesn't matter."

"Except it will when you turn into a Scottomb and I don't!" The dam I'd shoved my emotions behind ruptured, spilling out as volatile anger. "It'll matter when you die, and I go on living a lonely existence with a monster." I jabbed a finger into his solid chest, trying to move him, but he stayed rooted close.

Raiden's glinting silver eyes flashed, but he didn't answer.

Swallowing hard, I forced myself to say the words I hadn't wanted to say. "I'm going to go find Kai, he and I are going home." When he opened his mouth to say something else, I cut him off. "You have your duty here. To your king. I know how important that is for you."

My throat burned with emotion that I refused to let myself feel right now. I took a step toward the compound before feeling Raiden move with me like we were magnets irrevocably attracted to each other. Whipping around, I faced him again, and this time, I vowed it would be the last time. "Don't follow me. We won't see each other ever again after this. That's how it *must* be."

Raiden narrowed his eyes, the muscle in his jaw feathering like it did when he was angry or frustrated.

He waited for me to turn around before I heard his vow.

"Walk away as many times as you want, flower, but even in death you can't escape me."

Chapter 25

Ferrah

I found Kai laying on a mound of dirt between two female guards who questioned him. He was bloodied and even more beat up than when we'd attempted our reckless mission. But somehow, he wasn't already in manacles being dragged back to the dungeon for the crime he—we'd—committed.

"Sorry to interrupt, ladies, but we have to go." I helped Kai to his feet, and despite the shouts that followed us, we ran as fast as we could. To my complete and utter surprise, no one followed.

"Where to?" I questioned, and Kai pointed to the dark woods ahead.

Through dense trees he guided me to what I assumed were the tunnels. The first opening I found, we ran into, darkness enveloping us. My wrist communicator was still non-functioning, which meant I had nothing to offer by way of light.

"He's one of them? A soldier?" was all Kai asked when we made it past the castle and into the tunnels. I paused to lean against the wall, both of us gasping for breath.

The feeling of him watching me, waiting for a response, made me want to squirm. After debating whether I should give him one at all, I finally nodded. "Yeah," I said, knowing he couldn't see me.

He made a sound that might have been an acknowledgement, or it may have been an I-told-you-so. Either way, I chose to ignore it.

"Let's hope this tunnel leads to the sea, or we're going to have an extremely long walk north."

"We have to keep as quiet as possible," Kai said, his voice already a whisper. "It's like a Scottomb infestation in here."

I patted our one and only weapon. "If wrecking a hovercraft doesn't kill you, walk through the pitch-black tunnels until the Scottomb do the job."

Kai snorted a laugh. His fingers twined with mine, and my stomach dipped. But at least this way was easier than risking bumping into each other.

My other hand skimmed along the wall, careful not to create too much of a vibration that the Scottomb would pick up on.

We kept a steady pace, pausing only when absolutely needed. Kai's small grunts of pain told me we needed to find the surface soon so his wounds could be treated.

Distant howls rang out through the tunnels, too far away to be worrisome just yet. My eyes desperately fought to adjust to the complete darkness, especially with the danger I knew lurked up ahead.

A soft, salty breeze teased my face with delicate fingers, coming from the left.

"Do you feel that?" Kai whispered.

"Yeah, I think the tunnel forks."

"Let's bias to the other side," he suggested, and I nodded. The movement sounded almost as loud as speaking.

When he shuffled to the other side of the tunnel, I used my free hand to feel out in front of me so that I wouldn't smack into anything.

The wailing grew louder and my heart dropped into my toes.

"We have to run," I said quietly.

"Not yet, they'll know we're here," Kai argued.

Snarling echoed louder in the tunnel next to us. "They know, Kai, quick!"

He hesitated only a split click longer before taking off at a run, pulling me behind him. I pulled my echo blade free, illuminating its length. It stuttered and crackled before winking out.

"Oh Freeya, no." The blade had likely been damaged in the explosion.

I clicked the igniter again and it fizzled, trying to coat the blade in its energy. It was weak at best, but at least it held.

The cries of the Scottomb were deafening. If they hadn't known we were in the tunnels, they did now.

A ghostly form slid through the wall right beside me and I reacted just in time, slicing the blade through the screeching, monstrous face. Its body fell the rest of the way through, colliding with me. I stabbed its pale skin, between its ribs, a sharp sense of pity mixing with my need for survival.

Knowing what I did now, putting these creatures out of their misery seemed more like a blessing.

The only way to kill a Scottomb is to cut off their head.

My blade crackled again, threatening to leave us in the dark. I didn't have time to saw through the translucent neck. Especially not when a surge of Scottomb raced into the neck of the tunnel behind us.

"RUN!" Kai sprinted as though his life depended on it, with me at his heels.

The Scottomb gave chase, snapping eager, hungry jaws. They were possessed by their hunger. If we didn't find a way out soon, we would be torn to shreds down here.

Every time I felt their putrid breath on my back, I turned, cutting blindly through the air, hoping to at least slow them down.

Just as I brought my blade up into the jaw of a snapping Scottomb, one of them grabbed my wrist, yanking me back. Kai's grip on me fell away, and he turned, shock and horror filling his eyes.

"Run, Kai!" I screamed before my back hit the ground. My weapon severed the throat of one of the beasts that converged. Thick, dark blood rained down on me, spilling over my face and getting in my mouth.

I spat and choked on the taste of decay, unable to scream.

"Ferrah!" Kai's voice was so filled with raw terror that it made tears sting my already burning eyes.

Wildly I swung my blade left and right, kicking and thrashing. There were too many of them.

They weighed down my limbs, long, sticky tongues running over my flesh before they bit down.

The burning pain was too much. My scream stayed lodged in my throat, unable to find its way out when they tore into my flesh over and over.

The hand that held the blade slackened, and it fell uselessly into the dirt.

I could hear Kai screaming, but he sounded far away. Over and over they found parts of me that hadn't yet been ripped apart, but I couldn't feel a thing anymore.

I wanted to beg Kai to run, to get back to Freeya and to take care of Nona and Charle, but my mouth wouldn't work. A tear slid down my cheek, falling to the ground that was splattered with my blood.

My vision darkened, the end coming too fast. I had too much to say. Too much yet to do. I couldn't fathom that I'd never again hug my brother, or bake sweet treats with Nona.

Never again would Kai and I curl up in my living area just breathing each other in to remind ourselves that we weren't as alone as we felt. I'd never see Raiden again. Even if he had betrayed me, I was still so enthralled with his smile and the fact that he'd visited the border every birth-tide just to catch a glimpse of me.

He was imperfect in so many ways, but he'd somehow written him-self—flaws and all—at the center of my heart. I didn't know how to come to terms with that. Would he try to look for me again, only for me to never return to the border?

Maybe my body would be found, and he'd somehow know that I was gone. Would he grieve for the girl he saved so long ago?

A burst of light erupted above me, blinding me. With it came a deep, furious bellow. The tunnel trembled and darkness swallowed me up.

Only snippets of sound came in and out of time. Arms hefted me off the ground.

"Give her to me, I'll get her out," Kai snarled.

"You couldn't save her," the ruined, raspy voice snarled. Joy flooded my chest until I thought it would rupture. Pain sliced through my body anew and I struggled to breathe. "Hang on, flower," he whispered against my ear. "Don't you *dare* leave me yet."

The exhaustion was too heavy. No matter how much I wanted to open my eyes, sleep—or maybe it was death—kept pulling me away from Raiden. I wanted to get back to him, but I didn't know how.

"If I can't pull you from the afterlife, then I'll follow you into it, but we need you here. *I* need you." My body was jostled like Raiden was running.

Heat suddenly coated my body, setting every wound aflame, and a whimper escaped me.

"Skies, Ferrah," I heard Kai say, then to someone else he said, "Is she still breathing? She's so pale."

"Just barely," came Raiden's response. "This will help."

I didn't know what was meant to help, but the embrace of nothingness claimed me once again.

When my lashes fluttered open, the pale blue sky greeted me. Creaking and groaning accompanied the gentle sway of what could only be a ship. Slowly,

I moved to sit up, wincing at the stinging pain the action incited nearly everywhere. Even my bones felt like they had been gnawed on.

Flashes and bursts of what had transpired replayed in my head, ending with the fact that Raiden was here. Somewhere.

My gaze snagged on Kai who stood against the rail of the ship close enough to be seen, but too far for him to know I'd awoken. His back was to me, while his head hung in his hands.

I turned as much as my stiff body would allow, searching for Raiden, but he was nowhere to be found. Slowly, I got to my feet, ignoring the muscles that screamed in protest. When I was fully erect, my chest heaved with sharp, painful breaths.

My steps were slow as my equilibrium tried to account for the ship's movements. Just as I lifted a hand to touch Kai, he whirled, eyes wide.

"You're awake!"

"I'm alive," I answered in disbelief. "How?"

An emotion flickered over Kai's face before he smoothed it out, but I knew it had something to do with Raiden.

"Raiden showed up and killed most of the Scottomb. He got you out of the tunnel and on this ship after putting that healing stuff on your wounds."

I nodded in understanding. "Where is he now?" The hint of eagerness in my tone darkened Kai's expression further.

He sighed before looking back out at the vast ocean. "He told me what he did. His betrayal. He said that you told him you never wanted to see him again, so he thought it best if he left. I asked how he knew where we were, but he wouldn't say."

My heart fell slightly at knowing I'd driven Raiden away even after he'd saved me *again*. Kai looked to me as though expecting me to confirm what he'd said. I gave a shallow nod. The only answer I could give.

Looking around the ship, it was maybe half the size of the one we'd sailed from Golunfield on. "Are we headed back to the port city near the mines?" I asked.

"Yeah," Kai answered, sounding tired.

I placed a hand on the back of his arm. "When was the last time you slept?"

"In the cell."

"And how long was I out?" I asked.

"We'll be arriving in Golunfield in a rotation or two."

I blinked, processing his answer. "Two light-rises?" My reply came out shriller than I'd meant them to. I knew the Scottomb attack had been bad, but to have been asleep for two light-rises…?

Kai turned then as though he'd heard my thoughts. His eyes were swollen and his hair disheveled. He grasped my arms and pulled me into him, holding me to his chest. "You almost died, Ferrah. I thought you *had* died."

"I'm sorry," I whispered, emotion clogging my throat.

A dry laugh jolted his tall frame. "Don't be sorry. It's me who should be sorry. I couldn't do anything, I didn't have a weapon and there were so many of them I—"

"It's okay, Kai." I pulled back to meet his gaze. "I told you to run. I'm just glad they didn't get you."

He shuddered. "You were… There was barely anything left of you. Your face is still… healing."

I lifted a hand automatically, gingerly running my fingers around angry, swollen flesh. A grimace pulled at my lips. "I bet I look hideous."

Kai's eyes scanned me head to toe, taking me in. He swallowed hard. "Never hideous," he answered. "But even Raiden couldn't guarantee there wouldn't be scars."

I nodded, feeling a lump rise in my throat. It was silly, I knew, to be upset about scars when I'd survived an attack that would have killed me if not for Raiden. I wanted to thank him for coming to my rescue yet again. It seemed like he was always there when I needed him and in exchange, I'd sent him away.

His betrayal still stung, but the gravity of it didn't seem as severe as it once had. Too much had happened since then.

The ship's bell dinged loudly, sounding the warning that they were about to dock. I turned to the other side of the ship to face Golunfield and gasped.

Black smoke coiled above ruined buildings. The once vibrant town had been toppled. Hunks of stone and dust covered the streets. Nowhere did life stir; not a single fisherman reeling in his traps.

I covered my mouth with one hand, the other had clamped onto Kai's arm when my legs threatened to give out.

"What happened?" I breathed to the silent air.

Kai shook his head. "I don't know."

We shared a look of shock and pain. "Do you think the Council had one of the runners do this?" I asked.

His jaw was tight when he said, "Probably." It wasn't a stretch given that his mission had been to ruin the air strike base.

In all the aftermath I hadn't stopped to consider whether or not we'd killed anyone by what we'd done. My stomach twisted, but I couldn't bring myself to ask the question.

When the ship was secured to the shore, Kai and I were the only ones to get off. He carried my bag that was torn and fraying, but still contained everything we needed for the journey. I turned momentarily to watch the vessel sail away again before facing the wreckage of Golunfield. Part of me wondered if the Phantom knew about the attack.

If he cared at all that so many of his people had been murdered.

Was the attack retaliation for blowing up the mines?

We climbed over rubble, and I strained to hear signs of any survivors. Rock tumbled, sending up plumes of dust as we navigated the town. Though I didn't have every inch memorized, I faltered at the sight of Reya and Ferris' home.

Part of the stone steps laid askew, jaggedly cut down the middle. I stumbled forward, clawing my way up and over debris.

Arlakai's voice followed me. "Ferrah, don't."

I imagined poor Ferris and Reya, trapped together, and free-spirited Zaary who was too wild for even this thriving oceanic town being crushed to death. Even little Alvy likely didn't make it out alive. Like a switch activated inside me, I was possessed with the need to get to them. To pull their bodies from the ruins and bury them the way they deserved. Fingers digging, muscles straining, I ignored the jolts of pain the movements created.

I dug and dug, trying to shift as much as I could, but it may as well have been a mountain. Facing Kai I called, "Help me."

His expression was sullen. "Fairs..."

Grief for a family I barely knew burrowed into my very marrow. A tear slipped over my cheek, falling into the ruins. I ached physically and emotionally as Kai made his way to me.

Together we stood, staring at the place that had once been a home filled with love and laughter.

"We should go," he said after a while.

I nodded, forcing my body to climb the rest of the way out of Golunfield. The wall panels were mostly blown apart, the metal torn and warped like a giant fist had punched through them.

There was one, however, fully intact. Sounds of a creature snuffling and tearing into meat slowed our steps.

Cautiously, I peered around the slab of metal, finding a boar-like creature feasting on the bloody stump of a leg. The rest of the body was speared through with multiple spikes. In total, there were three hanging from the wall.

All of them in matching black jumpsuits with the Triste insignia on the shoulder.

Bile rose in my throat as I fully faced Imani's fierce, stunning face, along with Werea-Haot's two runners, Sandral and Jergo.

I sniffled before clearing my throat. "They were the ones that destroyed Golunfield."

"How do you know?" Kai asked.

In truth, I wasn't entirely certain, but this felt like a warning to any of the other racers not to mess with the citizens of Blood Valley. "The Phantom did this."

Kai reared back in surprise. "That's not possible, Fairy. We left Terrikult only two light-rises ago. He would have had to have been here when they attacked. *If* they even did it."

I turned toward him. "Who else could have done that much damage?"

He shook his head. "I'm not saying they didn't. Just that we don't know the whole story. We need to keep going though, or we'll never make it back."

Just that one sentence made my stomach clench. This year's run was so unlike the others that I couldn't help feeling as though none of us were meant to come back. I had no way of checking whether or not any of the others were still alive, but my best guess was that there were only nine remaining runners.

How would they know for sure if I killed the Phantom before anyone else had completed their mission? I hadn't taken the time to think through the details, and with each step toward the empire that had murdered countless people without a single thought, I couldn't help but feel like this year, there would be no winners.

Chapter 26

Ferrah

The trek around the gorge was grueling and long, but going through it wasn't an option without Raiden and a fully-functioning tent.

We did what we could to battle the dark's onslaught of blistering cold, by huddling close inside the defective tent that had been stabbed by the group of half-Scottomb. Our suits helped keep us from dying of hypothermia, but mine only pumped heat in certain parts that hadn't been destroyed by the Scottomb attack.

Fortunately, Kai's communicator showed the map, keeping us on target. Everything else came with a flashing error that read: Disconnected from Database.

Slowly, my wounds healed, and by some miracle I hadn't sustained any more.

When we stopped to eat and take a break on the thirteenth light-rise since leaving Golunfield, Kai consulted the map once more.

"We're past Werea-Haot and Maudeer. We have probably another four or so light-rises left."

I drank the last of the canteen and pulled out the handful of tablets left. "Good, because we only have enough water for one canteen a light-rise. And we're down to the last two nutrition slabs so we'll have to hunt in the dark or tomorrow. Any further north and there will only be kwipai."

Kai tilted his head back, eyes closed like he was relaxing, but I knew better. We were both exhausted and needed proper nourishment. Both of us had cut back on water and food, and it was beginning to take its toll. The sun bared down on us both, slowly sucking away the energy I needed to get up and keep walking.

Yet when Kai got to his feet several moments later and offered me his hand, I took it. He tugged me up, and I grunted my thanks, trying not to sway.

We walked for another rotation before dizziness crept over me. My vision swam in and out of focus. I stumbled and fell, my hands burning on the raging hot stone. But at least it hadn't been my face.

"Fairy," Kai said, concern etched into his voice, though it was hoarse from the lack of water.

"I don't think we're going to make it." My ears thundered with the rushing of my pulse. All I wanted to do was lay down for a bit. At least until the world stopped spinning.

"Get up, Fairs, I can't carry you."

It was the pleading that made me lift my gaze to his. Over his shoulder, a dark shape grew in the sky. The whirring that I'd thought to be the heavy rushing of blood in my veins grew more pronounced.

Kai's brows pinched, and then he turned, clearly hearing it too. He waved his arms above his head, giving out a triumphant laugh that was swept away by the hover-freight's spinning blades.

I saw Freeya's three-headed bear symbol and nearly sobbed with relief.

It landed a short distance from us, and several soldiers poured from the hatch. They rushed toward us, but I recognized one of them as Erina. Directly behind her was a hovering camera.

"What's going on?" I asked through dry, cracking lips.

"Let's get you both on board," she said in her usual, brusque manner. Several of the soldiers converged, pulling me to my feet. Already Erina had turned to stalk back towards the airship.

"Who won the Blood Run?" Arlakai called.

"You two did," Erina said over her shoulder. "You're the only two left."

My stomach bottomed out, the truth of that statement hitting me like a ton of bricks. Before I could ask how both Kai and I had won—especially when I hadn't completed my task of killing the Phantom, we were rush up the ramp of the aircraft, the door hissing shut a moment later.

The hands that held me upright shoved me roughly into one of the seats, and I grunted out a sarcastic, "Thanks."

"Get them hooked up to fluids and stabilized before we make it back to Freeya," Erina snapped. The cam bot was now nowhere in sight, which made sense. *At least Nona and Charle will see that I'm alive.*

A medic soldier knelt in front of me, her head bowed, a thick braid of golden hair draped over one shoulder as she pulled tools and a bag of fluid from her bag. Her sea-blue eyes darted up to meet mine once. Then twice.

I felt the sharp sting of the needle in my arm, then met the girl's gaze once more as everything blurred.

Darkness swept over me, cocooning me.

Shrieks, incessant and piercing, had my eyes flying open. My vision blurred and my stomach revolted at all the sounds. I recalled the airship picking up Kai and I, Erina announcing that we had won the Blood Run.

My body was reclined back against something marginally softer than the stone I'd grown accustomed to. Hard, coarse straps bound my wrists and ankles. I jerked against them, hoping for some give, but they were as rigid as the surface I laid against.

Blinking through the warped haze, at last my surroundings came into focus. A dimly lit room with white walls. Softly glowing lights.

Metal trays with tools and instruments I didn't recognize.

A lab, I realized with horror. *But why?*

The howls and cries of Scottomb still sounded from nearby, though I couldn't understand why.

Had the border been breached?

I looked down at my restraints, finding two tubes threaded into my veins. They were both filled with crimson, the flow sluggish. My stomach churned. What were they doing with my blood?

A door to my right slid open with a whisper. Two people stepped through. One was the same medic that had been on the hovercraft, the other an older woman. Her head was bent as she read something on a handheld device, either unaware or uncaring that I was conscious. The younger girl stared straight at me as though seeing a ghost. I stared back, before licking my parched lips.

"What are you doing to me?" I asked.

The woman with greying hair stopped walking in front of me, and slowly lifted her head to look at me. I might as well have been a projection on a communicator with how emotionlessly she looked over me, and then the screen beside me.

"You missed two of the aetharus injections. In order to ensure your well-being, you need to have your blood cleansed." She answered in a cold, clinical manner.

"Because the Lufarium is poisonous, you mean?"

The woman's eyes snapped to mine, surprise, quickly followed by a sneer of condescension passed over her lined face. "Yes, I'm sure the Phantom told you all manner of things while you were trying to seduce him."

I did the only thing that made sense. My head snapped forward, busting her in the face.

She screeched, calling me names I'd never heard before, though I was certain they were crass. Blood poured from her nose, but I didn't feel an ounce of remorse for the cruel woman. The timid medic girl from the ship simply watched in horror.

"I didn't try to *seduce* the king," I spat. "Unless burying an echo blade in one's chest is considered seduction, then by all means, I'm guilty."

She held gauze to her already bruising nose, and said, "Your hover bot was conveniently destroyed just after your little kiss with the Blood Dweller and before you arrived in Terrikult, then your communicator and tracking implant went offline too. The Council thought you to be dead at first, but when your devices showed signs of life again after eight or so light-rises, it was clear you hadn't been killed during your mission, and neither was he. Though for the sake of keeping the people of Triste calm, we have announced that your mission was completed and the elusive monster of the valley, dead. And soon, he will be."

For whatever reason, her words made my blood run cold. I shouldn't have felt anything for the man who tricked and manipulated me, but the pang of fear and dread swept through my veins nonetheless.

"Why say that I won the race then? Why not just make Arlakai the winner?"

"Because never have we lost so many runners in one race. The people were distraught. Especially with all the attacks at the borders. Not just Freeya, but each of the nations have had breaches. We needed to give them something to celebrate. And since the Phantom let you go, unharmed, you can bet that his downfall will be as a direct result of you."

"I escaped," I countered. There was no way that they could know he'd let me go. It didn't make sense.

She scoffed. "No one escapes the Phantom, and believe me, girl, many have tried."

I couldn't tell her that he let me go because of what I was, not because he cared for me. He wanted me to birth more Béchua in order to grow the population, nothing more. Though neither of those confessions would get me released from here.

"Well, I did," I said flatly. Letting my head fall back, I sucked in a deep breath, trying to calm my nerves. "I need to speak with the Empress, or even the Council."

"Oh you will. They'll collect everything you know about his lair, his armies, and the underground network that remains hidden to us."

Again, I wanted to clamp my mouth shut and refuse, but that wouldn't get Charle the surgery he needed. *You don't owe the Phantom any loyalty,* I told myself. But the words sounded hollow even in my own mind. Raiden's strikingly beautiful face filled my mind, and his crooked grin made my stomach swoop. If he knew I was about to sell him out, would he still look at me like that?

"Arlakai can help too," I said, suddenly feeling exhausted. "He was there, too."

"He is faced with fraud charges for switching places with the true selected champion of Freeya, but yes, I reckon those charges will mysteriously vanish if he can offer up enough intel to help Triste rid the world of the Phantom once and for all."

My ire flared. "It was better that he took that boy's place. He wouldn't have lasted a click out there."

The woman shrugged, checking the lines that went to each of my arms. "Maybe. But let's just say your futures rest solely on your continued cooperation."

"He can't be killed," I snarled, feeling a wave of anger that I didn't fully understand. "I stabbed him in the chest, and he pulled the blade free like it was nothing. If I can't kill him, then you can't either. And now I'm being punished for returning to my homeland after attempting what the Council demanded."

"You have it wrong, girl." she whispered, eyes flicking to a spot in the top corner of the room that I guessed was a camera. "You weren't meant to come back. No one was. All of you were given missions that would result in your deaths. But somehow, you and your friend made it back. That won't go over with the Council."

My blood ran colder than the storms that battered Freeya. They'd wanted us to die.

That realization was a slap in the face.

I was never meant to see Charle again. I wasn't supposed to be alive.

"You have to let me go," I said with urgency. When she began to shake her head, I leaned my head down, forcing her to see me. Really, *see me*. "Please," I whispered.

The medic shook her head, but this time I was fairly certain I saw a glimpse of sympathy in her eyes. "I can't, girl, and you know it. Now don't ask again."

My head fell back against the padded board in defeat. After a while of her bustling around and occasionally adding a syringe of fluid into one of my IVs, I asked, "Why are there Scottomb here?"

She started humming to herself, clearly done speaking to me, but my gaze landed back on the young medic who still watched me like I would turn into something terrifying at any moment.

A dinging sounded from the machine beside me, the sound making me startle.

The head medic swiveled to face it, a deep crease settling between her brows. With hurried steps, she moved to the machine, then halted.

She looked in my direction with wide eyes, then back to the machine. "That can't be right," she said with a tremor in her voice that set me on edge.

"What?" I tried to read the message on the screen before she jerked it to the side.

She picked up her tablet and began typing furiously, muttering under her breath. My pulse sped up, breaths coming faster.

When two other medics—both male—rushed into the room, reading whatever was on the screen, their eyes bulged before they looked at me like I was some sort of freak.

"What's going on?" I demanded, hoping the firmer tone would convince them to shed some light on the growing panic in the room.

"Should we tell the Council?" one of the men with a graying beard asked.

The head medic considered the question while staring at the machine that still beeped. Finally, she jerked her head in a nod. The younger girl took a step back, as though in fear. But of what, I didn't know.

Without further question, the two men bustled from the room as though it was on fire.

I gave an exasperated sigh when the door snicked shut, pulling the woman's attention back to me. Trying one more time, I asked, "What's wrong?"

"You're one of them," she breathed. It came out sounding both reverent, yet suspicious.

My mouth went dry, and for a moment I couldn't even remember how to breathe. I recalled what Raiden had said about the Béchua. How the Council had strung them up, using them to power Lufarium until their bodies gave out.

I struggled against my restraints, though it was all for not. They wouldn't budge.

"How is it possible?" the young medic questioned, her voice sounding small. Her eyes still never left mine. "There haven't been any around in centuries."

I didn't intend to tell either of them that they'd lived underground, killed off slowly as they were each hunted down. But my parents had saved me and my brother.

Charle! My heart spasmed with fear; it wouldn't take long for them to make the connection that Charle was also a Béchua. How long before they captured him and used him as little more than an object too?

My body thrashed harder, desperation shredding away all other thoughts. I had to get out. I had to get to Charle.

The older woman tsked before drawing up another syringe of fluid and inserting it into my IV. I screamed as she sank the plunger in, feeling the sedative spread through my body with a warm wave that made my stomach turn.

Fighting against the heaviness in my limbs I didn't stop struggling; didn't stop screaming.

Not when it weighted my muscles like hunks of Lufarium. Only when it claimed my voice and pushed my lids down did I go silent.

An angry tear slipped down my cheek, burning a trail to my chin before the room and the evil woman faded away.

Chapter 27

Ferrah

Chapter 27- Ferrah

*B*eep.

Beep.

Beep.

The sound wouldn't stop, and my limbs refused to cooperate so I could shut it out. An astringent scent filled my nostrils, causing nausea to burn its way up my throat.

I just need sleep. My desperation for silence made me want to throw something at whatever was making that sound.

So tired.

Hushed voices filtered into my foggy mind, jolting my memory of what had last happened into place. I strained to open my eyes, groggily blinking against the light.

"The connections are complete." A wispy, feminine voice spoke. "With one tiny crystal, her output of power will produce enough energy for the entire border."

Awed whispers ensued.

I pried my lids open with sheer willpower. The haze of my drugged state took several moments to clear enough to make out the ten or so people crowded around me.

One of them I knew with absolute certainty was the Empress herself.

"I didn't do anything wrong," I forced out between lips that felt too big, too clumsy. "Please don't do this."

The Empress was tall, her long white waves artfully tamed to one side. Her dress was crystalline blue—probably for the benefit of the Freejian people. She twisted her lips into a sickly-sweet smile. "No?" she strode closer, stopping just out of reach. The medic had probably relayed what happened when someone got too close.

"You forget, my dear, that all of Triste saw the Blood Valley boy with you. They saw you kiss him. Did you forget the rules of the race that is so integral to our empire?"

I thought for a moment before shaking my head. "I didn't break the treaty," my protest was slurred, sounding more like, "I dinnot brek the trety."

She lifted a perfectly sculpted brow. As though reading through the official treaty document, she recited, "Runners must not engage with citizens of Blood Valley in any way unless to save their own lives. If runners should pass through village or town, they may not ask for food, drink, nor shelter; and if it is offered, they must decline."

My mouth gaped like a fish.

"During your guard training, you were made aware of the treaty, were you not? I do believe every nation is meant to memorize its contents." She tapped a slender finger adorned with golden rings wrapped around her pale skin like serpents against her chin in false contemplation.

"I did nothing malicious." This time my words came out sounding more coherent.

"Betraying the Empires is an act of treason," she snapped, her façade of calm fell away like a mask torn from her face. Her delicate features twisted with disdain. "Let's go over your list of offenses then, shall we? You gave Freejian technology away to a village—"

"It was *water*, and I thought that boy was going to die—"

She continued like she hadn't heard my outburst, "You accepted aid from, *and aided* a blood-dweller even after him telling you that he would put Blood Valley over you..."

Rage swirled inside me like a growing storm that I was ready to unleash on the only person who had the power to release me. But I knew it was too late. She'd discovered what I was. There was no escaping what she had in store for me.

"You stayed in a city among the locals, taking whatever they offered, including passage to Terrikult. And those are just the infractions caught by your hover bot, which that blood-dweller you befriended destroyed for you."

"Stop calling him that," I snapped. "You know it's foul."

She smirked. "You don't deny any of the charges?"

I huffed a sigh of frustration, pulling at my restraints again, though I knew it was foolish. "Raiden didn't destroy my hover bot for *me*, he did it for his king, but that's beside the point. Why does Triste have such a terrible relationship with Blood Valley?" Before she could answer, I did so for her, "Because we treat them like they're less than us, and they hate us because we cut them off from trade, leaving them to their own devices. You destroy any thriving civilization you find. And then there's that little caveat that everyone seems to overlook that our power source has polluted and *poisoned* their people, and will continue to do so for as long as we keep using Lufarium."

The room held its breath several beats. I had to hope that what I'd said had made some sort of impact with the Empress, but when her smug smile only twisted into an ugly sneer, I knew I'd lost.

"Drug her and hook her up to the conductor grid. I'm told she has a brother too. Find him and bring him in."

My limbs began to quake. "No! Please! Leave Charle alone! He's unwell, please! PLEASE!"

The Empress leaned over me, looking triumphant. "You'll smile for the cameras, join in union with your precious Arlakai while we bleed every ounce of Lufarium from you and your brothers' veins." She lingered, letting her words sink in as I thrashed, trying to claw any part of her. Then she turned, marching from the room with the rustling of her gown and the air of superiority she never showed the people in her broadcasts.

Medics descended on me while I flailed and screamed, scorching my throat raw. The sedative hit my blood stream, stripping me of my fight until I sobbed. Helplessness overwhelmed me.

A click, followed by a sharp pinch in my forearm drew my bleary gaze up. The same device used to bury trackers under the runners' skin withdrew from me.

"What—?" The word came out garbled, but I couldn't make my mouth work to try again.

The sensation began as a slow itch spreading from my arm and in my veins. Thrumming heat filled me. At first it was euphoric. I strained against my bonds again, and this time I heard them groan. Then my blood turned hot, searing me until I couldn't hold in my screams.

NO! NO MORE!

It was burning me alive from the inside, magma roiling and scorching my throat, my lungs.

"Just a small pebble-sized piece for this trial, we don't want to introduce too much too quickly," someone said, and I barely heard the words.

The fire receded slowly, but it was too late. Darkness crept in and swallowed me back into the void of nothingness.

When I woke again, every part of me hurt. I felt drained, every movement taking concentration and effort I barely possessed.

The young female medic was the one to undo my bindings. She kept her head down while she did so, and only when each of my limbs were mine once more, did she meet my gaze.

"They want you to shower and get dressed," she said softly. "You and the boy have to give an interview."

I wanted to snort a laugh. Arlakai was hardly a boy. Instead, I grunted in response. I didn't have the energy for anything else.

The staff that cleaned me up and wrapped me in this horribly itchy dress led me through dimly-lit halls that lacked any sort of opulence. My shoes banged a horrible sound against the metallic floor. It added to the unsteady rhythm of my heart until we stopped outside a closed door.

One of the women in a sleeveless white tunic, still lined with fur stepped forward to type a key into the pin pad that opened the door.

An array of harried sounds flooded the hall before I was pushed through the opening. More men and women that bustled around the dark area turned their heads when they noticed I stood there, feeling defenseless without any sort of echo blade on my person.

"There she is!" One of the women whose face was painted in bright gold makeup rushed towards me, gripping my wrist and pulling me after her. I tried to dig my heels in, but there was no deterring this woman.

We rounded a long, pleated drape to reveal Kai waiting by the edge.

When our eyes met, my chest constricted with both relief and joy. His eyes shone with the similar emotions, everything suddenly whole and right between us again. I broke free of the woman's grip to launch myself at my best friend, my arms around his neck.

He wrapped his arms around my middle, stilling for a click before he whispered, "You're so thin."

I thought about making a snide remark about the food they served, but decided against it.

"Okay you two, that's enough. Arlakai, you'll go out first, answer a few questions solo, and then we'll bring Miss Zunnok out, okay?" Her voice was nasally, yet clipped.

We both nodded, and my eyes met his one last time before they pulled him away from me.

An immediate dull roar of applause and cheers rose up seemingly from nowhere. I stepped forward, peering around the pleated cloth. I saw Kai seated on a raised platform across from a woman who looked at him with dreamy eyes.

After the crowd below the platform settled, the woman began speaking to Kai, though I couldn't hear their exchange.

They went back and forth for a few snaps, the people looking on awed and cheered at various points. I so desperately wanted to know wheat Kai was saying, but then the interviewer rose to her feet, looking in my direction. Kai stood too, and I was suddenly being pushed out onto the stage. Again, the air was filled with thunderous adoration.

I focused on keeping my steps even despite the tremor in my muscles. Despite the crowd's enthusiasm, I didn't look their way, nor did I look for the bot that tracked alongside me, undoubtedly broadcasting my trek across the shiny platform for all of Triste to scrutinize.

When I was close enough, Kai took my hand and led me to the seat next to him, though he didn't let go after we were seated. Soon, the applause faded and then the starry-eyed woman in a white and gold uniform similar to that of the Guard, asked,

"How are you two adjusting from your time in Blood Valley? You looked ready to succumb, Miss Zunnok, towards the end, before the Freejian Guard brought you both back to safety."

My pulse quickened at the way story was being retold. I opened my mouth to answer, to set the record straight, when Kai cut me off.

"I can't speak for Ferrah, but I'm beyond grateful to the Council for intervening when they did." Pause. "I'm not sure we would have made it back if they hadn't." He sounded so genuine, so convincing that I couldn't help but cast him a sidelong glance.

"Yeah, it's rough out there," I added. "I'm still shocked that we survived the race, to be honest." *No thanks to the Council who are trying to kill me regardless.* Kai wasn't disheveled. He hadn't lost weight. They weren't torturing him. But for whatever reason, they were parading us around for Triste, as though that would smooth over the utter failure this birth-tide's race was.

The interviewer smiled sweetly at Kai, then turned her attention back on me. "Well while you were recovering, all of Triste got to hear about how Arlakai illegally traded places in the race to keep you safe. For many light-rises there was speculation throughout all of Triste if you two were the perfect match for unification, and now we all see just how in love with you he is. It's almost impossible to believe that you two will be unified in four light rises, it's all very exciting."

My smile fell, those words sinking in like acid on my skin. Kai and I were to be bonded in *four light rises?* He hadn't warned me, and for that I suddenly wished I could kick him. Kai's hand squeezed mine. A silent warning to comply. I nodded hurriedly. "He asked me that first night in the valley."

The reporter leaned forward, exuding no end of excitement. "I'll bet you said yes right then and there after his sacrifice to be with you."

I let out a nervous laugh. "Well, not right then, but when the sand whirlpool sucked Kai down, I..." My head turned to face Kai, a lump of emotion rising up in my throat at the memory. Pissed as I was at my best friend, the thought of losing him broke me in every way imaginable. We stayed locked in each other's gazes for an imperceptible length of time. His throat bobbed and I saw the love and affection he'd shown for me in Blood Valley.

I wanted to tell him that I loved him too, albeit a little differently. I wanted to tell him that I hoped we'd get a shot at that future. Because if the Council got their way, I'd die before we got the chance.

The woman clucked her tongue sympathetically, jerking me out of my thoughts.

"That's when you knew you didn't want to live without him?" The reporter supplied.

I nodded again, unable to speak, and cheers erupted all around us. The woman said something else, and the room descended into silence once more.

"I suppose you didn't know about this, since you were lost in the labyrinth beneath Blood Valley. Let's take a look at the footage."

My body jolted as I heard Raiden's murmured words, then on a projection above the gathered people, was me and Raiden just as he leaned in and kissed me. I felt Kai go still as everyone reacted with choruses of *oooo*, or boo's.

The interviewer sent me a sly smile, cleared pleased to bring such a scandalous thing up. "Will the kiss affect our bonded pair to be?" Though the question was for the audience, she looked between me and Kai.

I tried to offer a light squeeze, an unspoken apology, but he didn't react to me. However, he cleared his throat and said,

"The thing about Valley Dwellers is they like to stir up trouble. We saw that when they set up explosives right where we stepped into the valley, and we saw it with the villagers who would have taken everything we had to keep us from fulfilling our mission. But we know how Ferrah was betrayed by the dweller. Even I was imprisoned in the king's castle."

"That's true," the woman cooed sympathetically, earning sounds of pity from the people watching. Her words had soothed my apparent betrayal, but I knew Kai wasn't as unaffected as he made himself seem. When she rose to her feet, more applause rang out and filled the room to bursting. Kai thanked her, and pulled me up with him.

He led me back the way we'd come out, his hand on my lower back. My mind churned, and my stomach clenched.

For a brief moment, my thoughts drifted to Raiden, until I immediately shut them down. Kai was my future. Being bled dry for Triste was my future.

There would be nothing else.

Chapter 28

The Phantom

I paced like a wild animal, snarling orders at my captains to keep to the plan for now.

When I'd set her free, I'd known she'd return to her nation. I needed her as far away as humanly possible while we took Triste piece by bloody piece. She'd be away from the war until the last moment. What I hadn't expected was for Freeya to announce her and her companion as the winners of the Blood Run, and for the scheduled interviews to only include the boy.

He'd announced his impending union with Ferrah for the crowd to swoon over. It did nothing but leave an acrid taste in my mouth.

She was not his to claim. He knew nothing of mates and lengths I would go to keep him away from her.

Still, the cameras never showed her, promising that she was in recovery and would be released in time for the ceremony with the red-headed idiot. I had less than a lunar shift to keep that from happening.

Still, I couldn't shake the unease that something else was wrong. Ferrah was perhaps a little dehydrated and in need of an energy boost from Lufarium, but nothing that would keep her in lockup for six light-rises.

They know. They must have tested her blood and found the genetic marker.

Cold fury sluiced through my bones. "They'll kill her," I growled to the empty tent. *If they know, then they'll use her as a conduit until they overwhelm her.*

I wouldn't let that happen.

A ping from the broadcast interceptor in the center of my tent had me turning in time to see *her*. Her dark hair was styled into loose curls, a glittery blue dress clinging to her body. They'd dressed her up like a doll, but even through the grainy image on my projector, I saw her gaunt cheeks, and felt a rumble of rage vibrate in my chest.

No longer did I merely wonder if they knew what she was. They had already begun to drain her.

I took a slow step closer to her, wishing I could reach out and feel her soft skin beneath my fingertips.

"How are you two adjusting from your time in Blood Valley?" the interviewer asked, her false concern lacing her tone. "You looked ready to succumb, Miss Zunnok, towards the end, before the Freejian Guard brought you both back to safety."

Arlakai held her hand in his, smiling stupidly at the woman who asked the question.

"I can't speak for Ferrah, but I'm beyond grateful to the Council for intervening when they did." Pause. "I'm not sure we would have made it back if they hadn't." Emotion filled his voice and I snarled at his image. At the fact that he was touching what was mine.

Ferrah glanced to him, seeming surprised by his words, though she recovered quickly, a smile of her own tugging at her lips. It was as fake as the image Triste tried to project of her—their glittery champion.

"Yeah, it's rough out there," she said at last. "I'm still shocked that we survived the race, to be honest."

The interviewer shot first Kai, then Ferrah, a wide smile. "Well while you were recovering, all of Triste got to hear about how Arlakai illegally traded places in the race to keep you safe. For many light-rises there was speculation throughout all of Triste if you two were the perfect match for unification, and now we all see just how in love with you he is. It's almost impossible to believe that you two will be unified in four light rises, it's all very exciting."

Ferrah's smile slipped, and the nearly imperceptible squeeze of Kai's hand on hers had the expression returning. She nodded, seeming to come up with the right words. "He asked me that first night in the valley."

The reporter leaned forward slightly, intrigued. "I'll bet you said yes right then and there after his sacrifice to be with you."

Her throat bobbed before she let out a nervous laugh. "Well, not right then, but when the sand whirlpool sucked Kai down, I..." This time she turned her head to meet his gaze and my fingers clenched into fists at my sides. Even I could see the adoration she held for her... *friend*. When her words dissolved, the woman clucked her tongue in a sympathy.

"That's when you knew you didn't want to live without him?" The reporter supplied.

When Ferrah nodded, my jaw tightened too. *No, reickunteel, the mortal is nothing to you. And you're nothing to him. You'll see that soon enough.*

"Jasmynth!" I called for my soldier.

She rushed through the tent flap, ready for whatever command I would give. Her gaze went to the broadcaster, lingering on Ferrah as she answered some other inconsequential query.

"I'm altering our plan slightly and moving the timeline up. I have a wedding to interrupt."

Chapter 29

Ferrah

My heart still thudded behind my ribcage like it might hammer its way out. As I scanned the backstage area, eyes flickering through the hundreds of people who gathered to see me and Kai, I realized too late who I hoped to see.

Stupid. Raiden isn't here. The impossibility didn't stop me from wishing one of the faces would make my heart stop beating so fiercely.

Kai released my hand as soon as we were backstage. "I would say I'm sorry you didn't know about the binding ceremony, but I'm not the only one with things to be sorry for."

I whirled on him, a thousand shouts rising up my throat. My lips parted at the same time my gaze fell on the Empress, set away from the crowds and surrounded by her guards, but close enough to see. Her eyes narrowed on me—a warning.

"Yes, my one kiss with the guy who saved my life versus being told we'll be bonded in only four light rises. I didn't tell you because it didn't matter, but you could have warned me," I said, my voice pitched low and frantic.

His jaw flexed. After a long moment he said, "I'm sorry."

I didn't bother with a response. His apology was nothing more than a placating gesture, but in the end it didn't matter. Our futures were to be orchestrated by the Council.

Until my heart gave out, anyway.

One of the women who had helped get me ready for the interview flitted to my side, speaking too fast for me to catch all of it. Not that I cared to hear what she was saying anyway.

"It'll be a small affair, all things considered. The Council decided to broadcast the ceremony to placate the unrest in the nations." She clapped her long hands together excitedly, her golden ringlets bouncing with the movement. Her exaggerated makeup was glittery blue—to match the color of my dress if I had to guess.

I frowned at her words, glancing sidelong at Kai, who squeezed my hand again. A warning.

The woman continued to chatter about colors, flowers, and things that I couldn't focus on. I let the odd statement she'd made fade away beneath the twisting in my gut at what laid ahead.

Soon, I'd be bound to Kai.

Slowly the Empress made her way towards us. The sea of people parted to let her through, and the stylist mercifully went silent.

A cold smile teased her lips, the expression unable to meet her icy blue eyes. "Thank you, Resha. Please return Miss Zunnok to her quarters."

My heart dropped to my feet, chilling my blood. "No," I said with much more confidence than I felt.

The Empress lifted a single, pale brow.

"Not until I see my brother and Nona." I kept my stare leveled with the ice bitch who made a humming noise somewhere between amusement and thoughtfulness. Or maybe she was imagining all the ways she could have me killed.

After a moment, she said, "Resha, escort Miss Zunnok's family to her chambers for twenty snaps, and no more. Then she is to have her next... treatment."

The cold in my veins was replaced by sweltering heat. Anticipation and fear of the pain to come.

But at least I would get to see Charle and Nona.

Resha nodded energetically as she began to pull me away from Kai.

"Wait," he barked. I felt his eyes boring into me, but I didn't look back. He didn't need to see my fear.

I was in motion the moment the door hissed open, my bare feet slapping the cold stone floor audibly. But the sight that greeted me halted my steps.

Nona stood with eyes glistening in the harsh light. Beside her was Charle, in his automated chair. His frame was hunched, the pallor of his papery skin too grey.

"Charle?" I whispered, unable to keep the horror from my voice.

"Ferrah," Nona answered sharply. I jerked my gaze to meet hers.

"What happened?"

She sucked in a shaky breath. "They tried a new form of treatment that they warned might weaken him further..." Her words trailed off as a single tear slipped down her usually stoic face.

I pulled my attention back to Charle, who met my stare. Despite the weakened state of his body, there was a hard gleam in his violet eyes.

With a raspy inhale, his lips parted. "They. Hurt. You. Too." Each word took effort, and was almost too weak to be heard. Yet I understood that it wasn't a question.

My heart thudded painfully in my chest. The "treatment" they were using for Charle was not a treatment at all. They were draining his blood.

"Charle…" I swallowed hard before glancing sidelong at the camera capturing everything. There was nothing I could say or do, and it poured lava through my veins. I wanted to rip down the doors to this building and slice the Empress to ribbons myself.

I had only gone into Blood Valley and did what I did to try to save him, but instead I'd sentenced him to a worse death. The pain of them harvesting the raw energy from a Béchua's blood was excruciating. And I'd ensured that would be his end.

My hands squeezed into tight fists, my nails cutting through the skin.

Nona stepped forward, pulling me into a hug. Her lips brushed the shell of my ear as she whispered, "You need to get out. Run and don't stop running, girl. They're going to kill you."

My eyes widened. When she released me, a knowing look engraved into her features answered the question burning my tongue.

"Not at first, but yes." She nodded to punctuate her answer.

I cleared my throat, looking back to my brother whose eyes had begun to droop. "Is there any way you can… refuse this new treatment?"

Nona made a noise somewhere between disgust and amusement. "You know as well as I do that the Council's *generosity* will not be refused."

My gut clenched and I ached to pull my brother into my arms and hum the lullaby from the music box like I did when we were younger. Unable to stop myself, I reached for him, shocked when his hand trembled, fighting to lift. A wave of grief hit me as my hand embraced his. The bones protruded through his skin, but I fought to ignore the feeling. I desperately wanted to give him some of my strength. To pour out my energy into him, to give him more time.

My eyes closed so neither Charle nor Nona would see my heart breaking.

Charle's skin warmed under mine and a gasp made my eyes fly open again. A faint violet glow radiated from where our hands joined. I glanced to my brother, unsure if he was being hurt by whatever was taking place.

His head lifted from the seat back, as a deep breath filled his lungs. "Ferrah, stop."

Heat slid through my veins like boiled honey. I didn't let go, emboldened by his sudden show of strength.

When he tried to pull his hand away, I clasped down harder, willing more of my strength to fill him.

"Ferrah, stop!" He pulled his hand free with so much force, I cried out.

Dizziness crashed into me like a brutal wave, and I dropped to my knees, catching myself with my hands before my face could impact on the floor.

"Ferrah!" Nona cried, kneeling down in front of me. "What did you do?"

My neck strained to lift my head, and even then, my vision swam. I looked from her to Charle, finding his skin a healthier, golden hue and sighed with relief. To Nona, I said, "I gave him time."

"Not by killing yourself," Charle snapped, and he truly did look angry. "That was foolish. I accepted my fate well before you went into the valley. Don't risk yourself for me. You're too important."

Before I could answer the door slid open again, and the med staff rushed in. Darkness pushed in, but I forced it back, watching Nona and Charle be ushered out of the room.

"I love you both," I said, but my voice didn't project the way I wanted it to. And in an instant they were gone.

My body was hoisted up to the bed, straps wrapped around me like the spindly arms of a kwipai. The darkness crept ever closer, and my eyes grew too heavy to hold open before the Lufarium was injected inside me.

Then there was only pain in the emptiness of my mind before it dissolved to nothing.

Chapter 30

The Phantom

With a deafening blast, stone, dirt, and metal split apart, revealing a gaping hole. Soldiers poured down inside, flooding the tunnels that marched on Tiau.

I could hear their sirens and the shouts of terror as they realized they were under attack. Striding through the long stretch of tunnel, I thought only of how much closer I was to where I needed to be.

The Empress and the Council would be distracted long enough for a quick takeover.

Weapons clashing, and war cries filled the stale air. By the time light greeted me, the sounds of a struggle petered out, leaving unconscious and bleeding men on the ground.

Terrified eyes peered out of nearby homes, and a second wave of soldiers rushed towards us.

I lifted my hand, a cord of impatience coloring my tone as I said, "Sorry, but I really don't have time."

My power worked on them immediately, forcing them to the ground on one knee, their heads bowed. I hated to violate a person's ability to choose, but I needed to keep moving.

"Tiau now belongs to me, your king," I announced.

"Death spare our king!" Chanted my soldiers. It drowned out whatever protests the people of Triste might have tried to level at me. I drifted through their land, barely taking in the stunning mountains and healthy streams. All abundant land I planned to make smart use of.

The journey north felt longer than it truly was. Tiau fell easily. I slid under Auktraize, signaling only to collapse all of their tunnels at once as a warning that I would return. In L'Ogust, the air was crisper, the artificial cold grating on my nerves.

But soon I'd knock the walls down and let the natural climate of Triste take over. Ferrah would love the warmer weather, instead of being confined to snow and ice all year long.

I let my mind wander to thoughts of her and what our future together would soon look like.

And with each step closer I could practically taste her scent on the air, even though I knew my sense of her wasn't quite that strong. But my desire for her only grew from the first moment she crossed the border into my territory.

Now, there was nothing I wouldn't do to keep her.

Soon, she'd have to face that truth. Far sooner than she knew.

Chapter 31

Ferrah

*F*rost clung to my exposed nose, trying to seep through the fabric of my gloves to bite my fingertips. I shivered alongside the dozens of other cadets as we awaited orders.

In front of us was the entrance to a large trade tunnel, but the light didn't seem to penetrate the vast stretch below ground. The captain strode towards the tunnel, barking out in her usual manner,

"Cadets, the Scottomb have been unusually active at the L'Ogust border. Just in the past lunar shift, these tunnels have had a hundred breaches. We have no other way to get the supplies across the border, however. So follow me. And keep quiet or you'll become the Scottomb's next meal."

I opened my mouth to ask the very question that another soldier called out behind me. "Do we not have aircraft capable of going high enough above the ground to avoid the damned creatures?"

Captain Eris narrowed her eyes on the cadet. "Did you learn nothing in your classes? We would have to lower the shields that keep our nations safe to fly craft through. It would leave us exposed."

"Why have them go above the cities at all though?" the boy pressed. Finnigan, I thought his name was. "If the shields only went up as high as the tallest building, surely we could conduct trade up above instead of down below.

Again, our superior looked ready to make the cadet regret his line of questioning. But instead of directly answering him, she sneered,

"Stupid boy, do you not think the developers didn't consider that? That we didn't try such tactics at one point? Wherever there is a solid landing, the Scottomb can, and will, reach you. Even if that's high up in the air. Now let's get moving, it's a long journey."

A shiver of fear ran through each and every one of us gathered. I looked around at the other reddened faces stricken by that statement. No one seemed to want to move. Swallowing hard, I started after the captain, keeping my steps light. The sound of snow-covered boots crunching over the sleek stone made my jaw tighten.

How much noise was too much? Were they already above us, just waiting for an invitation to break through the tunnel? I'd heard of countless tunnel collapses, even before I joined the Freejian Guard. Now that we were about to enter with at least a dozen hovercraft of trade goods, the reality of the situation made my hands tremble. The older soldiers manned the ships while the rest of us would guard them.

At least those in the ships had extra protection if a tunnel collapsed.

Wordlessly, Kai's knuckles brushed against mine, a silent reassurance as he kept pace with me. Each step plunged us deeper into darkness, penetrated only by the hover craft's internal lighting.

My heart was a deafening cacophony in my ears, making it impossible to decipher how much noise I actually made. The curl of white plumes from our breath danced together in front of us.

Behind us, the soft whirring of the pods kept my jaw tight. My hands ached from gripping my echo bolt so tightly at my side.

We kept formation through the long stretch of tunnel, everyone teetering on the edge of madness. Were those howls above us the wind, or something else? Was that a *clink* deeper in the tunnel, or just a pebble kicked up by someone's boot? *Every noise set us further on edge. I tried to ignore it all. As long as the sirens didn't sound, we were safe. The tunnel was intact.*

"Is it just me, or is it getting warmer?" Someone whispered.

"Shut it," another hissed.

Captain Eris whirled, preparing to chastise us for speaking, when someone let out a quiet scream, tripping and bashing into me from behind.

I stumbled, gritting my teeth to keep from making a sound.

Everyone froze.

A look of horror slid over our leader's expression.

Directly above me, came a loud thump. *Then another. A bone-chilling scream even muted by the rock and electrified barrier that separated us from them, had me sucking in a breath.*

Kai pulled me sharply against him with one hand, his weapon lifted with the other.

"Quickly," the Captain whispered, "We're too far now to turn back, but we have to hurry."

My feet carried me lightly through the tunnel, the sound of our boots a now audible, steady rhythm. The thumping above us grew louder, their shrieks more deafening.

Dust rained down on us from above. I glanced up, spying the hairline cracks in the concrete.

Why hasn't the siren sounded? *I wondered with resolute terror taking hold in my veins. Kai seemed to notice them the same time as I did, because he grabbed a handful of my coat sleeve and yanked me after him, faster, overtaking Eris.*

Another tremble rocked the ground, and this time the tunnel cracked loud enough for us all to hear, sending a cascade of rubble down on us.

"Run," Kai bellowed.

We sprinted hard and fast, trying to drown out the Scottomb's desperate cries for blood. Another crack sounded, and a skeletal creature fell into the tunnel just behind me and Kai. I halted. Releasing my echo bolt on the sling that kept it to my body, grabbing instead for my blades.

Screams filled the cool, damp air, followed by the ear-splitting peel of the sirens.

I lifted my first blade, preparing to lodge it into the creature's back, when it vanished, though the girl it had been feasting on remained upright, her eyes rolled back in her head as her throat was torn open.

My stomach roiled as I let my blade fly. It met its mark, sinking into the girl who needn't suffer anymore than she already had.

Her body dropped like a puppet whose strings were cut, collapsing in a heap on the tunnel floor. More of the vile, reeking monsters poured into the tunnel. I threw blade after blade, hitting my targets before they managed to make themselves invisible.

Rushing forward, I collected the knives I could, preparing to throw them again, when Kai yanked me back again.

"We have to go!" he yelled.

I shook my head, trying to make sense of the melee in the darkness. Those in the pods began forcing their way through soldiers and creatures alike.

One steered himself with determination, mowing over three of our own people in his path. I wanted to scream at him to stop, even as he headed for me, but the pod halted and the air behind the driver shifted.

An ugly, wrinkled being with dead eyes appeared inside the aircraft without the soldier realizing until it was too late. It lunged, tearing the boy apart in moments. I turned away, letting Kai guide me in the opposite direction. Away from L'Ogust and back to Freeya.

"We're too far away," I mumbled, but I kept moving through the throng, skirting around rubble.

An inhuman cry followed us. I'd barely glimpsed the pale skin and wickedly sharp teeth before Kai spun. He shot two of the creatures that had chased us. The blinding light from the bolt making me squeeze my eyes shut.

My stomach churned over and over as we ran, leaving the sounds of slaughter behind us. Sooner than I thought possible, the mouth of the tunnel came into view, where dozens of soldiers poured in. They slowed when they saw us.

"Report?" one of the men in front barked.

"Tunnel breach, at least ten Scottomb were able to get in. We killed as many as we could and fled. I'm not sure if anyone else has been able to get away."

The man's eyes narrowed on us both as my stomach shot into my throat. Without warning I doubled over and emptied my stomach onto the ground.

"So you two left the rest of your squad to be eaten alive?" the disapproving soldier asked.

"No, sir. We fought our way out, but by the time we began our escape, most everyone was already dead."

"And the goods?" another asked. A woman this time.

Kai patted my back. When I was confident I was done regurgitating everything I'd had that morning, I wiped my mouth and straightened.

They were right.

We fled, leaving everyone to die.

"I don't believe any made it to the border," Kai answered.

A distant shriek in the tunnel told me we hadn't gotten them all.

"Get back to base, soldiers, and await orders," the terse man barked, his expression dripping with disdain.

I nodded, following Kai out of the tunnel. Once we were past the squad and on the snowy path, the world above us grey and angrily spitting flakes of snow to nip at my face, I choked out a sob.

Kai turned to me, his expression one of understanding. He drew me into him, the scent of blood and salt coating his usual comforting scent. "We did nothing wrong."

I snorted a humorless laugh through my tears. "They're all dead." The words burned my tongue. Shame and guilt wrapped my chest in a lethal vice. I hoped the pain of it would crush me. It was what we deserved for fleeing.

"We fought, Fairs," Kai said in a firm tone. "We didn't just run. How many of those bastards did we take down on our way to safety?"

When I didn't answer he pulled me back far enough to read his serious expression. "How many, Fairs?"

"I don't know," I muttered.

"At least eight of them. Just you and me. And there were thirty of us down in that tunnel. We did nothing *wrong. Do you understand me?"*

After a moment, I nodded.

His lips pressed to the top of my head and my lids fluttered shut. We stayed that way for several more moments. I let myself melt into the heat of him amidst the frigid cold. And for however long, I tried to believe my hands were coated in the blood of my brothers and sisters in arms.

That I hadn't grievously betrayed them.

Their faces surfaced in my mind in a dizzying wave, their screams as they were torn apart replaying in my mind.

I awoke with a jolt, a scream locked in my throat, but I wouldn't let it out. My limbs burned and ached.

A projection played in the corner where the older medic hunched over, watching the images play out.

Explosions rocked the ground sending soldiers in black and gold uniforms hurtling back. The scene changed, showing the dirty, tear-stained face of a child crying while a building in the background burned.

It changed again, this time to watch the opulent golden palace melt. The symbol for Werea-Haot turned to glittering rivulets until they began to run in different directions. After a moment, it reshaped into a coat of arms I'd only seen glimpses of. A bird with its wings outstretched, and a flower clutched in its beak.

The Phantom.

He was attacking Triste? To what end?

From the images on display, it looked as though he'd succeeded. Did he conquer Werea-Hoat? Were there others?

The door to my prison slid open and one of the servant women walked in. The medic jerked, promptly shutting down the broadcast and whipping to face her.

She inclined her head. "I was sent to get her ready for another appearance. People are starting to wonder where she's been." When she peered my way, her eyes widened slightly before she neutralized her expression.

The moment her words caught up to my foggy mind, I frowned. I'd given an interview what I assumed was only a light-rise ago.

"Well, get some food in her, or something, she looks like a corpse," the medic grunted, then stood, heading for the door the opened automatically. Before he vanished, his eyes locked with mine. "Your brother seems almost like a new person. Strange since his condition had been worsening for so long. Now he can walk. Fight." The glint of hunger in his gaze burned like a fire threatening to consume me.

I strained against my bindings, but my muscles were weak, my words even weaker as I rasped, "If you kill him, I swear I'll—"

The medic laughed before striding out the door, cutting off my fury like blade.

"Hush now, don't make a scene," the woman in the Empress' employ whispered as she hurried to release me.

The weight of my body fell into her, nearly knocking us both to the floor, but she somehow managed to keep me upright.

With a tsk, she said, "This is what happens when you leave someone unconscious for three light-rises."

My stomach swooped down to my feet, and for a breath, my vision swam. *Three* light-rises? That meant that the ceremony was the next light-rise. My heart picked up its sluggish pace, beating a bruising pace beneath my ribs.

I let the woman steady me again, and when she led me from the medical room and into a hygiene chamber, I asked in a low, hoarse voice, "Is Triste under attack?"

She froze. A few other girls were there to help dip me into the cubicle of water and dress me, but I ignored them. Before she could pass me off any of them, I grabbed the woman's arm, holding it as tightly as I could.

That forced her to meet my stare. A beat passed, then she nodded.

It was all the information I could glean while they all scrubbed and washed me, then slid another ornate gown over my head, this one a breath-taking silver with white beads clustered at the bottom. The sleeves were gauzy and light, hiding my pale complexion.

They didn't waste any time shuffling me out, through the silent halls of the ice palace, tittering to themselves about how handsome Arlakai was and how lucky I was to have won the race.

If only they knew.

It was clear they had no idea what I was, or what the Empress had done to me in secret. I supposed no one would learn the truth now.

I wouldn't survive a birth-tide at this rate. Neither would Charle, and I was certainly not going to be allowed anywhere near him after what I'd done.

When we arrived outside the silver doors, we paused, and the foolish girls finally fell silent. The doors flew open after only a beat.

A harried-looking woman nearly rammed into me, letting out a gasp just before grabbing my arm and pulling me after her. "There you are, you're late!"

I recognized her from the last time I took the stage. Wordlessly she hauled me through a set of dark drapes where a bunch of people looked over me, dabbing creams and powders to my face, brushing things onto my eyes and lips.

It was over almost as soon as they started, and then I was being led through to the area that, I assumed led to a stage. I could hear laughter and applause... a crowd of puppets who danced for their master.

"She's ready," the frantic woman whispered.

"Alright, people of Freeya, here she is, the Ice Champion—soon to be united for all of Triste to see—it's FERRAH ZUNNOCK!"

I barely registered my name through the thunderous cheers. When my feet didn't automatically move, the woman behind me gave me a small shove as the giant glittering doors parted.

Stumbling forward, into dazzling sunlight, I was nearly blinded. Somehow the volume turned from manic to downright chaotic.

I paused, trying to take it in.

The previous interview had been in an enclosed area with several hundred people, but this was...

Like the draw.

But I was on the Ice Palace's balcony, looking down at tens of thousands of Freejian citizens. The Empress stood at the edge, smiling back at me, with Arlakai by her side in his formal uniform, and the other Council members fanned out at either side of the doors I'd just come through.

The people below were held away from the courtyard by hundreds of Freejian Guard members. And as I sought out the faces in the push, I realized that not everyone cheered with joy. Some wept with abject terror in their eyes.

Did they know the Phantom had brought nations to their knees already? Was their fear for him... or something else?

But still they called out to me as if I could help them.

The Empress turned from me to offer them her fake smile. When her arms outstretched, the crowd quieted just enough for her call out,

"Freeya, you have no doubt seen firsthand the treacherous nature of Blood Valley; of the monsters who plague our borders and attack our people. But we have not just one Champion among us. Two of Freeya's bravest soldiers not only fought their way through the dangers of the valley but secured us our precious Lufarium for several birth-tides to come. And on their quest these two sought to be joined in union. To bring forth a new generation of soldiers who will protect our beloved nation."

A new round of cheers went up at the Empress' words.

My throat worked as I tried to swallow down the rage her lies incited. As though we were welcomed back to Freeya with open arms. And the Lufarium that she claimed we brought back was nothing more than mine and my brother's blood.

Though I couldn't help wrinkle my nose at her last statement. Any off-spring of mine would likely contain Béchua blood that the Empire would only bleed dry. There was no way Kai and I would be pro-creating. I was more than willing to bet I wouldn't live long enough to sustain a pregnancy anyway.

When relative silence fell yet again, several shouts went up from the crowd.

"What about the south?"

"When will you step in?"

"Are we next?"

I saw the Empress' jaw tick, though her placid smile remained. "The attacks in the south are well in hand. No radicals will be allowed to continue, I assure you. Peace will be restored in Triste, and Blood Valley will keep to its rightful place."

More applause and shouts mingled in the air before the Empress turned to me, snatching me by the wrist and hauling me towards the rail.

"And that is why we answer the violent acts committed by soulless mon-sters by ignoring their futile actions and, instead, showing that Triste will never be broken." She turned me to face Kai, his hands taking mine. He was warm, almost blisteringly hot. Was it him, or was I just that cold?

"Here, before all of Freeya, and the whole world, these two shall be bound this light-rise!" the Empress cried.

My stomach dropped and instinctively, I jerked my hands back, glancing at the Empress who shot me a look of warning. I took a wobbly step back, my breaths coming faster. Little puffs of steam gave away my panic.

Kai stepped towards me, taking my hands again, his grip firmer. "Hey," he murmured, so only I could hear. "I've got you." His lips tilted into a half smile; one that I knew was meant to be encouraging.

My heart raced, making my vision blurry around the edges. *This can't be happening now,* I thought desperately. *Not when I haven't had time to process this.*

Glancing at the Empress again, I read all that I needed to in her expression. *You will do this, or everyone you love will die.*

I forced myself to look back at Kai, to let his hold on me keep me from running away as fast as I could. *For Charle. For Nona. For Kai.*

"Please bring the ceremonial ribbon," the Empress ordered.

A man cloaked in black with silver thread stepped forward; his head bowed. On the plush, white velvet pillow was a silver ribbon, shining in the sunlight.

The Empress reached for it, her fingertips scarcely brushing the fabric when darkness washed over the balcony like a duvet.

Screams went up all around, followed by a few thumps and grunts. I felt someone move towards me and I thrust an elbow out. It connected with a snap of bone and a groan of pain.

"Kai?" I asked in horror. My eyes strained to make him out, but it was impossible.

A dark, rasping laugh sent a chill snaking down my spine. Then a brush of warm lips against my ear as a familiar voice said,

"Oh, *reickunteel*, how rude of you to start our wedding without me."

Chapter 32

Ferrah

S hadows darkened everything around us. Cocooning us so perfectly, I could hardly make out the skeletal face of the Phantom.

His body was solid and warm at my back, his arm wrapped around my middle and holding me there. My breaths came in jagged gasps as I tried to calm my racing heart.

Shouts of panic came from below, and somewhere behind us were the Empress's muffled screams.

Almost all at once the darkness receded, followed by a blinding bolt of violet light that struck the ground, eliciting more screams.

"Silence for your king," the Phantom said, and though his words were barely more than a whisper, the crowd obeyed. Fear was a tangible fist that held everyone by their throats, daring them to speak out and suffer the consequences.

Kai knelt several feet away, bound by thin black wire with his arms behind his back. His cheek and nose were slathered in crimson from my accidental blow. He glared up at the man who held me captive. Behind him, was none other than Isak, who held an echo bolt to the back of my best friend's skull.

"Now," the Phantom drawled, pressing his nose to my hair and inhaling softly. "For the union you all came here to see."

He made a gesture to someone I couldn't see, and then a cushion with a blood-red ribbon curled up on its center appeared in the hands of the soldier girl I'd met back in the Phantom's castle. *Jazmynth*.

He slid his free hand down to my wrist, yanking my sleeve up to my elbow, then wrapped his hand over my clenched fist, coaxing my fingers apart with surprising strength before winding his fingers through mine. The Phantom lifted our joined hands straight out. My brows lifted at the sight of his bronzed skin against my much paler arm as the woman said,

"Blood for blood, heart for heart. Joined together under the authority of our King, ruler of Krovaya, never to be cleaved apart, even in death. So shall these two souls be forever bound." She wrapped the ribbon around our two arms which glowed and burned against my skin. I hissed out a breath as the ribbon charred, leaving black ash on us both.

It was short and to the point, but I felt the weight of it in my chest, making my knees weak.

"NO!" Kai leaped to his feet, but he didn't get far before Isak cracked the butt of his weapon against his skull, sending Kai to the ground in a motionless heap.

"Kai—"

The Phantom's growl vibrated his chest. "I'm not a jealous man, but if you utter his name again while we're celebrating our vows, I'll have him tossed off this balcony, *flower*."

The shift in his voice.

That nickname.

Horror suffused my veins.

"No," I breathed. My eyes squeezed shut, a sudden flood of emotion clogging my throat. I was imagining it. I had to be.

With as much strength as I could muster, I whirled around, both hoping and dreading to see the boy I cared for. He kept hold of my wrist though, not daring to let me get far.

The king's skeletal features covered only half of his face, the other, unmarred and beautiful. A deceptive lie. Yet somehow an unsurprising twist that I felt I should have seen coming.

Raiden *was* the Phantom.

To conceal it from me, he hid behind a mask of sorts, but to his soldiers and his people, they saw the young, hauntingly striking boy I'd come to care for. The wicked king of Blood Valley was both the monster and the savior.

And now we were bound in some ancient ceremony that I had no desire to uphold.

A smooth, arrogant smirk tipped the corner of his mouth up. Triumph and something I couldn't read flashed in his silver eyes.

"I told you, you belong to me. And now you'll wear the proof of that on your skin forever." His ruined vocal cords made the words sound more like a prison sentence than... whatever it was supposed to be.

I looked down at my arm, finding the black soot still wound around my arm. Using my free hand, I tried to brush it off, but it wouldn't budge. I licked my thumb and scrubbed at the mark. Still, it remained inked onto my flesh.

My eyes widened, a sinking sensation pooling low in my gut. "What did you do?" I hissed.

His grin grew, though something softer entered his eyes. As though all of this was some sweet moment.

Slowly, as though awakening from a daze, the crowd began to stir. Shouts of fear and rage rang out over the murmurs.

"The Phantom has come to kill us all!"

"We must protect Triste!"

Several shots from echo bolts blazed past my head. The Phantom's lips turned into a snarl as he pulled me back to him.

My eyes went to Kai again, who stirred on the ground. He started to sit up when more blasts were shot our way. Confusion creased his brow before his expression smoothed to resolute anger.

"Fairy!"

The Phantom scoffed, and another blinding strike of unnatural lightning struck the balcony.

One moment the floor beneath my feet was solid, then there was nothing. We were falling.

Like Scottomb, we vanished.

From the castle. From Kai.

And from any semblance of freedom I'd hoped to possess.

Also By

The Weapon of Fire and Ash Series by Brittany Matsen
The Mark of Fallen Flame
The Spellcaster's Weapon
The Throne of Broken Bones
The Crown of Shattered Souls

Milton Keynes UK
Ingram Content Group UK Ltd.
UKHW010638271123
433341UK00005B/529